Lap Dog

The Shelter Series, Book Two

Kate Sherwood

About The Book You have Purchased

This story is a work of fiction. Names, characters, places, and incidents are either the product of the author's imagination or are used fictitiously to further the plot in this story. Any resemblance to actual persons living or dead, business establishments, events, or locales are entirely coincidental.

Cover Art by: A.J. Corza

website: www.ajcorza.com

Cover content is for illustrative purposes only and any persons depicted on the cover are models.

Formatting by: All Indie Publishing Services

website: www.allindiepublishingservices.com

Lap Dog

Tristan Beck sells his body for a living; Simon Yeung sold his soul for his family.

Simon's job is to make things run smoothly for his uncle's business, and he does his job well. When he's assigned to convince Tristan to work for a family ally, Simon develops a strategy and then implements it. Nothing personal.

But when "convincing" really means "forcing" it couldn't be more personal for Tristan and his friends. Tristan may be a prostitute, but as an independent he was in control—not of individual encounters maybe, but at least of his client list and what he was willing to do for them.

As Simon gets to know Tristan better, he begins to question his own beliefs, and when Tristan's friends get involved, Simon realizes that a family you choose can mean a lot more than a family you're born into. Thanks to Simon's actions, Tristan has to choose between staying with his friends or losing his freedom-- unless Simon takes desperate steps to free the man he's coming to love.

Word Count: 69,595

Genre: Gay Contemporary Romance

Warning: This book contains graphic language and sexually explicit content. Intended for adult audiences only. Not intended for anyone under the age of 18.

Chapter One

"WHAT THE HELL are we doing here?" Micah hissed, looking around with a mix of disgust and apprehension on his face.

Tristan Beck frowned at him. Micah was a friend, but that didn't mean Tristan approved of all his decisions. No more than Micah approved of all of Tristan's. "We're here for Shane. It's his thing—be nice!"

"In what possible world are we living, when Shane Black's 'thing' is a fucking Puppy Parade?"

"It's a *Christmas* Puppy Parade," Tristan said, trying to pretend that made it all more understandable somehow. He looked out at the bewildering scene in front of him: dogs of all shapes and sizes, most in some sort of festive costume, milling about a park lined with booths selling a variety of canine products. Somehow, it was a fundraiser for the veterinary clinic where Shane worked, but Tristan wasn't quite sure of the details. He'd come to show his support, and he'd probably end up buying something for a dog he didn't even own, just because it seemed like the thing to do. That was all he knew.

And then Shane himself was coming over, Dodger trotting happily beside him. The little dog had probably doubled in size in the last month or so, but he could still be easily scooped up with one arm, and absolutely expected the treatment whenever he met a friend. Now, seeing Tristan, he gave a happy yip and tugged at his leash, almost shaking his Santa hat free in his enthusiasm. At least seeing the pup gave Tristan a direction for his inevitable consumerism—he'd buy the little dog a Christmas present from one of the booths. Hopefully the clinic got a cut of the profits or something.

He crouched to greet Dodger and smiled up at the dog's owner. Shane had his own Santa hat on, perched at a jaunty angle that would have been enough to make most men seem effeminate. If Tristan had tried it he knew he'd have looked like the twinkiest twink to ever twink down the streets of Twinksville. But somehow on Shane, the hat, even slanted as it was, seemed masculine. Macho, practically. All just part of the Shane mystique, Tristan figured.

"Thanks for coming, guys," Shane said as Tristan stood up.

Shane didn't lean in for the hug or kiss that he would have offered just a month or two earlier, and Tristan tried not to miss it. Shane had a boyfriend now, and Noah seemed happy to believe that Shane had come to him as something damn close to a virgin. Or at least happy to believe that Shane wasn't still friends with someone he used to fuck through the mattress on a fairly regular basis.

Tristan was pretty sure that if he ever got a serious boyfriend he'd pull all the same defensive bullshit Noah was working on, so he tried not to bust the guy's balls about it. And he tried not to miss Shane's more physical greetings.

"It's a great event," Tristan said. He actually meant it. The whole scene was strange, hard to understand, totally foreign to his traditional view of the world—but, still, great. "I think the pugs dressed as elves are going to have to come home with me. Do you guys offer gift wrapping?"

"You don't even want to hear how much that lady charges for her dogs," Shane told him. "Unless you've got savings I don't know about, they're out of your league."

Tristan adopted a lofty tone as he said, "How disappointing," and was ready to move on.

But Micah had been quiet for too long, and now he chipped in with, "Maybe you could get one of your clients to buy them for you. You're running out of room for storing the rest of their crap."

From someone else, it might have been innocent. It wasn't like Tristan ever hid the way he earned his living: he was a whore, and a damn good one, and his clients expressed their complete satisfaction with gifts as well as cash. Nothing he was ashamed of, and if someone else, like Shane, had made the comment, Tristan would have laughed it off. But from Micah?

"I guess you've got the right system," Tristan said. "Better to spend all your money on shit to smoke or shoot into your veins, right? It's so bourgeois to accumulate material goods."

3

"Okay," Shane said quickly. "Not the best conversation for a happy, family-time Puppy Parade. Right?"

Tristan looked at Micah, and Micah looked back at him, long enough for the truce to be declared and approved. This was Shane's thing, after all, and Micah was having a good couple days, clear-headed enough to remember he cared about his friends and didn't want to hurt them. So Tristan said, "Puppy Parades? *So bourgeois.*"

And Micah said, "The proletariat shudders and cries in despair."

Shane just shook his head. "I never have any idea what you two are talking about when you get going."

"That's because you, my friend," and Micah stretched up far enough to throw an arm at least part of the way across Shane's shoulders, "are a true member of the proletariat."

"Salt of the earth," Tristan agreed.

"Okay," Shane said, clearly tired of the topic. "That's great. But do either of you know the guy over there in the black Benz?"

All the lightness fizzed out of Tristan's mood. The fucker had followed him here? Was there no damn limit? He refused to turn around and look, so he asked, "Young Chinese guy? Be pretty hot if he wasn't an obvious psycho?"

Tristan should have known better, because now Shane was frowning at him, protective instincts clearly gearing up. "You having a problem with him?"

Tristan forced a laugh. "No, it's not a big deal. I've got it under control." Shane's squint showed that he wasn't fooled, so Tristan let go of the act and said, "Seriously, Shane, this is not one you want to get involved in. The guy is connected. *Very* connected. You trying to scare him off isn't going to work, and it would get both of us in way more trouble than we've got now."

"What kind of trouble do we have now, exactly?" Shane's voice was dangerously calm.

"It's just a nuisance. He wants me to work for him—or for his dad, or his uncle, or whatever. They're a pretty big family, and they're connected to other families. You know?"

"Triad?"

Tristan shrugged. He really tried to avoid any association with organized crime, and in Seattle it wasn't usually that difficult. So he didn't know all the details, not for sure. But what he believed? "Maybe not officially, but I think they've got relationships in that area, yeah."

"So how do you want to handle it?"

"I want to ignore it and hope it goes away," Tristan said. It was true, although probably not all that likely to work.

Shane didn't look even remotely satisfied by the plan. "You're *sure* he's connected?"

"I'm not sure about Triad, but his family? Shane, he's driving a brand-new Benz around. Seem like a typical low-level pimp to you?"

Clearly it didn't, but just as clearly Shane wasn't willing to follow Tristan's forget-it-and-hope plan. "How long's this been going on?"

Tristan sighed. Now Shane was going to be upset because he hadn't been notified earlier. "His guy talked to me last week. Really polite, just a business deal. Said he could hook me up with new clients, take care of things for me. I said I liked being an independent, he said I should rethink that, I said no. Same guy showed up the next day with this guy along for the ride. A bit more pressure that time, and mentions of the family. And since then? Nothing big. I'm just seeing this guy around town, way more often than makes sense. He's not doing anything, just—watching. It's creepy, but not a big deal."

"I don't like it," Shane said, in a way that suggested he was planning to do something stupid.

"It's my deal, Shane. I'll handle it my way. If I need you, I'll let you know, but don't go charging into my business without me asking you to."

Shane looked ready to rebel. "Ignoring it isn't going to work."

Unfortunately, he was right. And, just as unfortunately, he was going to get himself hurt if he tried to take on the Triad single-handedly. So Tristan decided to play to his strengths. A sweet smile for Shane, then an even sweeter one as he jogged across the road to the Benz.

The driver didn't even look surprised to see him coming, which was a bit annoying. And the bastard didn't roll down his window, just left Tristan standing there in the street, waiting for him.

Tristan's already-fake smile was feeling completely frozen by the time the guy gave a tiny nod and then jerked his head toward the passenger side of the car.

That hadn't been Tristan's plan. He wanted to talk in public, not climb into the psycho's car. But he could hear Shane coming up behind him, probably after taking a little time to find somewhere safe for Dodger, now ready to start yelling or smashing headlights or whatever other nonsense he could think of. Tristan knew that would lead to disaster.

He hated his plan already, but he had to keep going with it. So he dodged past Shane in his full mother-bear protective mode, scampered around the back of the car, and found that the driver had leaned over and pushed the passenger door open. Tristan darted inside, yanked the door shut, and heard the lock click just as Shane's hand grabbed the outside handle. Oh, Shane didn't like this, and Shane was almost certainly right.

But Tristan's decision had been made.

The Benz glided out into traffic, away from angry Shane and disapproving Micah, and Tristan turned in the seat so he could get a better look at the driver. This was going to be interesting.

~*~*~*~

SIMON YEUNG BELIEVED in being prepared. His uncle, who ran the family business and had raised him since he was a toddler, also believed in Simon being prepared. Simon wasn't one of Frank Yeung's natural children, so he needed to be useful in order to be accepted. Frank had never hidden that truth, and Simon had never doubted it.

So it made no sense for Simon to be driving down the street with the beautiful blond whore beside him, because taking the kid for a ride had *not* been part of the plan. Maybe later, if the whore continued to resist the family's business proposals, he'd be taken somewhere private and taught a few lessons about gratitude and respect. But that wouldn't be Simon's role, and he certainly couldn't do it now, when there'd been hundreds of witnesses seeing the whore climbing into Simon's car, perfectly healthy. No, Simon's uncle would not be impressed with the way things were happening here. The way Simon was *allowing* things to happen.

"So, how've you been?" the whore asked, his voice deliberately saccharine and light. "What have you been up to? Stalked anyone interesting lately?"

"Not that interesting, no," Simon replied. "Just another spoiled little duck who doesn't have the sense to take advantage of someone's generosity."

"Not really generosity if you have to *force* someone to take it."

"So you agree that I *could* force you, if I decided to?" Simon glanced over to get a look at the whore's expression. This was an important point, really. Was he being rebellious because he didn't know who he was dealing with, or was something else going on?

The whore just raised an eyebrow, then pointed out the windshield of the car. "You see that little girl up there on her bike? Looks about eight years old?" He paused to allow Simon to find the child, then said, "*She* could probably force me into doing something, if we're just talking about playing rough. Seriously, I am not a tough guy, not at all."

"But you have tough-guy friends, and you think they can help you?" Simon asked, thinking of the punk who'd been chasing after the car.

"No," the whore said, just a little too quickly. "My friends aren't part of this."

"They will be if I decide they should be." So that was useful information. The whore was protective of his friends—a vulnerability.

"Jesus," the whore said. "Why is this such a big deal? I mean, I'm good at my job, sure, but it's not like I'm *that* good. If you're just looking to recruit a few new employees, I can ask around and see if anyone's interested. But as it is? You made an offer; I said no. Why can't we both just walk away?"

Simon needed to be smart about this, and there was nothing to be gained by getting into an argument. Still, if he could solve this whole issue right now, it would be one less headache for him in the days to come. So he drove with a little more purpose, but didn't bother answering the question.

"What, are you giving me the silent treatment, now?"

The whore waited for about half a block. "Seriously, we aren't even going to talk?"

Another half-block. "Well, this is totally pointless then, isn't it? Can you just drop me back at the park?"

They made it at least two more blocks before "Okay, it doesn't have to be back at the park. You can just let me out here—"

The car slowed for a light and the whore reached for the door handle. Simon reached over and caught his wrist. Warm skin, the bones close to the surface, but not as frail as the whore pretended to be. "Stay put," Simon said. "We're almost there."

"Almost where?"

"Where we're going."

The whore's body stayed tense for longer than Simon had thought it would, but his conditioning eventually kicked in and he relaxed. If something was going to be done to you no matter what you said, it was generally safest to resist as little as possible. A smart whore knew that. Simon knew it, too.

They drove silently for another few blocks before pulling into the parking lot at the motel. It was owned by the family, and they kept a room around the back for private business.

The whore didn't seem impressed. "A motel? Seriously? Okay, but I charge a hundred bucks an hour, two hour minimum. For you, though? Two hundred bucks an hour."

"I know what you charge," Simon said. "That's how I know it's stupid of you to be turning down our offer, since you'd be making more with us *and* having more security."

He pulled into the spot in front of the room and looked over at the whore, who was looking back at him, a squint pulling his finely arched brows into—well, into brows that were arched just as finely, but at a different angle. "So, seriously, we're here to fuck? Is that what this is all about?"

"Come inside," Simon said. It was strangely pleasant to have the whore off-balance and confused. Simon was supposed to do his job because it was his job, not because he enjoyed it, but there was something about this situation tempting him to mix a little pleasure into his business. But, no. Uncle Frank wouldn't approve of that, and, really, neither would Simon.

Still, he let himself fall behind the whore as they walked the few short steps to the motel room door and took a quick moment to admire the lean, lithe body in front of him. And when the whore stopped at the locked door and waited, Simon leaned over his shoulder to use the key card instead of edging around beside him. A good opportunity to be up close, to take an illicit sniff of the warm skin of the whore's neck....

But then the lock beeped and lit up green, the whore pushed the door open and went inside, and the moment was over.

Simon took a moment to collect himself before he stepped into the room and closed the door behind him. He was in charge of this meeting.

So he looked at the whore and didn't look away. He wanted to see the reaction. Then he pulled out his wallet, not even looking down as he pulled two bills from where the hundreds should be and took a half-step forward to drop the money onto the foot of the bed. The widening of the whore's eyes was satisfying.

"Take off your shirt," Simon said. His voice came out a little lower than he'd intended.

"One of the best parts of being an independent is that I can pick my own clients." The whore's hands didn't move to his shirt.

Simon just grinned at him. "One of the best parts of not being stupid is I don't talk business if I think someone might be wearing a wire. So if you want to talk this through, you'll need to get naked and watch me put your clothes and everything else you're carrying outside the door."

The whore frowned at him. "Who says I want to talk it through? I just want you to leave me the fuck alone!"

"And you plan to achieve that goal through persuasion and conversation, don't you? Isn't that why you got in my car?"

"I honestly have no idea why I got in your car."

"Maybe you just felt like wasting my time?" Simon let his gaze sharpen. He wasn't above taking advantage of the typical *gwai lo* attitudes—if racist whites thought Chinese faces lacked expression and could be cold? Well, he'd show them non-expressive and cold. But he didn't seem to be having much of an effect on the whore.

"Maybe. Maybe I feel like you're wasting *my* time, following me around like you have been."

Simon tamped down the flair of irritation. He was supposed to be calm and efficient; there was room for emotion in business, but only at the top levels. At Simon's level? He was a tool, and tools didn't get irritated. "Please, then." He gestured toward the door. "Don't let me keep you."

"And this is over? We're done, now?"

"The meeting? The meeting never really began, as I recall. So, it's almost a philosophical question at this point—can something that never existed be said to be over?"

"Not the meeting. The rest of it."

"I can't see why anything that happened this afternoon would have any impact on anything else that's happening in your life. After all, nothing really happened this afternoon, right? Are we back to the philosophy? Can something that never existed have an impact on something that does exist?"

"So, I get naked or you bore me to tears with cut-rate pseudo-zen bullshit?"

"What is the sound of one duck quacking, little duckling?"

"Enough with the 'duck' stuff. I know you're calling me a whore, but are you even *from* China? Or Hong Kong or wherever they use that word?"

"If I were, your comments about my zen bullshit would be really culturally insensitive, wouldn't they?"

"I'm honestly supposed to be culturally sensitive to some Triad-connected pimp trying to strong-arm me into whoring for him instead of for myself?"

"If you can't be true to your principles when you're angry, are they truly your principles? Or are they just some cut-rate pseudo-hipster bullshit?"

The whore stared at Simon, and Simon stared back. Finally the whore said, "What the hell do you know about my principles?"

"You live like a peasant even though you make enough to maintain a much higher standard. You spend time with people who are going nowhere, even though you yourself could have a bright future, and are, in fact, planning for one. And you refuse a valuable business offer, one that would actually help you earn that bright future, because you think it's more important that you stay independent." He'd already said too much, but he didn't think the whore realized it. Which meant he could stop talking and go back to his plan. He didn't have to continue improvising. "So I know at least a little about your principles. The part where you'd think you were culturally sensitive was just an educated guess."

"My friends aren't going nowhere."

What a strange part of the speech to focus on. But Simon had gotten past his burst of loquacity. "Time will tell," was all he said.

The whore was beautiful when his face was relaxed, smiling at his friends. But he was something else altogether when his eyes blazed as they did there in the dingy motel room. Something that would be burned into Simon's memory for a very long time.

"I'm done with you," the whore said. "This is over. All of it. I'll stop working altogether before I work for you, and maybe you're thinking that the cops won't do much to help protect a whore from a pimp and maybe you're right, but they'll do more to protect someone who *isn't* a whore anymore." He pulled the hem of his shirt up in a bravado display of his wireless chest. Listening devices were so small these days that the show meant nothing; the mike could have been hidden in countless places in his clothes, or on his body. But it was still a nice show. "I came to this meeting in good faith. But I guess it was pointless, because there's really nothing to talk about. There are no compromises to be reached. I won't work for you. Not ever." He stepped a little closer and practically whispered as he said, "I understand that it's not a word you hear too often, but you need to hear it now, and believe it." He waited for an appropriately dramatic moment, then said, "No."

He turned and started for the door. Simon said, "You know how to get in touch with me, don't you? When you decide you've changed your mind?"

"I'm not going to decide that."

"So you won't take my card with you? I really think it might be useful."

The whore was suspicious, now. He knew he was being set up, or maybe just bluffed, but he didn't know what to do about it and fell back on his obstinacy. "I don't need your card."

Simon nodded. "I'll tell you what. Tomorrow evening, say— eight o'clock? I'll send a car around for you. I think by then you'll realize that we really do have a few things to discuss. If you'd still like to try this without talking, that's your choice. But I think you'll get in the car."

"I think you're going to be really, really surprised," the whore said.

And Simon smiled as he again said, "Time will tell."

Chapter Two

As soon as he was out of the motel room, Tristan called Noah, since Shane still hadn't quite mastered cell phone usage. He *had* a phone now, but he never seemed to remember to take it with him anywhere. And, honestly, it was a pretty cheap phone and might not have been able to stand up to the decibels of Shane's current roaring.

"That was the stupidest fucking thing you've ever done!" Shane yelled. Tristan had lowered the earpiece volume before he even dialed, but he still had to hold the phone away from his head to avoid being deafened. "Jesus Christ, Tristan, it's bad enough you take chances with your clients, but this crazy fucker isn't even paying you, and you know he's trouble, and you still get in the car with him? How the fuck am I supposed to keep you safe if you do shit like that?"

Tristan thought about mentioning the two hundred dollars that had been thrown so casually on the bed; the Chinese guy had clearly been *willing* to pay, even if Tristan hadn't bothered to take the cash. But pointing that out wouldn't really help. "We've been through this before, Shane. It's not your job to keep me safe. I mean, I appreciate your help, *when I ask for it*, but I'm not Dodger—I'm not your pet. I make my own decisions."

"Stupid fucking decisions," Shane replied, but the volume was lower. Not because Tristan had actually convinced him of anything, just because Shane's temper was truly explosive—a powerful burst, but not something that lasted too long.

"Probably," Tristan agreed. "But I needed to do *something*, right? And I'm not sure what the smart decision would actually be in this case."

"I've been trying to figure that out," Shane said. "But my brain hasn't been working too well, what with me completely freaking the fuck out over your insane behaviour."

"No, Shane, this isn't your problem. Except—" Shit, maybe this was actually a good plan. "Except I might need your help in one tiny area."

"Tell me," Shane demanded.

"Okay, it's probably not a big deal." Tristan wasn't sure whether he was doing the right thing. He needed to play this carefully—he was trying to give Shane an outlet, not set him off on a mission of pointless aggression. "And he didn't make any threats or anything. But he's just—I don't know, he's *aware* of my friends. He knows I care about you guys. So this is just guessing on my part—probably total paranoia, really. But he can't mess me up too bad, not if he actually wants me to be able to work for him, right?" Of course, that was assuming this still *was* about working for the family, rather than just being made an example of. But it was an assumption Tristan really wanted to make. "So I feel like I'm kind of safe, almost. But if he wanted to make a point with me, without actually hurting me…"

"You think he'd go after—who? Micah? He's so fucked up sometimes he barely knows where he is. He'd be easy. The girls, maybe? Becky's at your place a lot, and Amanda almost as much. Trey would be a harder target, probably." He stopped for a moment, then said, "Shit. There's quite a few of them. It's a lot of people to look out for."

"And it's not your job to actually protect them," Tristan said hurriedly. "Number one, I'm honestly not sure this is a real problem. And even if it was, you can't protect the whole world. I know that. And I'll talk to people when I see them and make sure they know to be a bit more careful. I'm just saying maybe you could keep your eyes open. And seriously, Shane, these guys are—" He stopped. It wasn't a conversation he really wanted to have on the phone. But he wasn't sure when he'd next see Shane, so he might as well do it. "These guys are who you could be, if you hooked up with someone bigger. You know? They're no tougher than you, no smarter than you. But they will be better armed than you, and there are just so many more of them. I have no doubt you could take them on, one-on-one and with no weapons. But that's not how they're going to fight, you know? And if you piss them off? They could come after all of us."

There was silence on the other end of the line as Shane digested all of that, and Tristan took the time to look around. He'd been walking as he talked, but without any clear direction in mind. He hadn't been paying much attention in the car, either, and didn't really know what part of town he was in. "Look, I'm working in a couple hours and I need to go home and get ready. There's nothing about this that's an immediate threat, so you don't need to do anything drastic, okay?" He was essentially asking a bird not to sing, but finally he heard Shane's reluctant grunt of agreement. "I'll talk to people, you'll keep your eyes open, and we'll all live happily ever after."

"I don't like it," Shane grumbled.

"I know. And I promise, man, if I need you, I'll call you. So, actually it wouldn't hurt if you started *carrying your fucking phone.*" At least that would give Shane a sense that he was doing something, being proactive in some tiny way.

"I will," Shane promised. "And you'll use it, right? If you need anything, if things just don't feel right—whatever. You'll call me."

"If I need you, I'll call you," Tristan promised. It wasn't exactly what Shane had been asking for and they both knew it, but hopefully it would be enough. "Thanks, Shane."

"Be careful," Shane ordered, and then the call ended.

Tristan wondered how much of the conversation Noah had heard, and how he felt about it all. Noah was a bit of an enigma, really. Shane was crazy about him and that was enough for him to have a place in their group, but in terms of really understanding the guy? Tristan tried to imagine himself as he'd have been if his parents hadn't kicked him out when he'd told them their latest attempt to have him pray the gay away hadn't worked. But that wasn't enough, because even if they hadn't kicked him out, they'd still have been doing their thing, making it crystal damn clear that he was broken, damaged, and wrong in their eyes. As far as Tristan could tell, Noah had been raised in a family that actually accepted him as he was; it was cool, but kind of hard to really envision. So Tristan had trouble predicting Noah's responses to things, and wasn't sure just how he'd feel about his boyfriend being mixed up in something like this.

But that was something for Shane and Noah to worry about. Tristan had his own problems.

The first one was figuring out where the hell he was and how he was going to get home. He found an intersection and called for a cab, gave his home address, and let his mind run over the meeting with the Chinese guy. Damn, had he ever said his name? Tristan didn't think so. Maybe it was part of the image, trying to be all mysterious, or maybe the asshole just didn't have the common courtesy to introduce himself to the people he was trying to intimidate.

It was a waste for someone that arrogant to be so damn beautiful, but probably that was part of the arrogance. He had looks, he had power, he had money, so why *wouldn't* he be full of himself?

Tristan's phone beeped just as he arrived home, and he paid the driver then looked down at the text he'd received. It was from Gary, the guy he was supposed to be meeting in a few hours.

Have to cancel tonight. Something came up. Sorry.

Tristan made a point of finding something attractive about every trick; if he couldn't find anything, it was really hard to play his part as convincingly as he wanted to. Gary was middle-aged, overweight, and balding, but he had brilliant blue eyes, and he was sweet. Sure, he was into some pretty twisted shit, but he always had a general level of concern for Tristan's comfort, and he tipped well. And he'd never cancelled an appointment at short notice before.

I was looking forward to seeing you, Tristan typed back. It wasn't completely untrue; he'd been looking forward to getting paid, at least. *I hope everything's okay? Do you want to set another date?*

There was a longer pause than there should have been, and then the words *I'll get back to you* appeared.

Maybe he was just busy. Whatever had happened to make him cancel that night might still be going on. It wasn't anything to worry about. But Gary always wanted to plan things out. In the last two years, Tristan didn't think he'd ever had a time when there wasn't a date with Gary on his schedule.

A good whore can't be needy. A good whore needs to remember that he exists to satisfy the client, not to be satisfied himself. But clients like to feel needed, right? They like to be wanted. So Tristan let himself text *Is everything okay?*

And there was no answer. Sometimes, Tristan's imagination was a really useful tool, but right then, it was anything but. What the hell had the damn Chinese gangster been so smug about as Tristan had been leaving the motel? Had he known this was going to happen? Had they gotten to Tristan's clients, somehow? Either threatened them or just offered them a better product at a lower price?

The money they'd been offering Tristan had been good. Really good. If he'd trusted them to actually follow through on their promises, he would have been damned tempted to take it. So if they were paying whores that well, they couldn't have undercut Tristan with his clients, could they?

Not if they were trying to make money, no. But if they were just trying to make a point?

He felt like a tiny fish who'd somehow caught the attention of a shark. Maybe it would be hard for the shark to actually catch him, but if it just wanted to make his life miserable? That wouldn't be a problem.

So maybe it was time to do what he'd said he would. He climbed the stairs to his apartment and let himself inside. Maybe it was time to get out of the game. He'd figured he probably had another couple years in him, but maybe this was a sign.

Becks was sitting in the living room, watching TV. She looked stoned, as usual. "Hey," she said vaguely as he came into the room.

"Hey," he answered. He didn't have to play the gracious host to people who practically lived at his place, so that was all he bothered with.

Instead of talking, he headed into his bedroom, careful to shut the door behind him. He went to the far corner and was careful to lift the bedside table rather than making any noise by dragging it across the floor; he trusted Becks, more or less, but not enough to let her in on his secret. He hadn't even told Shane the details.

With the table out of the way, he dug his fingernails into the loose floorboard and pulled it back, then reached inside. He didn't need to count the money he had stashed in there; he knew how much there was right down to the last dollar. But it was comforting to—

His hand found nothing. The space between the joists was empty.

No, no, no.

He yanked the board harder, not worrying about noise anymore, and ripped it right out of the floor. He had a clear view now, and he ran his eyes and then his hand up and down the space. The empty space.

There was no way. It couldn't have been lost, couldn't have fallen through. Solid plywood below, solid two-by-sixes on two sides, and the stacked two-by-fours he'd added at either end of the space, paranoid that some marauding rat or something might get to his savings. None of that had been tampered with. The only way out was through the floor of his bedroom.

He pushed to his feet, sprinted to the living room, and saw Becks sit up in alarm. "Were you in my room?" he demanded. "Who was here? Who was in my room?" Micah was the logical suspect—he'd stolen before when he'd been desperate to support his habit. Had he left the puppy parade and come back to the apartment?

Becks blinked hard, then said, "The maintenance guys were here. The bug killers. What are they called?"

"Exterminators?" Tristan had lived in the building for over two years, complained about bugs countless times, and never gotten any attention. "Exterminators came? You let them in?"

"They said they were doing the whole building. They said they had to do it that way."

"Were you here while they were working?"

"No, they said it was poison and I had to leave for a couple hours. I went to Starbucks, and then walked around for a while."

Jesus Christ. Fuck. Shit, fuck, shit. Not Micah, which was easier to accept but harder to do anything about. "What company were they from? Did they leave a card or anything?"

"No." She frowned. "And it was weird, because Mrs. Moonie from down the hall came over and asked about them. She asked what you'd done to get them to do your apartment, when they didn't do hers. But they told me they were doing the whole building."

Shane stared at her and tried to make sense of it all. "What did they look like? Did you see their van, or truck?"

25

"I didn't see it. And they were just… guys. They were wearing coveralls." She frowned. "And they were all Chinese, I think. Like, speaking it, not just looking it."

He stared at her. There were lots of Chinese people in Seattle. If these guys were still speaking it, they were probably first generation, and first generation tended to stay with others from their old country, and maybe they started a business or got hired by someone who put them all on the same team, or—anything. It could all be a coincidence.

But he thought about the gangster, the smug confidence as he'd promised to send a car. That son of a bitch hadn't just scared off Tristan's clients, he'd stolen his life savings.

And Tristan had no way to get in touch with him until eight o'clock the next evening.

~*~*~*~

SIMON HAD BREAKFAST at the family home almost every morning. It didn't matter how late he'd been up the night before, doing family business, he was still expected to make an appearance.

He had three cousins, all of whom still lived in the home and came down for breakfast if they felt like it. Laurence was the youngest and still in college, but he spent most of his time drunk and hanging out with his friends; Michelle was in the middle and worked as a fashion designer, although Simon had never seen anyone wear her clothes unless they were getting paid for it; and Mitchell was the oldest, being groomed to take over the family business. He was the only one in the dining room when Simon arrived.

"I'm going to need your services this afternoon," he announced as Simon picked a plate up from the buffet table.

Services, not help. Mitchell would never lower himself to actually ask for Simon's help. Simon smiled blandly. "What will you need?" he asked.

"The contractors on the Capitol Hill project are behind schedule," Mitchell said. "I'd like you to take care of that."

The contractors who had been behind schedule on the last two projects. The contractors Mitchell had selected for a third project, against Simon's advice. But Simon had fixed things, more or less, the two times before, so now of course it was Simon's job to fix things again.

He'd taken an English literature course in his first year of college in order to fulfill some requirement or another, and he'd been in a study group with a girl who'd gone on and on about how stupid the characters were in the Jane Austen novel they'd been assigned. "Why do they put up with this crap from their families?" she'd demanded. "Why don't they just walk out and refuse to come back until they're treated better?"

Simon hadn't bothered to answer her question, but he'd had no trouble identifying with the characters in the book. No trouble at all. "I'll see what I can do," he said now.

"Of course you will," his uncle said from the doorway, his accent barely even detectable. He was the last one in the family to have been born in Hong Kong, and while he'd insisted that all the children learn both Cantonese and Mandarin, he rarely spoke either language himself. He was, as always, dressed impeccably in a dark suit and crisp white shirt, his greying hair smooth and tidy, his eyes sharp behind his wire-framed glasses. "You'll fix things because you're our fixer. Isn't that right?"

"I try to be," Simon said.

"It's too bad we have to work you so hard," Frank continued, and there was an edge to his voice that set Simon on guard. His uncle was angry about something, and that was never good. But he turned his gaze to Mitchell instead of Simon as he said, "It's too bad your cousin has to rescue you again, isn't it? Too bad you can't learn from your mistakes?"

Simon wanted to get the hell out of there, but it was too late. His uncle was giving this speech now because he wanted an audience, but not a large one. He wanted to humiliate his son without embarrassing the family. So the dressing-down would take place with a family witness, not in public. That was what his uncle wanted, and Simon knew better than to try to change the course of events now.

Mitchell, of course, glared at Simon as if this was all his fault. "Simon's *job* is to take care of these little details—"

"Managing that project is *your* job! Your only job. If your only job is 'a little detail', and you can't even get that right, what does it say about you?"

There was no way for Simon to turn this into anything but a negative. Family relations with Uncle Frank weren't a zero-sum game; just because he was angry with Mitchell didn't mean he'd be any happier with Simon. And being scolded in front of Simon would absolutely do nothing to improve cousinly relations that were already fairly strained. But things would just get worse if Simon tried to leave or, god forbid, intervene. So he scooped some fresh fruit onto his plate and stood awkwardly, waiting for it to be over.

Uncle Frank had a few more choice words to share with his son, and then he turned to Simon. "And you," he spat. "You're supposed to be helping David Chen's boy, not wasting time cleaning up after people who can't do their jobs. Have you got that situation under control?"

It wasn't the first time Simon had thought of the whore recently, but it was certainly the first time in a while he'd thought of him in a purely business sense. "I believe so, yes. We have a meeting tonight, and I think everything will fall into place after that."

"Good," his uncle grunted. "Chen's a dirtbag, running whores like a common criminal, but he's well connected and I want him on our side. You understand?"

"Yes, Uncle."

"So why are you waiting until tonight? Why the hell are you standing around here, eating my food, when you should be out there making Chen happy?"

It had been Uncle Frank who'd *taught* Simon to make a plan and see it through, damn it. And now the man wanted Simon to start improvising? "Everything's in place," he said. "I'm just waiting for the whore to be desperate enough to realize his mistakes."

Uncle Frank glared at him for half a breath, then nodded curtly. "Make sure it works," he growled.

The three of them sat at the table in stony silence until Aunt May arrived, all silk and perfume and cheek kisses, but with eyes just as sharp as her husband's. Just as sharp but, at least in Simon's experience, considerably kinder. She clearly noticed the tension as soon as she came into the room, but she defused at least some of it with a kiss to her husband's cheek and her son's temple, and then she sank into her seat at the end of the table and said, "Simon, bring me coffee, won't you?"

She wasn't treating him as a servant, she was including him in the group. She was doing it in a way that wouldn't anger her son or husband, of course, but he understood about that. Aunt May had kept him sane, growing up in this house, and he'd jump off a cliff for her if she asked him to. Fetching coffee was nothing.

So he added the milk and sweetener he knew she liked, then arranged a few pieces of fruit on the saucer and delivered it to her. He stayed on his feet after his task was complete.

"Thank you for breakfast," he said, just as he'd said pretty much every day of his life. "I'll speak to the contractors this afternoon, and I'll deal with the other matter this evening."

His cousin glared, his uncle scowled, and his aunt smiled serenely. Just another morning at the Yeung house. He made his escape, and as he sank into the plush leather seats of his Mercedes, he found himself thinking about the stubborn whore. So determined to be independent. What must that feel like? Was it lonely? Frightening?

Or was it exhilarating?

Lap Dog

Chapter Three

THE CAR WAS LATE. For more than twenty-four hours, Tristan had been rattling off the walls, snapping at his friends, refusing to tell Shane or anyone else what he was upset about, and waiting for the damn car to show up so he could go find that arrogant, thieving son-of-a-bitch and—do something. The last part was a bit shaky, really, but Tristan was too damn wired to even begin thinking of a plan. He needed his money back, he needed his clients back, and he would just have to make that happen.

And now the damn car was late.

Had he gotten something wrong? The bastard had said the car would pick him up at eight; that was definite. But maybe there'd been some confusion about *where* he'd be picked up? But where else, if not at home? At the motel? Shit, Tristan couldn't remember the name of the place, wasn't even sure where it was, other than a vague general idea about the part of town they'd been in. Was he supposed to be there?

No, that made no sense. Did it? No, probably not. Unless—

There was another damn black Mercedes, cruising down the street toward him. This one was a conservative sedan instead of the asshole's sportier model, with dark-tinted windows. Tristan took a deep breath and tried to look calm as the vehicle pulled to a smooth stop in front of him.

The man who climbed out of the driver's side was wearing a uniform that looked almost like a suit. "Mr. Beck?" he asked politely, as if he didn't know what Tristan was.

"Yeah," Tristan replied. He suddenly wished he was better dressed. His choice of clothing had been based on a general sort of *fuck him* when he thought about what the asshole would be expecting him to wear, but now his snug jeans and even snugger T-shirt definitely felt too casual. His leather jacket had been a gift from a client and had probably cost a lot, which was something, at least. And the driver already had the back door open and was waiting for Tristan to climb in, so he did what was expected of him.

There was no one else in the back of the car. Tristan's clients sent cars for him often enough that he knew the drill pretty well. He was essentially a product, and the drivers were delivery men. The vehicle was fancier than it might be for other goods, but that was for the benefit of the clients, not the product.

Tristan tried to come up with a plan as he was driven through the darkened streets of the city. He'd had two more clients cancel on him that day, neither with any explanation. If that was a sign of what was coming, he couldn't expect to make much more money from whoring. Which would have been okay, except his damn savings were gone. So he couldn't make money, and he didn't have the money he'd already made that would have allowed him to retire with a little dignity. He was backed into a corner, and he knew it.

He could leave town, go somewhere else, and start over. Back on the streets? That was how he'd started here, picking up random clients and sorting through them for the most palatable, most stable ones to become his regulars. But damn it, he was too old for that shit.

So maybe he'd find someone to work for. An agency, maybe down in Los Angeles, or in New York, or wherever he wanted, really. That wouldn't be so bad. Except he'd be leaving all his friends behind, and he'd be losing his independence, the one thing that had made him turn down the offer from these assholes in the first place.

And, damn it, he wanted his money back! He'd worked his ass off, he'd put up with a lot of shit, and that money was all he had to show for it. He knew better than to start whining about what was fair—the world wasn't fair, and only children believed that it was—but there was still something deep inside him that revolted at the idea of just walking away, just letting himself be robbed. It wasn't about justice, it was about not giving up. The world might not be fair, but that didn't mean he wouldn't keep fighting.

He looked out the window and realized they were heading into the financial district. Not exactly what he'd been expecting, not after the rundown motel of the previous meeting. He tapped on the opaque glass that separated the front of the car from the back, and it lowered as if the driver had just been waiting with his finger on the switch.

"Can you give me an address of where we're going?" Tristan asked.

And the driver did, casual and easy. Tristan typed the address into his phone and sent it to Trey. They'd set this system up well before Shane had entered the digital age and gotten a phone of his own, but even if Shane *had* been able to receive texts, it wouldn't have made sense to get him involved. If Tristan was going to something he thought was dodgy, he'd text Trey and Trey would just accept the information and not ask too many questions. Given the same address, Shane would probably charge down and try to fight his way to Tristan's side without further invitation. Definitely best to do this through Trey.

But unless the driver was truly clueless, the fact that he'd given the address so easily was its own kind of reassurance. And the building they stopped in front of seemed so glossy and respectable it was hard to imagine anything dangerous ever happening in it.

Stupid illusion, of course, and Tristan of all people should know that the wealthy were at least as cruel and twisted as the poor, but he pushed his fear to the back of his mind anyway.

The driver opened his door and Tristan felt a moment of self-conscious awareness. He was dressed like a street whore, about to go into a ritzy office building. Sure, it was after hours, but there'd be people working late. Respectable people with families and values and shit, people who'd look at him and know he was out of place and—

He stepped out of the car and shrugged his jacket, his only claim to moderate respectability, off his shoulders. What the fuck did he care if the assholes in this building didn't want to look at a whore? That was their problem, and maybe, if Tristan was lucky, it could be the Chinese asshole's problem as well. If the fucker wanted to deal with whores, he could deal with this.

Tristan's strut had a lot of slink in it as he headed for the front door of the building. He felt his shirt riding up to expose a little skin at his waist and didn't even think about tugging it back down. His skin was always pale, and even whiter now in the Seattle winter, and he had a quick, mad flash in his mind, a startling picture of how that whiteness would contrast against golden Asian skin.

Damn it, he hated his imagination sometimes.

The driver was coming inside with Tristan, which raised some questions about parking legalities but at least made it easier to figure out where to go. They cruised past the security desk with only a nod between the driver and the guard, then headed for an elevator, where the doors opened as soon as the driver hit the button. It was all so smooth, so easy. And these guys were just the *minions* of the rich, not even rich themselves. If Tristan worked for whoever the Chinese guy wanted him to, Tristan would probably make more than the driver or the guard, and he'd be one of the minions, one of the people benefitting from the halo of ease and efficiency that seemed to surround the very wealthy.

As the elevator whirred and rose, Tristan tried to remember why he'd refused the initial offer. More money, more safety, more ease. What had he objected to, exactly? Why had he been so damn stubborn and brought all this trouble down on himself?

The doors opened directly into a lobby, with a beautifully carved reception desk directly in front of visitors, couches backed by huge matching aquariums on either side. There was a polished blond woman at the desk, and her smile was cool and professional. Still no words, though, and no sign or anything to indicate the name of the company that owned this space. The blond hit a button, the glass doors beside her desk slid open, and the driver nodded Tristan through.

"Double doors at the end of the hall," the driver said, and Tristan was almost startled to hear a human voice.

He stepped through the doorway and the door slid shut behind him. He resisted the urge to turn around and see if he could open it. If he could, he'd feel foolish for having tried, and if he couldn't? Well, maybe it was better to delay that realization for as long as possible.

The hallway was long, but wide enough that it didn't make him feel claustrophobic even with all the frosted glass doorways closed. About half-way to the end he reached over and tried one of the doorknobs, but it was locked.

A rat in a maze. He was pretty sure there were cameras on him, recording his reactions in case anyone cared enough to ever study him.

And *this* was why he'd rejected the offer for an easier life. He didn't want to be a rat, or a cog in a machine, or an animal in a damn zoo. Maybe life was easier for birds living in a bird cage instead of the wild, but there was more to life than making things easy.

He turned back toward the double doors at the end of the hall and strode forward. More strutting, because if he was on camera, he might as well put on a worthwhile show. He'd make a grand entrance, and that would be something, at least.

But when he got to the conference room and the doors slid open before him, he stepped in and found the space empty. A wall of windows at one end, lots of modern furniture, glass and metal and monochromatic décor, but no people. So much for making an entrance.

He looked around, thought about leaving, and then remembered how much he needed his money, and his clients. He *needed* this meeting, and the bastard wasn't going to show up?

No. This was just another way to fuck with Tristan's head. Another way to get him off-balance and out of control.

He looked around the room and then strode deliberately to the chair at the far end of the table. It was the same design as all the others, but it had the wall of windows behind it so it seemed like the place where people's eyes would be drawn. Tristan bet this was the place the most important person sat in meetings. So he sank his ass down into the surprisingly comfortable seat, leaned back, kicked his booted feet up onto the glass table and tried to look relaxed.

He sat like that for twenty-five goddamn minutes. He knew the exact time because there was a clock projected onto the wall from some unknown source, counting it off down to the exact second, and he forced himself to stay completely still for five minutes at once, and then challenged himself to extend the stillness for another five minutes. The first five had been easy, but each successive round had made him more and more agitated, at least internally. His money. His clients. His future. And the asshole didn't even have the courtesy to be on time to discuss it all?

When the zeroes showed up for the twenty-sixth minute, Tristan pushed away from the table with so much energy his chair almost tipped over. He paced to the giant windows, looked out at the lights of the city, and tried to think of what should come next. He wanted to go, wanted to storm out and maybe smash a few things on the way, but where would that leave him?

A rustling sound caught his attention and he whirled to find the Chinese guy sinking gracefully into the power chair. Bastard had been watching from another room and snuck in when Tristan was distracted. Son of a bitch, he was smooth.

"Thank you for coming," the asshole said without even glancing in Tristan's direction. "If you'll come sit down, we can get started."

"We could have gotten started twenty-five minute ago," Tristan groused. He didn't leave the window.

"I don't see how," the guy responded. "I wasn't *here* twenty-five minutes ago, and I don't think I'm being arrogant when I say that I'm really a fairly important part of this meeting." He swivelled the chair around, finally, and smiled calmly. "But I'm here now, so if you'd like to sit down—"

"I've been sitting for a while. I'd like to stand."

"Of course." Tristan was pretty sure the rules of power dynamics said he should be the one in charge, since he was standing and therefore physically higher, but clearly the Chinese guy wasn't familiar with those rules. He seemed completely at ease, and completely in control. "I'm glad you changed your mind about coming to this meeting," he said smoothly. "Now we just need to find a way for you to change your mind about the other proposal in front of us."

"I changed my mind about coming to this meeting because you robbed me and you're scaring my clients away!"

"So the situation has changed, and now you need to re-evaluate your decision. There's no shame in that. The greatest strength of the human species is our adaptability, after all."

"You seriously think you're going to *force* me into working for you?"

"You wouldn't be working for me. This really isn't my line of business, traditionally. And I don't know that the word 'force' is appropriate. But I do think you're going to make a different decision today than you made a week ago, yes. Why wouldn't you?"

Tristan had no answer. The situation *had* changed. He *was* adaptable. He just—just couldn't bring himself to give in. So he tried to change the subject. "This isn't your usual business? You just decided to freelance a little?" And now that he started thinking, he realized this was something he should know. "Why? Why is it so important to you, so important to *anyone*, that I work for you?"

The man thought for a moment, giving the impression he was deciding whether to answer the question truthfully. Finally he gave a little shrug and said, "It's not important. Not to me, at all. To others? You'd be an asset, of course. You're attractive, and we've had reports that say you're good at your job. You're reasonably intelligent and could be trained to be much *better* at your job. But there are others out there who'd do just as well as you will."

Tristan wanted to demand more, but instead he waited, and his patience was rewarded with a gentle smile. Then the guy said, "People sometimes talk about 'face' as if it's a uniquely Asian concept, but obviously it isn't. Westerners know the importance of saving face as well."

"And this is about someone saving face?"

"Of course. You've been chosen; for you to reject the honor would be insulting to the one who made the choice. It would lessen his standing, and make it more difficult for him to do business in the future."

It wasn't exactly a new idea but it was somehow startling to hear it expressed so frankly. Which brought up another question. "Why aren't we playing the stripping game today? Why can you talk to me now when you couldn't talk to me yesterday?"

"This is a more sophisticated venue than yesterday. I don't pretend to understand the technology," and he gave an airy, dismissive wave toward the walls and ceiling, "but I trust it. This room is secure. You aren't transmitting anything." Then a half-smile. "But if you'd like to strip, I won't object."

"What's your name?" Tristan hadn't known he was going to ask the question and really wasn't sure why he cared, but for some reason, he did. He needed to personalize things, needed to remember he was talking to a human being, not a robotic representative of a faceless master.

And the question didn't seem to cause any surprise. Instead, the man rose gracefully to his feet and took three steps forward, standing in front of Tristan with his hand extended. "My apologies. If I'd known we were going to be spending more time together, I would have introduced myself at the first meeting. I'm Simon Yeung. It's been a pleasure getting to know you."

Tristan scowled at the offered hand and kept his own at his sides. "By spying on me. Stalking me. That's how you got to know me. And you're saying it was a pleasure?"

"Yes. Well, often it was boring. But there were moments of pleasure." Yeung dropped his hand with an expression that made it clear he regretted Tristan's lack of manners but wasn't personally upset by anything. "Have you stood for long enough? Would you like to come over and sit down and we'll try to sort all this out?"

"I'd *like* my money and my clients back!"

"Good. We have a good starting point. You've told me what you want, and you know what I want. So—let's talk about how we can both end up with what we want."

"I also want my independence and my freedom," Tristan added desperately. He felt as if this conversation was sliding away from him, slipping down a slope toward an inevitable conclusion.

Yeung nodded. "I understand. I think you may need to sacrifice a little of that in order to achieve your other goals, but let's talk about ways to make sure the sacrifice is minimized."

The words burst from Tristan's lips. "This is my *life*. You're talking as if it's nothing important, just a puzzle to be solved, but that's bullshit. You've backed me into a corner, and now you're acting like you're a fucking good guy for opening up a tiny door that lets me get away from you? You're a fucking psychopath!"

Yeung didn't even blink. "I don't think this will be your life, Tristan. It will be a few years of employment. That's all."

Tristan wanted to cry. He wanted to let himself crumble to the floor and curl up and start sobbing. But if he did, fucking Yeung would probably just sit there and do some paperwork or something until Tristan was done, and then they'd start this whole damn conversation all over again.

"Sleep deprivation," he said. "That's why you made me wait until tonight for this meeting. You knew I wouldn't be able to sleep last night. And making me wait—obviously a power thing. Being in your offices, the way this place is designed, so cold and everything—it's all about making me crazy, right?"

"No, not crazy. That wouldn't do any good for anybody. But, yes, I did want to give you enough time to realize how serious this is. How serious *I* am."

"You've got a way to twist everything around, don't you? A way to make it seem like you're the good guy, and I'm being unreasonable."

"This really isn't about good guys or bad guys. It's just business. Someone made you an offer, and under the circumstances at the time you refused the offer. So I changed the circumstances."

"And if I walk out of here? If I decide I'd rather give up all my money and give up my clients and start fresh somewhere else? Then what happens?"

Yeung frowned. "Then I'd have failed, and I'd have to pass the job along to others. I can't predict what they would do, and I'd prefer not to speculate. But, really, Tristan. There was a significant amount of money in that envelope. Knowing what I do about your income and expenses, I can say it must have taken you several years to save that much. Probably your entire career. So if you walk away from your savings, and from the friends you've made here in Seattle, it would be as if you were throwing away years of your life. You'd have nothing to show for your time but some memories. I don't really think you'll choose to do that, not when the alternative is just to continue doing work similar to what you've been doing all along, for another few years, still with all your friends and the life you've built for yourself here. It wouldn't make sense for you to walk away."

Tristan had spent years trying to curb Shane's instinct to respond with *Fuck You* whenever faced with anyone more powerful than himself. But now, in this cold glass tower with this impossibly smooth man and his completely amoral logic, Tristan felt the same impulse. *Fuck you, Simon Yeung. Why? Because fuck you.*

But that wasn't going to get him anywhere. He needed a plan. He needed to think. He needed to—god damn it. Did he need to give in?

Chapter Four

EVERYTHING WAS GOING according to plan. The whore was no longer stubbornly defiant; now he was desperate, just as Simon had intended. If he'd been a different sort of person, someone who took satisfaction in his work, he'd be anticipating imminent satisfaction. As it was, though? He made the next move because it was the logical thing to do. That was all.

"I can arrange to have your money paid back to you," he said. "Not all at once, but as bonuses for good work. And your clients? Most of them won't be able to afford your new rates, but if you have a few favorites, I could see about giving them a discount. It would be your choice who should receive that favor."

"How did you scare them away? Are they going to *want* to come back?"

"There was no fear. Simply—well, I'm sorry to say it, but we offered them a better product at a lower price. An introductory deal, of course, although I'm not sure we mentioned that to them."

The whore didn't like that, Simon could tell. It stung his pride to think of his clients preferring someone else. And it was his pride that was getting in the way of changing his mind about the job offer. "I could arrange to have you meet the young men we found for them, if you like. You could learn from your competition and become *better* than them. You clearly have the raw materials— your face, your body, your mind. You just haven't been exposed to the proper resources. You could become truly magnificent, a polished diamond in a beautiful setting."

"Things get cut away when a diamond gets polished, right? They slice off the parts they don't want and just keep the parts that are pretty for other people."

Simon's smile was genuine. "You're quick. Smart. That's good, you know. It'll be very useful."

"But not smart enough to outsmart you, right? I'm not smart enough to think of a way out of this."

"You already have thought of a way out of it. You could run. You'd have to go pretty far, and you'd have to be pretty careful, but you could run and hide, if you thought it was best. So, yes, you've outsmarted me, if that's the choice you decide to make. I just don't think it's the choice that would give you the best outcome. But it's up to you to decide that, ultimately."

The whore was pacing now, his body a bright presence blotting out the darkness of the nightscape behind him. "Does none of this bother you? I mean, you're essentially forcing me into prostitution, and that's just all in a day's work for you?"

"You've been a prostitute for almost four years, according to my research. Full time, at least. Maybe you dabbled a little before that? I didn't bother to dig all the way down to your traumatic childhood. But let's not pretend I'm corrupting an innocent, here."

"What if I told you I'd quit? If you give me my money back, I'll retire. Would that work? You could tell—whoever—that you chased me out of the business. Wouldn't that be enough?"

It would be so simple if Simon could just agree to that, but he shook his head instead. "No. It wouldn't be enough. They don't want you out of the business, they want you *in* the business."

"And it's your job to make that happen."

"I think maybe you've personalized this a bit too much." Possibly because Simon had gone out of his way to be seen while he was following the whore, for some reason he still didn't understand. He'd *made* the whore think Simon was the enemy. "This really isn't about me. It's barely even about you. This is all much larger, and we're just—"

"Cogs in a machine, rats in a cage, animals in a zoo." The whore sounded bitterly amused.

"I was going to say 'very small parts', but your more figurative language is fine, if you prefer. The point is, it's not a contest between you and me. It's between you and a much larger body. And between you and them? I'm sorry, but there really *is* no contest. They win. That's the way it is."

"So it makes sense that it isn't personal to *you*. But you really expect it to not be personal for *me*?"

Well, that was a good point, but not one that Simon could really afford to entertain. "It's business, isn't it? Sometimes in business, we do things we don't enjoy. You must have—I'm sorry if I'm being insensitive, but in your working life, you must have found yourself doing things for money that you wouldn't have done if there weren't money involved? This is something similar."

"So if I'm a whore, that's it for me? That extends to every aspect of my damn life?"

What was it about this creature that got under Simon's skin? Why did he want to argue with him instead of just handling him? He tried to control his urges as he said, "I really don't think it's my place to speak to every aspect of your life—do you? I'm talking about business."

The whore didn't say anything for a moment. He looked out the window, and Simon took a moment to appreciate the view. The whore was almost as tall as Simon, but thinner, and his skin and hair were so light he sometimes seemed ethereal. He destroyed that illusion as soon as he opened his mouth, of course, but proper training would teach him to keep his mouth closed, at least for purposes of communication.

Strange that Simon found himself thinking about that as something regrettable rather than an obvious improvement.

Then the whore turned around, and it was as if the lights in the room dimmed. As if the stars themselves, twinkling behind him, were lessened. Because the whore had somehow made himself glow from within, calling all light to him, leaving none for any other source.

Fanciful nonsense, of course, but Simon couldn't deny the way his breath caught and his pulse quickened.

The whore took two steps forward, two steps closer to Simon, closer to a fire that threatened to burn out of control, but he still seemed cool and untouchable. "You've done an excellent job," the whore purred. "You've caught me. Trapped me. You're very good at what you do."

And it was as if the extra words slipped into Simon's mind unbidden. *You're valuable. You're worthwhile. I care about you, just for you.* Sentimental bullshit, but still, he could almost hear the whore crooning the words into his ear.

"You've won," the whore said. "If that matters to you? I surrender." And there, only a step away from Simon, the whore fell to his knees. "I submit," he whispered, and Simon's cock pulsed in time with the words.

Then the whore said, "Can you help me? Can I be yours, instead of theirs?" and Simon's mind returned to his body. Of course the whore would try this. Simon had *known* the whore would try this, and he'd thought he'd been prepared. He just hadn't realized how very good the whore was. Watching from a distance had taught Simon some things, but not *every* thing. He'd never felt the beam of charisma shot in his direction before, and it was enough to make him re-evaluate his earlier promises. Was there anything Chen's whores could teach to this magical creature, any way for him to become a more polished gem than he already was?

"What would that mean?" he asked. He knew he needed to resist. He *was* resisting, really. It just might look like capitulation from the outside. "If you were mine, what would that look like?"

"What would you want it to look like?" the whore asked. He seemed so sweet, so sincere. "What could I give you? What could I do for you?" He'd somehow shuffled closer, far too close for Simon's peace of mind, and as he reached his hands out to rest gently on Simon's thighs, it was almost impossible to keep intelligent thoughts at the forefront. "I'd be yours, Simon. What would you want from me?"

It was the use of his name that brought Simon completely back to himself. "What would I want that I couldn't get for two hundred dollars an hour?" he asked, pretending to consider it. "I can't think of anything, really."

"Two hundred dollars an hour buys you an act," the whore said. "What I'm offering is the real thing. Genuine gratitude, and genuine submission."

Simon's laugh was a mark against his professionalism, but at least he resisted the urge to reach out and touch the whore's face. "Grateful, maybe. But have you ever been genuinely submissive toward anyone in your entire life, little duck?"

"You'd be the first." Velvet over gravel, soft but firm: the whore's voice cut through Simon like a laser beam.

"This is your final effort, then?" Simon asked. He couldn't recall a time he'd had to fight harder to maintain the calm façade. "We've had the anger, the desperation, and now we have the seduction? When this is over, you'll accept that it's time to discuss things like adults?"

The whore drew back as if he'd been slapped, but then forced a smile onto his sculpted face. "Everything I'm suggesting here is *definitely* best suited for adults."

"No," Simon said. Amazing how difficult it was to express that one syllable. "Neither one of us is in charge of things, but that doesn't mean we're on the same team. Not at all. So I appreciate your offer, but if I feel the need of your services, I'll arrange them through traditional channels."

The whore's eyes narrowed. He'd abased himself and it had done him no good; of course he was angry. Simon genuinely wished he could find a way to make this easier for him, but possibly the kindest thing was to be quick and firm. "Stand up," he said. Not quite an order, but close enough.

Close enough that of course the whore couldn't follow it. But he couldn't stay on his knees, either, not now that his offer had been rejected. So he rolled to the side a little, shifted onto his ass and sprawled there on the polished floor, legs spread in a casual invitation for Simon to lower himself and nestle between them. Damn. Not easy to resist.

But Simon managed, and leaned back in his chair again. "Fine. Don't stand up. Play with little rebellions if you want to. But the big rebellion is over." He reached into the breast pocket of his jacket and pulled out a folded sheet of paper. "This is your schedule for the next two days. Wardrobe, hair—I don't know or care what it all is, I just care that you show up on time and are reasonably cooperative while you're there. You have a meeting with your new employer Wednesday afternoon—it's all written down."

"And if I don't show up?"

"I've already told you. If you don't show up, it's out of my hands. And I don't want to speculate about what will happen. But I should let you know—when I was watching you over the last week? I was taking notes, and I've forwarded them to interested parties. So everywhere you went, everyone you saw—all your friends—they aren't a secret. You understand what I'm saying?"

The whore rolled to his feet, fast and aggressive, and leaned over Simon. "You're threatening my friends, you son of a bitch? No. Don't you dare. They aren't part of this! This is between you and me."

"No, it's not." Simon stayed completely still in his chair, refusing to lean away or drop his gaze. "This is between you and a large, powerful, unforgiving organization. It's not even an organization I work for, most of the time. You need to stop focusing on me as a person, and start focusing on me as a messenger. Do you understand that? Do you understand the message I'm giving you?"

"Pretty fucking convenient for you to be able to separate yourself from it all like that. Is that how you're able to sleep at night?"

"I'm beginning to think you're *willfully* ignoring the truth in order to focus on insignificant details. How I sleep or don't sleep doesn't matter. You've been chosen to become part of an organization that doesn't take 'no' for an answer. That's all you need to be thinking about."

For a moment, Simon thought the whore's fury would overcome him. It was fascinating, almost hypnotic, to watch his eyes blaze with righteous anger, and then to see the rage—not dispel. No, it would be a mistake to think the rage was gone. But the whore controlled it. He pushed it away, saved it for later, and finally frowned in seemingly genuine thoughtfulness. "So that's that?" he asked. "There's no way out?" He sounded like a child being forced to confront the hard truths of life, and it made Simon want to comfort him. But that wasn't the job he was there to perform.

"You've built it up into some sort of epic struggle, but it really isn't. You'll make more money, you'll be taken care of, and you won't be doing anything any worse than what you've already been doing for years. It's a good opportunity for you." Simon tried to make his smile look encouraging, but it didn't seem to have any effect on the whore. So he tried, "And I'll give you your money back. Weekly bonuses. Say a thousand dollars a week to start, every week that you're cooperative. If you're really good, I'll double it. You'll have your money back in no time."

"You think I'm going to thank you for bribing me with my own money?"

"It *was* your money, but it isn't anymore. It's mine now, unless I decide to give it back to you."

"So you're a thief on top of everything else."

"I'm a very bad man," Simon said calmly. "And after tonight, you won't ever have to see me again. I'll have someone else give you your bonuses."

The whore stared, clearly trying to think of something more to say and coming up dry. So after a polite few moments, Simon pushed himself to his feet and said, "I'll walk you out."

"I can walk myself out."

"Offering to walk you out is a polite way of telling you it's time to go."

And the anger that hadn't really gone away flared up a little. "Yeah, your manners are fucking impeccable. You're a real gentleman."

"Time to go, little duck."

"Go to hell," the whore spat. But it was empty bravado and they both knew it. Simon had won, and the whore had lost. It didn't matter that Simon got no real benefit from the victory, didn't matter that the whore's loss would lead to him having a safer, more prosperous life. There was a principle involved, at least for the whore.

The whore still had the luxury of principles. Simon had left his behind ages ago, if he'd ever had any to begin with.

"I'll wait, then," Simon said now. "I have some work to catch up on. You can show yourself out when you're done doing whatever it is you're doing." And then, just because there was still a gleam of something wild in the whore's eyes, Simon added, "Any damage to the facility will be deducted from your little nest egg. And be careful—this furniture may look simple, but it costs a lot to look so plain."

"You're a soulless corporate drone," the whore growled.

The conversation was over. There was no more business to conduct, no more goals to reach. So there was no good reason for Simon to respond with "There's my little hipster, coming back for a visit."

"You're going to add 'patronizing' to your list of bullshit qualities?"

"I believe in being thorough. There's no point in only having *some* of the bullshit qualities on my list. I want to collect them all."

The whore frowned at him. "Does anything get to you? Is there anything I could say that would make you angry, or make you actually *feel* a damn thing?"

"I'm a soulless corporate drone. I'm not programed to feel, am I?"

Something in the whore's expression changed, and after a moment he said, "I don`t know which of us I feel more sorry for."

"And I don't know why you're bothering to feel sorry for either of us. We're both fine."

"You really believe that?"

And right there in the corporate boardroom of his uncle's business headquarters, facing down this angry, frustrated young man, Simon was actually tempted to tell the truth. What would happen if he shared his real beliefs, his own frustrations? What would it be like to have real friends, people to trust and support him the way the people in Tristan's life seemed to—No. Not "Tristan". That was unwise. This entire line of thought was unwise, almost disloyal, and by this stage of his life, Simon really should know better.

"I believe you'll enjoy your new job as much as you enjoyed your old job, and be better compensated for it. Beyond that, my beliefs are not important."

The whore looked disappointed by the answer, and Simon felt a completely irrational pang of guilt. After everything else he'd done to this kid, his conscience decided to give him a hard time about refusing to have a caring-and-sharing session?

"You never want to be something different?" the whore asked, his voice almost as seductive in its honesty as it had been in its sexuality. "Something better? This is it for you?"

Simon stood up. The meeting was over, and he'd only been indulging himself by dragging it out. Now that it was no longer enjoyable, there was no reason for him to stay. "As we agreed, you can show yourself out. Remember what I said about any damage being deducted from your bonus fund."

The whore was still fairly close to him on the floor, but he pushed his chair back enough that he could stand without risk of contact. "Remember: this is the last meeting between you and me. If you make further intervention necessary, it will come from someone else, someone much less likely to be patient with your nonsense."

And that was all. The whore didn't answer, just sat there on the floor and watched as Simon made his escape. He headed through the single door at the back of the conference room, made sure it was closed behind him, and then took longer than he should have needed to collect himself. It was over. It was taken care of.

He looked at the computer screen in front of him, showing the live feed from the cameras in the conference room. The whore was still sitting there, trying to figure out how to pull everything together and go on with his life, changed as it was after his meeting with Simon.

It made absolutely no sense that Simon felt as if he needed to make a similar adjustment in his own mind.

He'd done his job. He was done with the whore. Done with Tristan.

Completely bewildering how empty that realization made him feel.

Lap Dog

Chapter Five

TRISTAN SHOULD HAVE been stronger, and smarter. Maybe not in the meeting with Simon Yeung; there really hadn't seemed to be any room for manoeuvering there, and trying any harder than he had would have just resulted in even more frustration and humiliation. But at least he should have been smarter when he'd gotten home and found a room full of people in his apartment.

He could have said he was tired and gone straight through to the bedroom. Shane might have followed him in, but Shane was easy to handle; Tristan tried not to do it too often, but one flash of sad puppy dog eyes was all it took to have Shane totally preoccupied with fetching blankets and fluffing pillows instead of asking difficult questions.

So there was really no excuse for Tristan's decision to collapse onto the floor, lean back so his head was resting on the couch somewhere between Shane and Noah's thighs, and yell "It's fucking bullshit," so loudly that Dodger shied away and had to be coaxed back to exchange proper canine greetings.

Even after that, Tristan could have escaped without explaining. It was his apartment, after all, and if he wanted to be alone, he'd be alone. But that wasn't what he wanted. It wasn't smart, not at all, but he was too tired, too defeated, to care. He needed comfort from his friends, and the only way to get it was to tell them the whole story.

Shane got up part way through and started pacing, and that was definitely something Tristan would have to deal with eventually, but he let himself put it out of his head for the moment. "I think I have to do it," he said after he'd told the whole story. "I can't see a way out. And he's right, really. It's not that bad. I mean, more money, safer… that's good, right?"

"If it was good, you would have chosen it in the first place," Shane growled. "If this was what you wanted, you'd have had it."

"I don't know," Tristan said. He was pretty sure he'd changed his mind about wanting comfort; he just wanted his bed, now. Well, what he really wanted was his bed with Shane in it. Not for sex, just for warmth and snuggling and feeling safe with the arms of an animated teddy bear wrapped around him. He looked over at Noah, feeling almost guilty just for having the thought, and found Noah looking steadily back at him. Jesus, were pre-vet students trained to be mind-readers?

Maybe they were, because Noah smiled almost sadly and then said, "You look like you need to be put to bed. You want Shane to tuck you in?"

It was either a generous offer or a weird kind of taunt, making it clear that Shane was Noah's to lend as he saw fit. But, no, there'd been no sign of Noah being that kind of a dick ever before.

Tristan was just being over-sensitive. He forced his own smile and said, "You're right, I'm tired. But I'm sure I can make it on my own."

Noah leaned forward and spoke a little more quietly. "Shane's going crazy, trying to think of something to do. Let him do this." A pause, then a bashful shrug. "I trust you both. And I'm going to be right out here. There's a limit to how much I should expect to have my insecurity humored, isn't there?"

"No, there's no limit," Shane said. He crouched down so he was somewhere between Noah, sitting on the couch, and Tristan, still on the floor. "If you're not okay with it—"

"I *am* okay with it," Noah said firmly. He ran his hand through Shane's hair, down over the tattoo on his neck, and rested it there, a comfortable, gently possessive claim.

"Come with us," Tristan said. "It's not like we're going to be fooling around or anything." Not that Tristan *or* Shane hadn't been part of sexual combinations far kinkier than a threesome between friends, but Noah didn't really seem that adventurous, so maybe a little reassurance would be appreciated. And Tristan really didn't mind the idea of Noah coming along.

He pushed to his feet, waited for a moment of silent communication between Noah and Shane to conclude, then held out a hand to each of them.

"The Emperor summons his favorite concubines," Micah mumbled from the corner, but Micah had been fucked up when Tristan had arrived and didn't seem to have come down since, so he could just as well be talking about his favorite hallucinations as anything happening in the room right then.

And everybody else was pretty used to seeking and accepting whatever comfort they needed from whatever source would offer it, so they sure weren't going to judge Tristan for taking advantage of an opportunity.

Shane's hand was warm and strong, Noah's cooler, less confident, but still there. Dodger muddled around their feet, clearly insistent that whatever was happening, he should be part of it.

"I have to leave in an hour or two," Shane said as Tristan tugged them toward the bedroom. Shane was still spending his nights at the veterinary clinic and tried to be there from shortly after midnight until dawn. "But we can put you to sleep, okay?"

"And you can leave Noah with me," Tristan teased as he closed the bedroom door with his foot and then toed off his shoes.

Shane looked startled by the very suggestion and Noah stood on his tiptoes to kiss his cheek. "You trust me, don't you?" he asked, and then he grinned at Tristan and jerked his head in Shane's direction. "Big spoon, I'm assuming?"

"Ideally," Tristan said.

Noah gave Shane a gentle shove toward the bed. "Your snuggling duties await."

"What about you?" Shane asked.

Noah looked at Tristan, who looked back at him and said, "Ideally?"

"Sure."

"Ideally...the bad part about being the little spoon is that your tummy gets cold. So..."

"If you'd prefer Dodger, he's pretty good at tummy warming. I can just sit on the floor or—"

"Dodger's my second choice," Tristan said. He actually probably would have preferred the pup, who *was* an expert tummy warmer, but he'd been the one to drag Noah into this, so he should be as good of a host as possible. "If you'd be happier on the floor, I totally understand."

Noah took a deep breath, then smiled. "Okay. Three spoons. And a pup at our feet, I expect."

There was some squirming, some rearranging, and quite a bit of laughter, but eventually all three of them settled down. Tristan's bed wasn't big enough to *sleep* three, not if the sleepers wanted any kind of personal space, but it turned out to be just fine for three people to snuggle together, even when one of the three was as big as Shane.

Tristan couldn't remember the last time he'd felt so safe. An illusion, of course; nothing that was happening that night would do a damn thing to protect him from Yeung or anyone else. But it was a *nice* illusion, and he let himself enjoy it. The next day, he was pretty sure he was going to have to follow the instructions on the papers Yeung had given him. He was going to have to let himself be primped and pampered and turned into whatever version of a perfect prostitute Yeung's masters imaged for him.

But right then? Snuggled in his bed, with two good friends and a warm, happy puppy? For right then, everything was okay. And Tristan had always been pretty good at focusing on the happy present when the future was too bleak to consider.

~*~*~*~

SIMON HAD BEEN productive over the last couple days. Of course, he was always productive, but even by his own high standards, the last few days had been an achievement. He'd gotten reports that the stubborn whore had shown up for his fittings or haircuts or whatever had been on his schedule for that day, *and* he'd solved Mitchell's problem with the contractors, and he'd tidied up several other minor issues along the way. He was doing well.

He wondered what it would feel like if doing well were enough. He thought about the constant itching in his brain, the need, the reminder that he could never do well enough to actually satisfy anyone, including himself. He thought about what it would be like if all of that just ended.

Then he poured himself a fourth glass of Scotch and walked over to the wall of glass at the end of his living room. His apartment was close to the family offices, of course, and this window looked out over downtown, the same direction as the window in the corporate boardroom. He was looking at the same city lights, the same distant stars that the whore had seen the night before. What did lights look like through the whore's eyes? Simon suspected they were somehow more beautiful, more remarkable.

He turned away from the window just as the buzzer sounded. The one that told him someone was at his door, not downstairs with the doorman.

A neighbor, then. Not that Simon ever shared more than the basic courtesies with his neighbors, but maybe it was time for that to change. He tapped the screen to activate the camera outside his door.

And he saw the whore's large friend. Shane. That was his name. He was outside Simon's door. Simon's home, not his office. Shane was inside the building, and he looked determined.

The jump of excitement in Simon's chest was alarm. That was all. It wasn't anticipation, wasn't joy to discover that the whore— Tristan—wasn't completely out of his life yet. No, it was just a recognition that this was a dangerous situation.

That justification would have made a hell of a lot more sense if Simon's next move had been calling building security. Instead, he set his glass on the table that served as a bar, and headed for the door.

The friend looked understandably surprised when Simon opened the door. Well, understandable in that he should have known Simon would have cameras and some sense of self-preservation. But if he hadn't expected Simon to answer, why the hell had he snuck into the building and rung the damn bell?

"Shane, isn't it?" Simon asked. "Please, come in." Because it totally made sense for him to invite a probably violent thug into his personal space.

Shane looked about as surprised as Simon was feeling, but after a moment, he stepped through the doorway and then seemed to push himself further into the apartment. Simon followed along behind him, knowing the whole situation was dangerous and stupid, and still not doing a thing to change any of it.

They both stopped in the middle of the living room, and the friend turned to face Simon. "We need to talk," he said.

Simon nodded. "If you say so. Please, sit down. Can I get you anything? A drink?"

The friend had clearly been expecting a different sort of welcome. "No. I don't want your drinks."

"You don't mind if I—" Simon said, and gestured toward the half-full glass on the console.

The friend seemed bewildered. And that was good, Simon told himself as he retrieved his glass and took a sip. Keeping people off balance was his specialty; a gentle shove at just the right time could do more to change a position than a brutal tackle at the wrong time. So it wasn't bad that the friend didn't really know what was going on. It was good, really.

"So," Simon said as he settled himself into one of the leather armchairs that flanked his gas fireplace, "How can I help you?"

The friend frowned. "You have cameras," he said. "And you've been spying on Tristan. You know who I am, and you knew it before you opened the door."

"Yes, I recognize you. But that doesn't actually help me understand why you're here."

"You have cameras," the friend repeated. "You should turn them on."

"Turn them on? They're on. I did see you before I opened the door. This isn't a camera issue."

"No, I mean you should look at them. There's a camera in your parking garage, right? You should look at it, now."

Simon thought about refusing. He had a rough idea what was happening now, and it would probably make sense to minimize the impact of it by refusing to play along. But there was a sick sort of fascination to the idea of doing his part, a strange kind of justice that he probably deserved to receive. So he stood up, set his glass down, and crossed over to the screen fixed to the wall by the front door.

A few taps and he had the garage camera active. His Mercedes, sleek and dark and efficient, as usual. But there weren't usually five people wearing hoodies, with scarves over their faces, standing on all sides of the vehicle.

He saw one of them glance down at a phone in his hand and looked over to see the friend shoving his own phone back into his pocket. Simon didn't need to see the tallest of the hooded assailants raise a baseball bat in order to know what was about to happen.

He reached out a steady hand and tapped the screen, turning the image off, then returned to his seat, retrieving his Scotch along the way.

"Is there an actual point?" he asked as he sank into the soft leather. "Your friends damage my car. I get it. But do you understand that I have insurance? And that even if I didn't, I'd just have to report the breach in security to the building management and they'd pay for the repairs out of *their* insurance? Alternatively, I could skip the insurance stage and just deduct the cost of repairs directly from your friend's bonus account. If they do enough damage I might need to buy myself a whole new car, and that would eat up most, if not all, of your friend's precious savings. Do you understand all of that?"

Simon sipped his drink as the friend processed the information, then continued. "And do you understand that even if none of that was true, even if this *was* a devastating blow you were landing and it truly hurt me very much—do you understand that it wouldn't make a bit of difference? The people in charge of all this don't care about me any more than they care about your friend, or about you. If my car is destroyed, they'll buy me a new car if it suits their needs, or ignore me completely if *that* suits their needs. But they won't be significantly affected, one way or another."

"And what if it's not just your car that gets damaged?" the friend asked.

He really was very large, and he had a truly impressive glower. Possibly Simon was going to regret opening his door as easily as he had. But he told the truth. "If more than the car is damaged, they still won't care. You could beat me—kill me—and they would possibly regret that they'd lost a useful tool. That would be all. But in the meantime, the police would be involved, and as we've already established, there are cameras all over this building. You'd be caught, and charged. Your friends in the garage would probably be charged as accessories. All of that, and your friend would *still* be expected to show up for his appointments tomorrow and his meeting tomorrow night. And he'd still face the same consequences if he didn't show up."

The friend stared at him. "So that's all. That's it. There's no way out."

Simon's smile was inappropriate, but completely genuine. "You sound like your friend. Like Tristan."

"I don't give a *fuck* who I sound like," the friend spat. "I came here for a reason. You need to figure out a way to help him! You need to tell us what to do, and we'll do it."

"Because it's so terrible for him to work for someone else? Because making a little more money and having a little less control is so completely unthinkable?"

"Because it has to be his *choice*," the friend said, his voice almost a yell. "Because what he has to do for a living is bad enough, but at least he *chooses* to do it. He gets to control that much of it all. But you're trying to take even that away from him."

Simon nodded slowly. There was no point in arguing about who it was, exactly, who was taking the whore's control away. Someone was, and Simon was the personification of that someone. "I understand," he said. "But there's truly nothing I can do."

"Have you even *tried*?"

"You mean, have I done anything as clever as breaking into a secure building and committing several crimes—vandalism, uttering threats—in a completely pointless way? No, I haven't done that. I suppose I'm just not as good of a person as you are."

"You could try to talk to them, couldn't you?" The friend was desperate, now, and it was too reminiscent of the whore's reaction to leave Simon unmoved. "You could tell them—something. I mean, whatever you are, whatever you do, you're not nobody, right? You've got some pull. You could use it."

"For your friend? I should use any small influence I have to make things better for someone I barely know, someone who sends thugs to my home to try to intimidate me?"

"No," the friend said. "He didn't send us. He doesn't know we're here. He'd—he'd freak out if he knew." The friend frowned as if thinking it through. "That's what you don't understand. He wouldn't freak out because he'd know this wouldn't work. I mean, he's not stupid—probably he'd be pissed about that, too. But the thing you don't get? Is that he'd mostly be upset because he doesn't want any of us involved with you guys, for *us*. He doesn't want us to take any chances for him. Even though shit like this is pretty much all I'm good for—I'm not smart enough to help him, or whatever, so all I can do is rough stuff—even though he knows that, he still doesn't want me to do it. Do you understand what that's like? For him to care about what's good for *me* more than what's good for *him*? That's the kind of thing he cares about. That's why when I got this stupid idea to come over here I had no trouble finding people who were willing to smash up your car." He thought for a moment, then shrugged. "Partly because nobody likes a young guy driving a fucking Mercedes, but mostly for Tristan. You know?" The friend stared at Simon, his eyes fierce and intent. "You got anyone in your life who cares about you that way?"

Simon should have called security long ago, and he certainly shouldn't have let this guy into his apartment. There was no real way to explain the decisions he'd been making lately, and that worried him. But not as much as he was worried about the true answer to the friend's question. Because, no, there was nobody in his life who cared about him enough to risk themselves for him. Aunt May would come the closest, he supposed, but her first loyalty was clearly to her husband and children, and…

And they were likely to be the source of risk, if Simon didn't watch himself.

"It's very touching that you all came," he said. "But I think you've misjudged the situation. I'm honestly not the decision maker in any of this. I have very little influence. Probably none at all."

"But you haven't even tried to find out," the friend said. His voice was almost gentle, as if he were correcting a small child. "That's all we're asking for—we're just asking you to try."

Such a sweet message to be accompanied by home invasion and car destruction.

"It's time for you to go," Simon said. "And make sure your friends are on their way as well. The cameras in the public areas of the building have people monitoring them, so you all will have been seen coming in. If security hasn't already made it to the garage, they'll be there soon."

"They should already be gone," the friend said. He pulled his phone out of his pocket, glanced down, and nodded. "Yeah, they're clear." He looked back up and frowned. "How come you're being—" He stopped, clearly searching for the right word. "I mean, you're being—more than nice, really. You don't seem pissed about the car or anything."

"I told you. Insurance will cover it, and if it doesn't, I have your friend's nest egg to crack open. This isn't a problem for me."

The friend nodded slowly. "It'd be a problem for you if I beat you up, though."

"Yes, that would be unpleasant. But you know it wouldn't make any difference, right? If you get bad news in a letter, there's no point beating up the mailman."

The friend thought it through, then shook his head. "This whole thing is so fucking stupid. There has to be something we could do."

"You could contact the police and see what they have to say. But obviously that would only work if your friend admitted to some illegal activity of his own. And the police always want proof, which your friend likely won't have. And…" Simon was strangely reluctant to say the next part, the most important part. "You need to remember that you're dealing with a large organization, here. The best you could hope for from the police would be help dealing with one very small part of that organization. Which would leave all the other parts still functioning, and absolutely interested in making an example out of someone who ratted them out." He watched the friend's expression. No surprise, no extra fear. He'd known all of that all along. Of course he had. "So—I'm not really aware of any reasonable options for your friend, I'm afraid."

"We're not giving up," the friend said as he headed for the door.

We. Such a simple word, used so casually by this intruder into Simon's ordered life. It wasn't clear how many people were included in the term, but even if it was only two of them, only the whore and the friend, it was still more than Simon had.

"Okay," he said. "I understand. And, honestly, I wish you luck. But you need to be careful. Coming here tonight was not smart—it could have ended up with a lot of arrests. But trying something like this on a different target? It could have been deadly. You understand that, right?"

"Are you seriously pretending you care?"

"I don't like it when things get messy. That's all."

The friend took a dismissive look around the apartment. "Yeah, I can see that." His hand was on the doorknob, now, but he was twisted far enough around to fix Simon with a hard stare. "I'm still not sure I shouldn't be beating the shit out of you."

"I'm still not sure I shouldn't be calling security or the police on you and your friends."

A pause, then a sudden grin that transformed the man's face from thuggish to something much more innocent and appealing. "So, we're both not sure. Nice to have something in common, right?"

And with that, he was gone, leaving Simon to deal with whatever had been done to his car, and whatever had been done to his calm philosophy on life.

Chapter Six

"WE'VE BEEN REALLY busy the last couple days," the woman said. One of her hands was nestled right up in Tristan's crotch, her knuckles brushing against his balls, but she seemed completely unconcerned about it. "Thirty-one," she called over her shoulder, and pulled the tape measure away from Tristan's body. "You guys have some big party on Friday, right? A show or something?"

Tristan didn't want to be there, didn't want to be having this conversation, didn't want to be one of whoever "you guys" were. He didn't want any of it, but it wasn't this woman's fault, so he tried to smile as he said, "I have no idea, really. This is all—it's a bit up in the air. I'm still working things through."

She nodded. "We've had a couple guys like you in the last few days. I guess they did a big recruitment drive or something. Some of the regulars are saying the party is, like, an initiation or something." She grinned and waggled her eyebrows. "Got to break you all in, he said."

Tristan couldn't tell if she was just being chatty or if she was actually taking pleasure in his discomfort. He inexplicably thought of Simon Yeung, the man's calm responses to whatever Tristan had thrown at him, and smiled politely. "I'm afraid I have no new information for you."

She looked disappointed, but he couldn't tell if it was because he hadn't added to her gossip reservoir or because he hadn't responded to her taunting. Either way, though, he figured he'd won. One tiny victory to balance against all the recent losses.

Like the unwanted haircut he'd received the day before because his current look hadn't matched the stylist's vision for him. The waxing, the plucking, the massage with essential oils that would have been blissful if he'd been able to get rid of the image of himself as a piece of meat being marinated before consumption. The removal of the two earrings he'd worn in his right ear since he'd left home for good, replaced with a single diamond stud.

None of it was bad, he kept trying to tell himself. It was all just surface stuff, and he'd never been too caught up in what he looked like. And it wasn't like he hadn't always made a conscious effort to present himself the way his clients wanted. He'd dress up for some of them, dress down for others, trying to match their desires. The only difference now was that it was someone else making the decisions. That was all.

Yeah, that was all. Just the complete loss of his personal autonomy. Not a big—

His thoughts stuttered to a halt when the woman who'd been measuring him came out of the backroom carrying a hanger with—Jesus. Tiny scraps and straps of black leather, huge metal rings that looked like they were designed to be attached to something, pointy studs on what looked like the inside of the clothes, so they'd be pressing into his skin… and the woman smirked as she saw his reaction. Yeah, she'd wanted to scare him earlier, and she was happy to be getting a response now.

So he smiled again. "Is it a retro party? People aren't still wearing that sort of thing un-ironically, are they?"

Her frown was his reward, and he realized how much easier all this was when she was being unpleasant. If she'd been sympathetic, or gentle with him, he wasn't sure he'd have been able to stay strong.

"This is very *au courant*," she snapped.

"Oh. Is it?" It probably was—he certainly was no sort of an expert on bondage wear, or fashion, or anything else. But he'd be damned if he'd admit that to her. "I guess Seattle is—well, it's a beautiful city, but not really known for—but, never mind. I can just *tell* myself it's a retro party, right?"

Her scowl deepened. "This was designed based on pictures from a party in New York last spring!"

Tristan was starting to feel a little guilty, but not guilty enough to stop. So he nodded slowly. "Last spring. Yeah, okay. That explains it. But, don't worry, I'll wear it with enough attitude that people will be wondering if *they're* the ones who are behind the times. It'll be fine. Let's try it on."

There was no point being modest, not when he was about to put that outfit on, not after all the invasions of the day before, so he stripped down right in front of her and let her strap him into the outfit. He could tell she took some extra pleasure in tightening things with an unnecessary level of roughness, and he made himself focus on that. Much better to think about this woman, with her frustrations and resentments, than to worry about the *other* people who'd be seeing him dressed like this. Touching him, controlling him—it wasn't like he hadn't had clients who liked to hurt him, but he'd always *known* those men. He'd chosen them, at least to some extent, and he'd laid out ground rules before anything started. He hadn't been in control, exactly, but he'd been the one to decide to give up the control, and that had made it bearable. This?

The woman cranked the leather g-string so hard his balls groaned in protest, and he wanted to thank her. Yes, think about the current problems, not the larger ones yet to come.

Or maybe think about the problems of the night before, when Shane and a bunch of others had disappeared for a couple hours and come back to the apartment looking like they'd just found out the truth about Santa Claus. None of them had said where they'd been, and Tristan honestly hadn't pressed as hard as he should have. He had enough problems, and didn't really think he could handle taking on any more.

So he squabbled with the woman outfitting him for the event he didn't want to think about. It wasn't really a solution, but at least it was a distraction.

~*~*~*~

DAVID CHEN'S OFFICE was in Chinatown, and came complete with a bunch of kitschy, Americanized versions of Chinese design—dragons everywhere, painted landscapes on fabric panels, and bamboo growing inside and out. Chen had left China as a little boy, as far as Simon knew, but apparently he was hanging on to at least one version of his heritage with significant enthusiasm.

The receptionist was tall and blond, wearing a red silk blouse with black pants, and nodded a bow to him as he approached. "Mr. Chen is expecting you," she said. No further recognition, no acknowledgement of their previous meetings, the times Simon had paid her significant bribes in order to be given access to her boss's appointment books and records. Good.

Simon made his way back through the maze of cubicles and small offices, trying to retrace his steps from his one previous visit. The Chens were a different sort of family than the Yeungs—less established in the Seattle social fabric, less conservative, less careful. That made them useful; they could be the ones taking the chances, while the Yeungs sat back and took a share of the profits. And the Chens were ambitious, with illicit contacts that could be very useful, especially when the Chens were willing to serve as a buffer, ensuring the Yeungs kept their hands clean. Well, all the Yeungs except for Simon; he could get a little grubby, if it served the family interests.

Simon found the office in the back corner and knocked, heard a shouted "Come in," and stepped into relative peace. This space was less cluttered, dominated by two overstuffed leather couches and an ornately carved wooden desk with a short, fat, middle-aged man behind it.

"Simon Yeung," David Chen said. He stood up and made his way around the desk, extending his hand in greeting. "I'm glad you've come. My son says things are going much more smoothly with his little project since you got involved. You really do have a knack for solving problems, don't you? I'm glad your uncle was kind enough to loan you to us."

"I was pleased to be of service," Simon said.

"But you don't come to me now looking for more thanks, do you?" Chen waved Simon toward one of the couches and took a seat on the other one himself.

"No. As I said, I was pleased to help; no thanks are necessary. I just—well, I have a bit of a strange request. I should stress that I'm asking for myself, not for my uncle. This is a private matter."

Private. Ridiculous. Absurd, and maybe even shameful. Certainly nothing Simon would be able to justify or explain to his uncle, should the older man find out. Which he almost certainly would. The whole enterprise was madness, and Simon felt as if he was standing somewhere at a distance, watching the impulsive creature who'd taken over his body make nonsensical decisions. At the same time, Simon knew he could take control back any time he wanted to, and he chose not to. So he couldn't disown this madness, not if he was being honest with himself.

"I'm intrigued," Chen said now, and the glow in the man's eyes made it clear he was telling the truth. He had Frank Yeung's nephew before him, wanting something, and a man like Chen would see many ways to turn that situation to his favor. "How may I help you?"

It wasn't too late. Simon could make something up, some little favor, maybe a request to help him obtain a gift for his uncle or some other simpering gesture. But he remembered the friend's question from the night before. *Have you even tried?*

"It's a peculiar request," he said. "I know I'm not in a position to be whimsical, or to expect anyone else to care about my strange ideas. But—I wondered if you might find the situation just as interesting as I seem to."

"I'm finding it very interesting so far. Please, continue."

Not too late, not too late. But, damn it, *have you even tried?*

"The prostitute," Simon said, and the die was cast. "The stubborn one I was dealing with. He—intrigued me. There was a quality to him, something I hadn't expected to see, and it's made me—conflicted, I suppose. I appreciate that your son did him an honor by selecting him to be part of his enterprise, and I believe the prostitute understands that now, too. But as I was working, I saw some very interesting things, and I believe that he may be better suited to a different line of work. I've been thinking about taking on an assistant, and despite his background, I believe he might be the person for the job." Simon cast his eyes toward the floor. "Although of course I would never mention such a possibility to him without your permission."

Chen was quiet for too long. There was a rhythm to conversations like this one, and Simon had learned to feel it like the beat of his heart. But this time, there was no answer when there should have been one. No gentle inquiry, no counter-offer, no attempt to negotiate. Just silence.

Finally, Simon looked up, and saw Chen grinning at him. No, not just grinning, *laughing*, his shoulders shaking in silent mirth. "You think he might be 'the person for the job'?" Chen finally said. His voice was light and teasing, but there was a sharpness as well. "There's 'a quality to him'?" Another bout of laughter before Chen said, "You think we don't know about you? About your *preferences*?" He shook his head as if amused, but also a little disappointed in Simon's naiveté. Then he squinted thoughtfully and said, "You don't know, do you?"

Simon tried to sound calm and controlled. "Know what?"

Chen's smile widened. "About a year ago, your uncle and I had a meeting. He was looking for new ways to take advantage of my family."

"I'm sure my uncle would want to be fair," Simon started, but Chen raised an imperious hand.

"Your uncle wants to be *rich*. Richer than he already is. *That's* what he wants."

There was no point in arguing, not when they both knew the words were the truth. So Simon just waited, and eventually Chen nodded.

"He thought it might be good to set up a more permanent alliance between our families, and I have daughters. Of course his own son could never lower himself to marry into a family like mine, but your uncle mentioned you as a possibility, and I had my people do a little research."

Simon nodded slowly. He would admit to nothing, but he wouldn't hide, either.

Chen's smile was almost gentle. "So when your uncle came back to discuss it again, after I'd learned a little about you, do you want to know why I rejected his arrangement?"

Because it's the twenty-first century and nobody arranges marriages anymore? But of course, men like Chen and Simon's uncle arranged whatever the hell they wanted. "I assume you found me unsuitable," Simon said, only a little stiffly.

"Of course I did." Chen watched for the reaction, then smiled again. "Because you have no money! Your uncle *brags* about what a tight leash he keeps you on. He pays for your apartment, your car, your credit card bills, barely gives you any cash at all! He's not stupid—he knows money is power, money is freedom, and he doesn't want you to have either. You think I want my daughter married to someone like that? You think I want her living like a dog, begging for scraps from someone's table?"

Simon had no idea how to respond. He supposed he should be at least a little insulted to be dismissed so easily, but nothing Chen was saying was untrue, and it was certainly more socially acceptable than what he'd *thought* Chen was going to say. "I'm not sure how that ties in to the current conversation," he managed.

Chen frowned. "Oh. I've gotten ahead of myself. I should have told you what *else* my investigators found. I wouldn't want my daughter married to someone who likes men, either. And you're right, that's the important point right now. I know you're not interested in the whore because he would be a good assistant; you're interested in him because you think he'd be a good cocksucker. Or maybe you already know he is; I don't need to hear details. But the point is, you want to take a whore from *my* public stable and put him in your own private barn, and you want me to be fine with it."

"No." Simon tried to let the truth of the word show in his face. "I won't deny that he's attractive. Of course he is—that's why he's valuable. But I'm honestly not looking at him as a prostitute. I wouldn't want—" What? Wouldn't want the whore on those terms? That was the truth, but probably not something that Chen would understand or find persuasive. "I wouldn't want to steal from you. I wouldn't want to show you any discourtesy or disrespect. I honestly think it may be time for him to be useful in a different way. That's all."

"That's all," Chen said, his eyes dancing with amusement. Simon was getting a little tired of entertaining this guy.

"I thought we could discuss the idea. I wouldn't expect you to make any sacrifices on my behalf, but I hoped there would be something we could negotiate."

"Negotiate? We've already established that you have no money. And there's no way your uncle is going to give you cash so you can buy yourself a whore. A *male* whore. So what do you want to negotiate with?"

"I have—skills. If I had an assistant helping me, I'd have more time, and the time I don't spend on my uncle's projects I could spend on yours." Simon leaned forward a little. This was the delicate part, and he needed to make sure Chen saw his sincerity. "Your business is very profitable; that's why my uncle wants to be involved. But it's not always—tidy. And I'm very good at making things tidy, keeping things quiet. If you want someone to act on your behalf, someone to help you establish business of a different sort, at least on the surface, I could be useful."

"You have your MBA," Chen mused. "Your uncle paid for you to go to school for a long time."

"My uncle is a very generous man."

Chen snorted, but wasn't rude enough to disagree out loud. "You think having a fancy degree means you can do things I can't do?"

"I think you're a busy man, and you shouldn't be bothering yourself with details. But you need someone you can trust to take care of them for you."

"Someone I can trust? Frank fucking Yeung's goddamn nephew? You're saying I should trust you?"

"I would owe you. It would be a matter of honor for me to repay you."

"Honor. Don't give me that old country bullshit. This is America; honor doesn't mean shit. And I'm not sure it meant much in China, either."

"My reputation means something. It would be—" The right word was *inefficient*. It would be inefficient for Simon to make an enemy of David Chen. But that wasn't the word that would get Simon what he wanted. "It would be stupid of me to cross you."

"And how's your uncle going to feel about you working for me?"

"If there were ever an issue in which you and my uncle were in conflict, I would have to work for my family. We would have this agreement from the start, you and I. But for all other matters? I don't think this would be any of my uncle's business."

Chen leaned back in his chair and actually steepled his fingers like a cartoon villain. He looked at Simon for longer than was comfortable, then shook his head. "No. It's tempting, I admit it. But, no. Not because you wouldn't be of service, but because your uncle wouldn't approve, and it's more trouble than you'd be worth for me to piss off Frank Yeung."

"If I can make that work? If I can get him to agree, would you be interested?"

"If you can get him to agree? Then you'd be a miracle worker, and I'd absolutely have a use for you."

Simon nodded. It was something. Not much, but at least he had a next step. "I'll be back in touch, then. Thank you for your time."

Simon exchanged a few more courtesies and then left the office.

He could quit now, he realized as he walked down the sidewalk toward the loaner car the body shop had provided. He'd made an effort. He'd done more than made any kind of sense, so whatever guilt he'd been feeling, whatever little identity crisis he'd gone through, he could leave it behind and get back to his normal life.

But he didn't want to. Partly because of the wh—no. If Simon was going to do this, he should do it all the way. He should admit that his interest in all of this was partly because of *Tristan* himself. The mix of defiance and vulnerability, the quick wit, and, of course, the beautiful face and body. But there was more to it than that. Simon wanted to find a solution to this problem for himself, and for Tristan's stubborn friend, and for—for all of it. He wanted Tristan to be free because the world would be a better place if he was.

It was a dangerous indulgence to continue with this quest. But he was already planning his next step as he pulled out of the parking spot and headed out into traffic.

Lap Dog

Chapter Seven

THE KNOCK ON THE door was startling. It shouldn't have been; Tristan's apartment was like Grand Central Station most days, with people coming and going all the time. But this was a triple knock, bam-bam-bam, not the double-double combo Tristan's friends used. And really, just about all the regulars were already there, pigging out on the pasta Noah was getting good at making in large quantities. So maybe Tristan was just surprised that someone new was arriving.

But probably he was completely on edge because he'd had two absolutely demeaning days in a row, hardly slept since the weekend, and had nothing but more trouble to look forward to in the coming days. Yeah, probably that was it.

No one else seemed to even notice the knock, so Tristan pushed himself to his feet and headed for the front door. He opened it without looking through the peephole and then almost swung it shut again.

"What the hell are you doing here?" he demanded. "You can't seriously want *more* from me."

Simon Yeung didn't seem surprised by that greeting, but then, he never seemed too surprised by anything. "I was hoping we could talk. I have a proposal for you, but I'm not actually sure you'll be interested. I thought we should discuss it before I took it any further."

"And if I'm not interested, what are you going to steal from me *this* time?"

"If you aren't interested, I'll walk away. No repercussions. Actually everything would be significantly easier for me if you aren't interested, so I promise, I won't even try to sell the idea too hard."

Tristan was standing still, trying to figure out what the hell was going on, when he heard Shane's voice from behind him. "What the hell are you doing here?" It was belligerent Shane, angry Shane, ready-to-start-trouble Shane.

But Yeung didn't seem even a little alarmed. He just looked over Tristan's shoulder, his gaze level, and said, "I'm trying."

And for whatever reason, that seemed to be enough to calm Shane down. He still prowled closer, always so light and graceful for someone his size, but he didn't look like he was ready to pounce, not anymore. "Have you got a plan?" he asked.

Tristan felt a bit out of the loop, but he didn't object, just listened as Yeung said, "Maybe. Something worth talking about, at least. I was just telling Tristan that he may not be interested, and if he isn't, there won't be much more I can do." He turned his attention back to Tristan as he added, "And even if you are interested, there's no guarantee I can make it work. It's a long shot, really. But I thought I should at least come over and discuss it with you."

"Why?" Tristan asked. "I mean, why are you doing any of this? I thought you were done. You won, or whatever. Why are you still involved?"

Another look between Yeung and Shane. "Your friends care about you," Yeung said. "It's—intriguing, I suppose. And it's a challenge, finding a solution to such a difficult problem. I like a challenge."

"Good," Shane said quickly. "Liking challenges is good."

But Tristan wasn't quite ready to move on to that part. "What do my friends have to do with any of this?" he demanded.

Another damn look between the other two men, and Tristan started to feel like he wasn't really a very important participant in the conversation. But then Yeung shrugged and said, "My motivations aren't important, I don't think. Let me present the idea to you, and you can tell me what you think."

"Not inside," Shane said quickly. "Everyone in there is pretty hostile. If you go in, you're not going to come out in one piece."

"The roof," Tristan decided. The landlord and the tenants waged a constant battle over roof access, the landlord padlocking the door, one tenant or another cutting the lock and opening it up, then the landlord finding another lock and the whole cycle starting over. Tristan was pretty sure they were at an *unlocked* stage, and it hadn't been raining the last time he'd been outside.

Shane took about two steps to get down the hallway and grab his and Tristan's jackets from the hooks on the wall, and then he was back, clearly not planning to let Tristan out of his sight while Yeung was around. As much as Shane's protectiveness sometimes chafed, right then, Tristan was glad of it.

He led the way up the stairs and down the short hallway to the utility room, then up the ladder and out onto the crunchy gravel of the flat roof. The stars were out, not bright against the lights of the city, but still there, and he breathed in the cool, damp night air and tried to organize his thoughts.

"What's this all about?" he asked, and Yeung nodded an acknowledgement of the question.

"You don't want to work for the Chen family," Yeung said. "I can understand that. So I'm trying to find a way for you to not have to. But as I've told both of you several times, I really don't have much influence over these decisions."

"But you have a plan?" Tristan asked. He felt stupid for feeling hopeful, but there was something about Yeung, his calm intelligence, that made it seem as if he could probably make anything happen if he applied himself.

"I have a proposal," Yeung said. "There are three people who need to agree to it, and I have the tentative approval of one. You're the second. The third will be—the third will be very challenging. And there's no point even approaching him about it if you aren't interested."

Tristan leaned back against the brick hutch that covered the ladder opening and tried to look nonchalant. "Okay. Hit me with it."

"There's no solution I can find that will take you back to where you were before this started," Yeung said. He sounded almost apologetic, which was a bit unusual, coming from him. "I can't find a way for you to continue in your regular line of work, as an independent, in Seattle. That won't work."

"It should be his choice," Shane growled.

"Yes, that would be lovely," Yeung replied with just a little too much patience, "but as I said, I can't find a way to make this happen. I'm looking at what *can* be, not what *should* be." He waited for more objections, but Tristan didn't have any, and apparently Shane was at least temporarily quieted as well.

"The alternative I've come up with is for you to leave the profession entirely," Yeung said, "which I believe was something you were originally considering. The problem will be—well, I've had to come up with a *reason* for you to leave the profession. It can't just be 'because you feel like it'. You understand that?"

"None of this can be about giving me what I want," Tristan said. It wasn't as if the concept was unfamiliar to him, considering how he'd been making his living for years. "It has to be about giving someone *else* what he wants."

Yeung nodded approvingly, and it was absolutely stupid that Tristan actually felt a quick burst of pride. As if Tristan cared what this bastard thought about his ability to understand the situation.

95

"Yes. Someone else. And in this case, the only 'someone else' I could come up with was myself."

And Tristan was again startled by his own reaction. The idea of being a kept boy instead of an independent whore? And, more importantly, being kept by someone young and handsome, someone intelligent, with no known kinks that would be dangerous? It should have been a relief, not a disappointment. "I see," he said carefully.

Shane frowned and said, "Would that be better? I mean, you still wouldn't have your freedom, right?"

Tristan thought about the previous couple days, the fittings and the preening and the talk about the party. Yes, it would be better to do whatever he could to avoid that. And he had his mouth open to say so when Yeung replied to Shane.

"Being employed isn't quite the same as losing your independence, I wouldn't think."

"So he can quit? You ask him to do something too weird, or you want to hurt him all the time or something, and he can walk?"

Yeung turned from Shane to Tristan and said, "I haven't made myself clear. I apologize. I wouldn't be hiring you to perform sex work. I'm interested in hiring you as an assistant, someone to help me with various business matters. Clothes on."

"Why?" Tristan demanded, looking for the trap. "I have no education, no relevant skills—why the hell would you want me to do a job like that?"

"I have no idea," Yeung said, and his voice was a little more brittle, a little louder than Tristan had heard before. Then a breath to compose himself, which apparently worked a hell of a lot better for Yeung than it ever did for Tristan. "I suppose I'm feeling charitable," he continued more calmly. "And even without formal education, you seem intelligent. Trainable. I'm hoping that will allow you to do well in my field." He stopped, thought for a moment, then said, "Mostly, I believe I'm doing it because I set myself to solve a problem, and this is the only solution I could find."

"It's that important to you? Solving the problem?"

Yeung nodded slowly, maybe bitterly. "Are you familiar with the phrase *raison d'etre*? In my case, I think it applies literally. Solving problems is my reason for being."

"And you want to turn him into one of you?" Shane burst out. "*That's* your fucking solution? One way or the other, he has to join the fucking Borg? Either as a drone or an assistant, he must be assimilated? Resistance is fucking futile?"

Three *fuckings* that close together meant Shane was building up to one of his explosions, and that wouldn't be good for anybody. Still, Tristan couldn't ignore the truth of his friend's words. "He's got a point. And, honestly—morally—I'm okay with being a whore. I know some people don't like it, but I don't really give a shit what some people think. *I'm* okay with it. But what you do? I don't—I mean, at least as a whore, people *like it* when I fuck them. You know? But your job? You're fucking people over, and they don't like it. *I* didn't like it. I'm not sure I can really be part of that."

Yeung stared at him, and it was chilling to watch the expression on his face change. It was subtle but clear as he shifted from open and calm to closed and—well, closed and something Tristan didn't want to look at too closely.

"It's not a personal judgement," he said quickly, but of course it had been, and of course Yeung wasn't going to pretend otherwise.

"So you're not interested," Yeung said, his voice dangerously cool. "Good. That's good." He turned to Shane. "So there will be no more visits, no more vandalism. I've offered your friend an alternative, and he has rejected it. It's beneath him, and he'd rather be cruelly fucked by random strangers than be associated with me. You heard him make that choice. I will not need to take the chances I was prepared to take or undergo the inconveniences that would have been inevitable. I won't need to worry about the difficulties of a whore being asked to—well, being asked to be exactly what he is. This should have been over days ago, and I apologize for wasting everyone's time with this silliness."

Yeung stepped back toward the door, toward the ladder, and Tristan wanted to reach out and catch him, keep him from going until there'd been apologies and thanks and—and what? How did Tristan see that exchange ending, exactly?

He had no idea. So he let Yeung go, watched him turn and slide down the ladder so quickly it almost looked like he was falling. And then it was just Tristan and Shane, alone on the roof.

"What did he mean about vandalism?" Tristan asked.

Shane winced. "He was pretty cool about it, actually. But—I don't really think we should expect that level of coolness again. You know?"

No, Tristan didn't know. He didn't know what Shane was talking about, but more importantly he didn't know how to explain his own feelings. Was he honestly feeling *guilty* because he'd— because he'd hurt the damn feelings of the trouble shooter from the organized crime family who'd robbed him and forced him into an unwanted contract with people who were going to violate him in any way they wanted? Was guilt really an appropriate response?

Of course not. Not rationally.

But there'd been something about Yeung's face as Tristan had refused to work with him. Something real, and vulnerable, and strangely heartbreaking.

For the first time, Tristan found himself wondering who Yeung was, beyond being an agent for a crime family. How had he ended up doing what he did? What had his choices been? Why had he made them?

Would Tristan have done differently if he'd been in Yeung's place?

"I seriously wish I had a time machine," he groaned. He could go back to when things were simpler. Easier. "Also, you're really going to have to tell me what the hell he was talking about with the 'vandalism' stuff."

"Well," Shane said reluctantly, "that was a bit of a mistake. But—no harm done, long term. Right?"

"I will absolutely not agree to that until you tell me what you're talking about." Easier to be testy with Shane than to think about Yeung.

Shane sighed. "Let's go inside. There are more people to share the blame in there."

"You go on in," Tristan said. "I'm just going to chill out a little."

"You sure you don't want company?"

"Yeah," Tristan said, and Shane gave him a quick, fierce kiss on the temple, then turned away and climbed down the ladder.

Tristan stayed on the roof and looked at the stars. So distant, so cold. So beautiful.

No, damn it, he needed to keep his head in the game. He needed all his strength to deal with the days to come; he couldn't let himself be distracted by regrets or curiosity or whatever this strange fascination was.

Simon Yeung was gone. Tristan needed to let him go.

~*~*~*~

IT HAD BEEN SO long since Simon had felt angry that it actually took him a few moments to identify the emotion. Stomping down the stairs of the disgusting tenement where the whore and his fucking naïve friends chose to spend their time, throwing the front door open and taking a breath of clean air and *still* not finding the sense of calm that usually enveloped him. It took him that long to realize he was angry. He'd reached his rental car, the piece of shit he was driving because the whore's delinquent friends thought they were fucking heroes, yanked the door open, and thrown himself into the driver's seat before he realized the emotion that was bubbling *beneath* the anger, the emotion the anger was helpfully disguising.

He was hurt. The whore and the thug had hurt his feelings. "Jesus Christ," he muttered. How pathetic he was.

He took a deep breath, almost choked on the air freshener the body shop clearly used to pretend their loaners had that "new car" smell, and deliberately blew the air out, trying to send some negative emotions out with it. Another breath, just like Aunt May had taught him when he'd been a little boy. "Breathe in life and peace," she'd told him. "Breathe out anger and sadness."

He had no idea if it had been genuine Chinese wisdom or just some hokey new age spiritualism, but it had worked for him, back then. It had helped him deal with the pain of being abandoned by his parents, and the frustrations of living with his demanding uncle and resentful cousins. And it helped him now, at least a little, sitting in the car, breathing in and out, trying to control his thoughts and emotions.

He stayed parked until he was calm enough to drive safely, then slipped the car into gear. He'd planned to drive aimlessly, but somehow wasn't too surprised to find himself pulling through the gates of his aunt's home. His uncle and cousins' home too, of course, but he knew the family schedule well enough to predict that he'd be able to avoid them. The family rarely ate dinner or spent the evenings together unless they were entertaining.

He parked in the shadows beside the garage. Not sneaking, exactly, but not advertising his presence, either. Kind of handy to have the rental to avoid instant identification.

It was drizzling again as he made his way around the side of the house, down the stone staircase into the formal garden, and then around past the reflecting pool. The family didn't like to swim, so the reflecting pool had been his main source of aquatic fun as a child. He paused for a moment, thinking about the plastic wind-up toys he'd raced from one side to the other, the boats made of folded paper, the coolness of the water on his calves as he'd gone wading.

There had rarely been anyone to play *with*, but he hadn't had a miserable childhood. It was important to remember that. He'd been safe, and clean, and educated. His uncle had fulfilled every moral obligation to the son of his worthless brother. Simon owed him for that.

He stopped outside the conservatory door and tapped gently on the glass. There were security cameras and a guard always on duty, but nobody would have bothered to notify his aunt that Simon was there; he was too frequent a visitor. He didn't want to startle her. Another gentle tap and he pushed the door open, stepped through the graceful archway of vines the gardener had somehow persuaded to bloom even in the cool darkness of winter, and found Aunt May, serene as always, reclining on her delicately carved divan.

"Simon," she said, no hint of surprise. "It's lovely to see you. You don't visit as often as you should."

From some, it might have seemed like an attempt to make him feel guilty, but from her, it was just a recognition that it would be better for *him* to come by more often. She patted the spot by her feet on the divan, and even though he was a grown man and really should find his own chair, it felt right to take the spot he'd sat in so often as a child.

He'd seen her just that morning, but that had been with others around. Now, with just the two of them, he wondered how long it had been since they'd had a real conversation. "I hope you're well," he said. It was absurdly formal, but her smile was gentle in response.

"I am. And you?"

Stupid to be shy about it now. He'd come over for a reason, after all. But he felt suddenly foolish, weak, immature. He'd gotten his feelings hurt and gone running to his surrogate mommy? Really?

"Nothing to complain about," he said.

"Complain? No, you don't complain. But that doesn't really answer my question, does it?"

He smiled. "You're too wily for me."

"And you're too wily for me, when you want to be. But here you are, letting that clever façade drop, letting me see that you're not happy." She paused, then said, "*Finally* letting me see that. It's not an opportunity I feel I should let pass. So, I'll ask again, Simon, and this time I'll expect a more complete answer. Are you well, Simon?"

It felt like an absurd self-indulgence, as if he were giving in to the hipster nonsense he'd accused Tristan of spouting, but he said it anyway. "I'm not really sure what that means, to be 'well'. I'm fine, physically. I'm—safe. Comfortable. So I suppose I'm well."

"But something has happened," she said, still calm. "Something that's made you realize that while you may be safe and comfortable, you're not—what? Happy?"

Something? Some*one* had happened. Well, someone and his annoying bruiser of a friend. "It's childish," he said.

"Well, you didn't have much chance to be childish when you actually were a child, so maybe it's fair for you to make up for that now."

He laughed, just a little. "You're determined to have me whine at you?"

She didn't say anything, just waited patiently.

It didn't take too long for him to break. "I'm honored to be part of the family business." True or not, he needed to say it.

"But—I don't have—there isn't any room for—" He stopped. Was he really going to complain to her that her husband didn't let him do what he wanted? That the man who'd given him so much wasn't giving him a little more?

He stood abruptly. The conservatory, warm and humid as the tropics, felt claustrophobic, as if the air itself was weighing him down. "I'm sorry. I'm fine. Truly, I'm well. I don't know what's gotten into me."

"You're twenty-eight years old," his aunt said quietly. "I expected us to have this conversation a decade or more ago."

He nodded. "Yes, you're right. It's immature. I apologize again. I shouldn't have disturbed you."

He'd taken two steps toward the door, planning to turn when he got there to give his goodbye, when Aunt May said, "Simon." She waited for him to freeze, then added, "Come over here and sit down. We're not finished yet."

He returned to the divan like a little boy being summoned to a well-deserved scolding.

His aunt waited until he was settled at her feet, then said, "You never rebelled. I kept waiting for it to happen, but it never did. And now? I'm not sure I can really even call this a rebellion— certainly not a vigorous one. But I'm going to give you the speech I came up with then, just because it's a lovely speech and it seems a shame to waste it."

A rebellion. Was that what he'd been contemplating? Surely not—not him. But he didn't argue with her, and when she was satisfied that he was listening, she began.

"Your parents were young when they came to us for help. They'd married without family support, had a baby far too soon, and found themselves overwhelmed by poverty and immaturity."

Nothing new there, but his aunt didn't generally speak for no reason, so he waited, and she continued. "There were three options your uncle considered; well, three options he *claimed* to consider, but I think possibly the third one he only pretended to think about. The first, of course, was to turn them away. Your father had defied his family when he'd married someone unsuitable, so why should his family help him get out of the mess? The second option was to take you in, as they requested."

Again, nothing new, except—"What was the third option?"

"The third option, the one I'm not sure your uncle really considered, was to *help* them. Not by taking their child away but by giving them work, and a home, and a chance to grow stronger instead of weaker." Simon wasn't looking right at her, but he could see her shake her head in his peripheral vision. "He could have done that, but he didn't."

She sighed. "And maybe it's just as well. Maybe it would have been even worse for your father to be turned into Frank's shadow than it's been for you to be treated the same way. I'm not sure. But the point is, the support you've gotten from your family? The home, and the rest of it? It came at a cost. I know you know that, but you think the price is your eternal loyalty. And I'm telling you this now so you understand: you paid the price when you were a small child, when your parents were sent away from this house, leaving you behind."

For someone generally considered to be a quick thinker, it took far too long for Simon to process what she was saying. Not the words, and not the facts behind them, but the emotions they evoked. His parents could have stayed? They'd been sent away, rather than running? And his uncle could have stopped it.

He'd never asked too many questions about them when he'd been a child; they were gone, he was here, and it was made very clear that he should be glad of it. But his aunt's words felt true, and important.

But important how? "I have a good life," he said slowly. "A nice car, a nice apartment. My work is—I'm well suited to it."

"When you were little, you used to love to paint," Aunt May said quietly. "And you'd tell me stories. Beautiful stories, with magical creatures and adventurous children."

"When I was little I'd pull my shoes and socks off every time I had the chance and run around barefoot, no matter where I was."

He could feel her smile more than see it. "Yes, you did," she said. "And maybe you should do more of that, as well as more of the creative side of things."

He sighed. It was a game, and not even an especially pleasant one. They were pretending his uncle was someone else, pretending their *lives* were something else. "You know that wouldn't be allowed," he said quietly, and her feet tensed against his thigh.

"You've done your time," she said, quietly but firmly.

"I'm still of value. Still useful. Even if I don't stay out of gratitude, I'll stay because—of other reasons."

He'd stay because his uncle didn't accept being crossed. He might have shifted his business into the more legitimate world, but he'd kept his contacts in the criminal underworld, and he'd use them if he had to. He probably wouldn't *kill* his brother's son. Probably. But if Simon left the family business he'd be penniless, unable to protect himself from whatever short-of-killing punishments his uncle devised. When Tristan had refused to obey, Simon had stolen his savings and his business; in a similar situation, Simon wouldn't have those assets to lose, but his uncle was certainly in a position to ensure that he never *gained* those assets. And that was the mildest response Simon could imagine.

He pushed himself to his feet. "There's no point in this," he said. "It doesn't make any difference."

His aunt was quiet for only a moment, and then she said, "Sometimes everything seems to be out of our control. I know that. But we can still control our own minds. Our own thoughts and attitudes. Maybe you need to keep working for your uncle; you know more about that side of things than I do. But you don't need to be grateful for it. That I know."

"And you think it's actually going to be *easier* to keep going as I have been, with a different attitude than what I've had?" He shook his head. For a wise woman, his aunt could sometimes be quite naïve. She seemed to have no idea about the powers of denial.

But she didn't sound doubtful as she said, "Easier? Maybe not. But the easy way isn't always the best way, Simon. You know that."

He wasn't really sure he knew anything of the kind, but he nodded anyway. "Thank you for seeing me," he said quietly, and started for the door.

"Any time, Simon. I mean that—come see me whenever you need to."

He managed to make it out of the conservatory without hearing any more of her gentle proddings or troublesome ideas. His aunt had been raised in a wealthy family and married, with that family's approval, into an even wealthier one. She'd been sheltered her entire life, expected to be little more than an ornament. She didn't know, didn't understand.

But her words stayed with him. *The easy way isn't always the best way.*

He supposed it was true. The easy thing would be to walk away from Tristan and his problems and never look back. But would that be the best thing?

Lap Dog

Chapter Eight

THE LEATHER OUTFIT was just as revealing, just as demeaning, as Tristan had known it would be. It might have been something different if he'd been wearing it for someone he knew, but for strangers? For businessmen, packaging him as a commodity? His stomach was churning with disgust.

There'd been a sort of going-away procession when he'd left the apartment, with Shane glowering, Noah hovering, and the rest of the gang watching anxiously. Micah had offered Tristan two little green pills. "If you need a little escape," he'd whispered. "One to take the edge off, two to take off entirely."

Tristan had been tempted. But he'd never needed drugs to deal with his job, never let himself give in to the temptation of "taking off". Then, after he was driven to the mansion where the party was taking place, escorted to the back room and handed his little outfit, he'd wished he hadn't been quite so quick to refuse the assistance. And after strapping himself into the—damn it, he was just going to abandon all pride and call it a damn bikini, because that's essentially what it was, with straps across his chest instead of triangles of fabric—he'd thought about asking around, seeing what he could find at the party that might help him out. Hell, yeah, he wanted to take off.

He wasn't into the leather scene, but that wasn't a big deal. He hadn't been into a lot of things his clients had wanted in the past, and he'd been able to get through it all. But he'd always been able to walk away.

He nervously adjusted the straps, trying to find a position that didn't make them dig into him so hard. Yeah, he'd been able to walk away, to get the hell out of any situation he didn't like, knowing that the only repercussion would be losing one client he didn't want anyway. He'd only taken advantage of that freedom a handful of times, but the security of knowing he had the option? He hadn't realized how important that had been until he'd lost it.

And he could have escaped. If he'd let Simon Yeung help him out, whatever that would have looked like, whatever it would have meant, at least it wouldn't have been *this*. But Tristan's morals, or, more likely, his pride, had gotten in the way. Better to be a victim than a victimizer? Did he really believe that? And was he ready to deal with the consequences of his beliefs?

"Let's go!" a strident voice rang out, and Tristan turned to look at the tiny blond woman in a tight-fitting business suit who was barking out orders. Apparently she was the Mistress of Ceremonies for the night's events. Tristan had the feeling she was taking the *Mistress* thing a little too seriously. "I want you all lined up, I want you all gorgeous, I want you all fabulous and ready to go!" She strutted around the room, slapping a crop against her boots, and paused when she got to Tristan.

"You're one of the new boys," she purred. "The stubborn one. We have something special for you tonight."

"I appreciate the thought," he managed, and she gave him an incredulous look before stalking off to stare at someone else.

Tristan looked down at himself. If there was someone in the crowd who was into humiliating people? Clearly, Tristan would be a fucking bullseye for that sort of thing. He didn't have a really clear idea of what was going to happen when he and the others were let out into the main part of the house, but he absolutely knew that whatever it was, it would be controlled by someone else, not him. He was just expected to go along with it all, because that was what he was there for.

Because you're a whore, he reminded himself. *That's all you've been for years. Don't get melodramatic about this.*

That's what he told himself. But at his core, the part that was screaming at him for having refused Micah's pills, he knew that this night was different from all the ones that had gone before. Different in a terrible, hopeless way.

SIMON'S INVITATION TO the Chens' party had come only that morning, and all day long, he'd told himself he wouldn't be attending. There was no logical reason for him to be there, after all.

His work was complete, he'd done enough extra to appease even the most onerous demands of his conscience, and Tristan clearly had no interest in ever seeing him again. There was absolutely no reason to be there.

But still, he somehow wasn't surprised to find himself showering and shaving, pulling on a conservative dark suit, and heading for the parking garage. He was still driving the loaner, and he found himself starting to miss his own sleek ride. He could have gone for a drive that night, could have tested the Mercedes' handling on the Olympic Peninsula loop and let himself be distracted by the ocean and the stars and anything else that wasn't a stubborn, sullen whore who wouldn't let himself be rescued.

But, no. Simon wouldn't fool himself like that. Even if he'd had the Mercedes, even if he could have gone for the best drive in the history of solitary automotive escapes, he wouldn't have chosen it. Not when seeing Tristan Beck was his other option.

So he tapped the address from the invitation into his phone and followed its directions east, across the bridge over the lake, and then out into what was starting to feel like wilderness before his GPS told him he'd arrived. There was a uniformed man at the gate who took Simon's invitation, checked a list, and then shone a flashlight into the back seat of the car, clearly looking for any uninvited guests.

"Want me to pop the trunk so you can look in there?" Simon asked.

"That's not necessary, sir. Enjoy your evening."

It was too dark to see the man's face, but had there been a bit of a smirk in his voice?

No, that was just Simon's paranoia at work. A party like this, or like what Simon *thought* this party was like, would be costing the Chens a lot of money, and they'd have paid attention to every detail. All staff would be discrete and respectful.

He reminded himself that his rationale for showing up, the thin justification he'd been able to come up with, was to observe and learn. The Chens were allies now, but they could be enemies in the future. He needed to gather intel, just as he always did. He'd learn about their ways of doing business, look for weaknesses, and be ready to exploit them as needed. That was what he'd tell his uncle if it ever came up.

He tried to look casual as he handed his keys to the valet and jogged up the wide staircase to the front door. The house was modern, with a lot of windows, but blinds were down on all of them, only glowing light escaping to the driveway. And the foyer, once Simon was admitted, didn't give away much more. There were staff members in black clothes, one to take his coat, another to offer him a drink, and then David Chen himself appeared, his son trailing along behind him.

"Simon," Chen said, his voice warm and welcoming. "I'm so glad you could make it. I know it was a little last minute, but William—" and he stepped aside, bringing his son further into the conversation, "will introduce you to Alicia, our client relations manager, and once she has a better idea of your interests, we'll be happy to include you in further events."

"I appreciate the thought, but I think tonight is probably a one-time visit for me."

Chen stepped a little closer so only Simon and William could hear him say, "Finances don't need to be a concern. I'd be happy to take care of that. And if you're worried that your uncle might not approve, I assure you, discretion is one of our most valued services. Isn't that right, William?"

"Of course," William agreed.

So that was unfolding about as Simon had expected. Men like Chen—men like Simon's uncle—damn it, men like Simon himself—they didn't issue random invitations or do much of anything just to be nice. Chen wanted to have something to hold over Simon's head. A financial debt, a secret that could be told, or even just a way inside his brain. It could all be useful to Chen, and damaging to Simon.

Still, he let himself be led further into the mansion. Around a grand staircase into what could only be described as a ball room, with a soaring ceiling and a peaked glass roof. It must cost a fortune just to heat the place, and Simon wondered again about the economics of the business.

There were about thirty well-dressed men in the room, standing in small clusters around—Simon swallowed hard.

It wasn't his thing. He had no interest in causing or feeling pain, didn't want to humiliate or control his partners, certainly didn't want to be humiliated or controlled by anyone else. But the scenes were so overtly sexual, so *unashamedly* erotic, that he felt as if he'd been wearing a blindfold all his life and it had just been taken off.

Onc of the groups was clustered around a wood-and-metal framework, maybe eight by eight feet, with huge, industrial-strength bolts and reinforcement all over it. There were chains, strong enough that they might have come from a shipyard somewhere, hanging from different parts of the structure, with heavy metal cuffs at their ends. And, of course, there was a human being, a young, beautiful man with skin darker than the iron shackled around him, stretched out and naked and exposed.

In a different setting it could have been an art installation, some statement about the dehumanizing impact of industrialization. But in this space, with the men staring at the display, with the floggers or whips or whatever the hell they were hung out by the side of the frame in anticipation of something more? It wasn't the sort of sex Simon imagined, certainly nothing like he had ever experienced, but it was sex, all the same. And none of the men watching seemed even a little embarrassed.

There were other displays set up around the room, and each one had a little cluster of men around it, sipping their glasses of scotch or fine wines, chatting a little, but mostly just watching.

"Where do you get your clientele?" Simon asked, trying to activate his brain instead of his cock. There couldn't be this many rich, kinky gay men in Seattle, could there?

"There's a fairly lucrative travel sideline," William said, his enthusiasm winning out over his discretion. "We have guests tonight from New York, Dubai, London, Hong Kong, Vancouver, Los Angeles—all over. And we have connections with similar businesses in all of those places and are able to offer our local Seattle clients access to events in those cities."

And the business was sex. Gay sex. Kinky gay sex. Simon felt like a naïve child. It wasn't like he hadn't known this sort of thing was happening, but knowing about it in the abstract and seeing it in person were apparently two very different things.

Then he remembered the real reason he was there, and suddenly arousal wasn't an issue anymore. *This* was what Tristan was being forced into. Whatever he'd been doing before, whatever his clients had wanted, it had been small-scale, not this commercialized, corporatized, multi-national system.

"You have more than one room operating?" Simon asked, still trying to sound only mildly curious.

Chen's smile made it clear he wasn't fooled. "This is our main display area right now. There are private rooms elsewhere, of course, for those who wish."

Did that mean Tristan was in one of those private rooms right then? What was being done to him, and by whom?

Simon fought to keep his expression neutral. "It's a very interesting event," he managed.

"I think you'll be even *more* interested by what comes next," Chen said and he nodded to a woman across the room, who reached out and flicked a panel of light switches on the wall, throwing the room into darkness for about a second before turning the lights back on.

"I know many of you have been waiting to see our newest arrivals," the woman said, her voice carrying through the room without apparent effort. "If you'd like the chance to see them first, and, of course, to take part in our traditional auction for their first night's services, please join me in the library. I think you'll be very pleased with our offerings."

An auction. Simon's stomach churned. It was as if he'd been transported back in time. Would the prospective buyers look at the teeth of the new "offerings"? Would they test their muscles, judge their ability to work? To withstand?

And Tristan would be one of those offerings, there because Simon had connived to put him there. And Simon didn't have the money, didn't have the power to do a damn thing to change it. He had Tristan's savings, of course, but—did it make sense to spend that? Was it right? Was it what Tristan would want?

Somehow, Simon didn't think so. Tristan had worked hard to save that money, and Simon could blow through it all pretty quickly, trying to delay the inevitable moment when the money ran out and Tristan was still in Chen's power, only now without any savings to help him get on with his life afterward.

So Simon didn't have money, and he didn't have power. His uncle hadn't seen fit to grant him either of those tools. But his uncle had let Simon train his brain. And if that was all Simon had, then that was what Simon would use.

He clamped down on his natural reactions and took a moment to consider what Chen would want to see. He'd invited Simon there because he wanted something, wanted to uncover something. Not strength; that was the last thing Chen would find useful. And not revulsion, certainly; that was what Simon's uncle would expect Simon to display, for the homosexuality, if not the commercialization. No. Chen wanted to see something different from Simon, something he'd think he could use.

So Simon turned to the older man and let just a little light shine in his eyes, just a little hint of lust and avarice. "He's been used before," he said. "It's not as if he's a virgin. He shouldn't be *too* valuable, should he?"

Chen shrugged. "Our clients are very wealthy men, and your little friend does have a certain quality to him. Something—well, as you say, he's been used before, but he somehow doesn't *seem* it, does he? There's something about him that still seems pure, isn't there? We have clients who like that sort of thing very much. So—" Another shrug, this one accompanied with a satisfied smile. "I expect the price will be more than worth the trouble it took to get him here."

Simon let a little of his real anxiety show on his face. A little, but not too much. Chen wouldn't believe it if Simon suddenly melted down into a big pile of emotion and compassion. No, he had to play this just right. And, of course, he had to be aware that Chen was playing him in return.

"Shall we go watch?" Chen asked, his hand just grazing across the small of Simon's back. "It's always very dramatic. And, honestly, with your friend being somewhat less than enthusiastic? That makes it so much more interesting—a sullen angel instead of a sweet one."

Simon didn't let his hands clench into fists. This wasn't something he could hate Chen for, not until he was through hating himself. So he allowed himself to be guided into the library, a room about as large as Simon's entire apartment, with one of those balconies running around the entire space, half-way up the two storey walls. The walkway widened at one end, giving enough space for the woman from the other room to gather her charges together.

And there Tristan was, standing above the crowd, off to the side, looking as if he were trying to wish himself away. He was wearing some outlandish, ridiculous concoction of leather and metal, so over the top it almost seemed like a parody. But then Simon remembered the black man in the other room, stretched out and exposed, chained into whatever position his controllers wanted. He'd been wearing something fairly similar, and it hadn't seemed at all ridiculous, then.

Simon let himself take a long look. He let Chen *see* him taking the long look. This was a negotiation, and Simon had made his interests clear. But if he gave away too much, too soon, he'd look weak, and he wouldn't get what he wanted. So he made himself look away, and took a moment to study the other men in the room. "No confidentiality concerns?" he asked. "If these men can afford what I assume you're charging, they have reputations to uphold. Even if you and your staff are discreet, they aren't worried that one of their compatriots might not be?"

"It's actually a valuable networking opportunity," Chen said. "Several of them do business together, after meeting at events like this." He paused, then said, "It's the twenty-first century, Simon. Men don't need to be ashamed of wanting what they want."

And that was the invitation. Simon snorted. "Ashamed? Maybe not. But *wanting* doesn't do much good, all on its own." Invitation to a deal.

And Chen nodded his understanding. "Not all on its own, no. But someone like you? Someone with skills, and connections?" He looked up at Tristan, then back at Simon. "I was disappointed when you told me we wouldn't be working together. I'd thought of several projects where I could use someone like you."

"I was disappointed as well," Simon said. Maybe he should have been honest and told Chen that Tristan had been the one who'd backed out, but he wasn't quite ready for that level of humiliation. Much easier to let Chen believe Simon's uncle had been the problem. And better, too, because if Chen thought Simon was angry at his uncle, he'd expect Simon to be more open to whatever he was about to propose.

But Chen surprised him, which wasn't a good thing. Instead of making his offer, he just turned to his son, murmured a few words, and then turned back to look up at the balcony.

William Chen spoke into a transmitter on his wrist, one that had been hidden beneath his jacket, and the woman on the balcony looked down, clearly getting the message in her earpiece. There was a moment when it seemed as if she wanted to ask questions, but instead she nodded, turned, and gestured to Tristan. She seemed to be sending him back through the doorway at the rear of the library. Sending him where, and why?

Simon realized that David Chen was watching him react, but with so little understanding of the situation, he couldn't really figure out what response would be best. So he went with honesty. "I don't understand what's happening," he said.

"Because you've been raised with a transactional understanding of human relations," Chen said regretfully. "You can't accept that sometimes you are given something with nothing being taken in return."

Simon frowned at him. "I'm going to need you to spell things out a little more clearly."

A sigh, showing that Chen was disappointed by Simon's lack of understanding, but unfortunately not surprised. "You may have him. For this evening, at least. For long enough to decide whether you want to find a way to keep him longer term."

"For free," Simon said, testing for the trap. "My gratitude, obviously, but nothing beyond that? No actual bargain?"

"Your gratitude is sufficient. This is not a transaction, it is a gesture of goodwill."

It was hardly unheard of. Simon's original service for Chen had been just such a gesture, after all—his uncle had received no direct compensation for loaning Simon out. But these gifts were given at the higher levels, from one leader to another, not from a leader to a mere tool.

"I can't do anything to compromise my loyalty to my family," Simon said.

"Of course not. But your family and mine are not enemies. We are not even rivals. There's no reason you should not accept a gift from me."

Well, the gift was a human being, so of course there was a reason, if anyone was being at all ethical about things. But, of more direct concern, the gift was a *male* human being, gifted for the purposes of sex. Simon's uncle would *not* approve.

But Simon had paid his debt to his uncle when he'd lost his parents.

It was strange to think that, and Simon felt guilt creeping up his spine. Then he thought of what he'd done to trap Tristan Beck, and his worries about his uncle turned into a few drops in a huge ocean. He was making himself vulnerable, giving the Chens power over him, and he didn't even hesitate.

"Thank you," he said. "I'm truly grateful."

David Chen's smile was as sweet and innocent as a man handing ice cream to a child. "Enjoy," he said. "He'll be waiting in your car."

Which should have been good. It should have been a solution. But as Simon started for the front door, still a little dazed from the quick shift in fortunes, he remembered that the last time he'd seen Tristan hadn't been exactly friendly. In fact, *no* time he'd seen Tristan had been friendly. Simon might be taking some weird sense of responsibility for the guy, but as far as Tristan was concerned, Simon was an evil corporate drone.

Excellent. That made everything just a little bit more complicated.

Lap Dog

Chapter Nine

WHEN TRISTAN HAD still been living with his family, his mother had often complained about being on her last nerve. He'd never really understood what she meant, not until this moment, sitting in the passenger seat of some stranger's car, waiting for he knew not what.

They'd put his real clothes in a paper bag and given him a baggy jumpsuit to zip over his bondage wear and he thought it should have made him feel better to be more covered, but then he'd started thinking about prison uniforms and wondering who else had ever worn this suit and whether that person was okay now, or was still in trouble. The valet who'd driven the car up to the main doors of the house hadn't even glanced toward him, and it had made Tristan feel as if he were invisible, maybe already dead and just a ghost, and it hadn't been as upsetting a thought as it should have been. Yeah, he'd burned through all his available nerves, and there was only one left, and it was charring in the middle. He wondered what would happen if it snapped.

He tried not to look toward the house, tried not to anticipate the man who would soon be coming down the stairs toward him.

Where that man would take them, and what he'd do to Tristan once they got there.

He should run. Middle of nowhere, jumpsuit over leather, bare feet stumbling through the darkness. He didn't care. He needed to get the hell away from all this, and he didn't care if he got eaten by a bear, it would still be better than—

The driver's door opened, and even before he saw the man's face, Tristan recognized the lean body, the grace and economy of movement as he slid into the driver's seat. "You?"

"You need to be quiet for a bit," Simon Yeung said. "I need to think."

"About what? What the hell is going on?"

Yeung twisted the key in the ignition and threw the car into gear almost violently. "Is that really your version of being quiet?"

So Tristan tried. His last nerve was still stretched, still smoking, but it didn't seem to actually be on fire, and it was entirely possible that a few of the others were starting to grow back together, stretching tentative nerve-fronds across the abyss toward each other—

"I can't take you home," Yeung said. He sounded frustrated. "I'm not exactly sure what's going on, but I need to look as if I'm—enjoying you. It would be rude otherwise. I need to make it appear as if you're a welcome gift."

"A *gift*? You didn't pay for me?"

"Fuck, no," Yeung said. He glanced into the backseat for a moment before returning his gaze to the road. "Don't flatter yourself. You made it totally clear you didn't want to work with me, so let me make something totally clear to you: I don't fuck whores. I don't pay for sex. I don't like this BDSM bullshit, and I think you look like an idiot all dressed up like that."

"I'm wearing a jumpsuit," Tristan protested. It probably wasn't the part he should be focusing on, but it was the easiest point to rebut.

"And what's underneath the jumpsuit?"

"A lot of weird shit that *I* don't like either. It's not like I dressed *myself* for this."

Yeung didn't answer, just kept driving, and eventually Tristan said, "So, where are we going? You can't take me to my home. So are we going to your place?"

"No."

"Are we going to Disneyworld?"

Yeung sighed. 'Maybe we'll just keep driving. Do you like driving? Oh, wait, probably not. We're burning fossil fuels, right? Feeding the military-industrial complex with our dependence on the oil cartels? We should be walking, or riding horses or some other crunchy granola bullshit."

"You're really angry tonight." Possibly that was something Tristan should have kept to himself, but apparently having only one nerve left didn't leave him any extras with which to control his mouth. "I don't really know what's going on. But you got me out of that party, somehow, and apparently it wasn't because you want to drag me off to your dungeon to squeeze my balls in a vice, so, seriously—thank you. Whatever we're doing? Even if we're consuming fossil-fuel at a completely irresponsible rate? I'm down with it. It's a huge improvement on the way I thought I'd be spending my night."

Yeung didn't answer for a while, but when he finally did, he sounded calmer. "Do you have your phone with you? Find us a motel. Something not too expensive. And we'll only be paying for one room, so make sure you find one with two beds. And room service, or at least a restaurant nearby. I'm hungry."

One of the nerves that had been trying to regrow twanged its ends farther apart at the mention of a motel, then let the tendrils join and strengthen as Yeung bitched about beds and food. This wasn't something sleazy. Weird, but not sleazy.

"We're taking a road trip," Tristan said, mostly to himself. "There's probably a reason for it, but I don't need to know, necessarily. I'll just focus on the positive, how 'bout that? I'll find somewhere with a really good restaurant, because I'm hungry too. And you're paying, right?"

"Somewhere cheap. I mean it."

"I've seen your car, man. And I made Shane tell me about the trip to your apartment—you're living on one of the top floors of one of the nicest buildings in town. So how come you're so worried about money all of a sudden?"

"I guess I don't have to be—we can just spend from your savings, right?"

Well, that put things in a different perspective. "I'll find somewhere cheap," Tristan said. "But, speaking of my savings—I don't suppose you'd be interested in giving any of that back? I think there was mention of bonuses for working hard. I showed up tonight, you know. I wore what they wanted me to, and I left the party with some guy I barely know, just like I was told to."

Yeung didn't answer for quite a while, but finally he said, "Look in the glovebox."

It seemed too easy, but Tristan reached forward anyway, depressed the little button, let the door fall open, and saw a familiar envelope on top of all the other papers in the compartment. He reached for it, telling himself it was just an illusion that the envelope looked as thick as it had been when it had been nestled under his floorboards. But his fingers closed around the paper and felt the weight of it, and when he pulled it out and looked inside, the money all seemed to be there.

"I don't understand," he said.

"I told you, I was trying to help. You didn't like my last idea. So this is the next idea." Yeung glanced over at him, and said, "You take your money and get the hell out of town." He looked back at the road and added, "I know we agreed that wasn't a good option for you. But that was before we—well, it was before *I* really understood. I thought—I don't know what I thought. It doesn't matter. The point is, you don't want to do the one thing I could think of that might get you out of this and let you stay in town, so you should get out of town. You can keep your principles intact and start over somewhere else. You've got enough money to pay for a couple years of school, probably. Or you could just get a job. A regular job, and use your savings to put a down payment on somewhere to live."

"And my friends?" Tristan asked quietly.

"You'd make new friends. And this bunch could go visit you or something. I don't know. Look, Tristan, you're not going to get everything you want here. That's just not going to happen. But that doesn't mean you have to give up entirely."

"You said you passed information along. You said—you implied—that they might go after my friends if they couldn't find me. Isn't that still true?"

"I could try to protect them."

"How? I thought you were powerless in all this, just another pawn like me. You're just the messenger, right?"

There was a muscle in Yeung's cheek that twitched when he was trying to control himself. High cheekbones, strong jaw, golden skin, and a tiny, twitching muscle. "I couldn't guarantee anything. But your friends can look after themselves."

"No, they can't. Not against something like this. And they shouldn't have to. This is my mess, not theirs."

They drove silently through the night, and for the first time, Tristan found himself trying to understand Simon Yeung. What the hell was motivating him? What was he looking for, and why did he seem to be having so much trouble finding it?

"You got me to do what you wanted, before." Tristan wasn't sure if Yeung was listening, and certainly wasn't sure if he'd deign to answer, but he continued anyway. "It didn't seem like it was even difficult for you. But now—it seems different, now. You seem frustrated. What's different?"

Another several moments with no answer and then, snake-fast, Yeung's hand shot out and grabbed the envelope out of Tristan's lap. He tossed it easily to his other hand, slipped it down the far side of his seat, and kept driving without even looking over.

"Okay," he said. "I'll get rid of the differences. I'll stop trying to do what you want, because clearly what you want is stupid and self-destructive. So, back to the old way. You have no money. You have no clients unless you accept the control of your evil corporate overlords. And I know things about your friends, things that would make their lives much more difficult. I've got the video recording of their vandalism, and of the other one breaking into my building. And I can find other tools as well, just as I found tools to use against you. So, if you don't respond to reason, it's time to respond to threats. Get the hell out of town."

It was all said so calmly. Yeung *was* back to the man he'd been at the beginning, and it was only then that Tristan realized how much their interaction had changed. Somewhere over their past few meetings, Yeung had shifted from presenting himself as cool and in charge to something much more human. Until now. "So as soon as I have a thought of my own, that's it?" Tristan demanded. "If I don't do exactly what you say, you cut me off?"

"When did you stop having thoughts of your own, little duck? I must have missed that millisecond of lucidity and reason."

"It's unreasonable of me to want my independence and freedom?"

"It's unreasonable of you to ignore reality and do nothing to help your damn self, but still bitch and moan about other people not helping you in the exact—and impossible—way that you want." There was a little heat coming back into Yeung's voice, but then he caught himself almost visibly, shook his head, and continued in a quieter tone. "So, you tell me. What's your next step? Should I just drive you back to the party and thank them for the gesture but tell them I'm done with you?"

Tristan's stomach clenched in rebellion at the thought. No. As complicated and frustrating as things were in the car, driving around with Yeung was still so much better than being at the party or whatever would have come *after* the party. "No," he said, trying to sound as if the very idea hadn't sent a wave of revulsion and fear through him. "I don't want to go back there."

"Okay, then. You want your freedom and your independence. For the next few hours, at least, you have it. What do you want to actually *do* with that time? How do you want to make things better?"

"I don't know!" That last nerve was stretched taut again. "Is that what you want to hear? I'm sorry I'm not the great Simon Yeung, master of planning and strategy! I'm sorry I don't have everything under control like you do."

"Do ducks not have *ears*?" Yeung retorted. "I've told you—I have no power. Nothing is under my control except *me*. I don't make the rules for the game, but at least I play it as well as I can. You're refusing to play, and you seem to think that if you do that, it will all just go away. But it won't. They've noticed you, and they want you on the board, so you're on the board. Wishing otherwise won't change a damn thing."

Tristan wanted to argue, but he couldn't find anything to say. Yeung was right: wishing wasn't going to do anybody any good. "Maybe I *do* have to go back," he whispered. He was talking mostly to himself, but he knew Yeung could hear him, and that was okay. "If those are my choices—run away and put my friends at risk, stay and work for you and become part of the machine, or work for them? Maybe working for them is the best option."

"It may make your decision easier if you know that working for me is no longer an option. I'm not sure it ever really was; it was an idea, but I didn't have my uncle's agreement, and I'm not sure I would have been able to persuade him. But now? After tonight? No. Now that the Chens made me admit I see you as desirable— whether it's true or not, I made it seem true when I accepted you as a gift—I can't go back to saying I just want an assistant. And they won't let me take you as a whore."

Tristan hadn't realized how tense his body was until he slumped in defeat and felt his muscles relax. "So. That's it, then? Only two choices now, and one of them means my friends might get hurt."

Yeung looked over at him. Again, Tristan felt as if he could actually *see* Yeung arguing with himself internally, but it wasn't clear which side had won when he said, "Did you find anywhere for us to go? We aren't being followed, as far as I can tell, but that doesn't mean they aren't tracking us somehow. Hell, maybe you're wearing a bug. But assuming you aren't, they won't know we're up to anything as long as we keep things looking as they'd expect. So a motel would be good."

"Isn't a motel a little low-rent for someone like me?" Tristan asked, trying to reclaim at least a bit of his spirit.

"Yes. But not for someone like me. They know I can't take you home where my uncle might find out, and they know I don't have any money of my own. So a motel is fine."

"You're actually taking a lot of risks with this, aren't you?" Tristan felt stupid for not having realized it earlier. "For no real reason. The easiest thing for you would be to walk away and go back to your life. Right?"

"You would think that would be easy," Yeung agreed. "But I'm actually finding it fairly difficult. Still, let's look at one problem at a time. We need somewhere we can talk, and sort things out. We can make a new plan. So, first step: find us a motel, please."

For the first time, Tristan didn't resent the way Yeung was taking charge. Maybe because he'd explained his reasoning, maybe because he clearly did seem to be trying to help, but mostly because he was risking things himself, by doing all this. The motives for that were still unclear, but the outcome didn't seem to be. For whatever reason, Yeung had committed himself to helping Tristan out. That meant they were in this together. Strange as it was, it seemed to be true. At least for the time being.

THE MOTEL TRISTAN FOUND would have been perfect, if they'd actually been heading there to engage in whatever illicit activities one engaged in with a bondage-dressed whore. Simon wasn't sure what could be done without elaborate frames and equipment, and didn't really want to find out. But the setting surely seemed right; an almost abandoned motel, and he'd asked for the room furthest from the office, so nobody would have been able to hear—and his mind shut down there, because the sounds he was imagining weren't screams of pain but moans of quite a different kind.

No, he could not afford to make this damn situation any more complicated than it already was.

He returned to the room after a trip to the vending machines that provided the only food, since the restaurant was closed for the night, and found Tristan changed back into his own clothes, jeans and a sweatshirt about five times too big for his slight frame. Simon was pretty sure the hoodie belonged to the thug friend, and wondered whether Tristan wore it when he needed comfort. It wasn't a thought that should have made him feel jealous.

Simon needed to get his mind back on the task at hand. He shut the door behind him and tossed two bags of potato chips and two chocolate bars onto the bed, then set two cans of soda somewhat more carefully down beside them. "Brain food, hopefully," he said. "Eat if you're hungry. And figure out what your goals are."

"Goals?"

"Not some stupid go-back-to-the-good-old-days stuff. Something that we could possibly achieve, given the current reality."

Tristan frowned as he picked up a bag of chips. Hopefully he was thinking of a goal, not planning another damn rebellion.

Simon took the other bag and opened it for himself, then removed his suit jacket and settled into the only armchair in the room.

"I don't know what's realistic," Tristan finally said. "You're the one who knows these people. What are my options?"

Great, another chance to have a suggestion shot down. But Simon tried to see things from Tristan's perspective. "You'd been saving money. Why? What were you saving up for? Just a rainy day, or something specific?"

Tristan didn't answer right away, making it clear there still wasn't much trust between them. Tristan didn't want to tell his secrets to a virtual stranger, and that made sense, so Simon sat, looking as non-threatening as he could manage, until Tristan finally spoke. "I wasn't totally sure. I used to think I'd go back to school. But—I don't know. It seems like—" he shoved a few chips in his mouth, almost certainly to give himself time to think rather than because he was hungry. "It's like I'd be setting myself up to live a lie, I guess. I mean, if I went to school, got a profession or something, started a regular life—would I tell people what I used to do? Like, I couldn't be a teacher or something, not knowing that the next parent who walked into the classroom might be a former client. But something less sensitive? Like, could I just work in an office somewhere?"

"Couldn't you?" Simon asked. "Just leave it all behind and start over?"

Tristan almost smiled, but he didn't look happy. "That's just it. Leave it all behind. Start over. When people asked what I'd been doing for those years, make something up, or be vague. Keep my new friends away from my old friends, or to be totally safe, cut off my old friends entirely. Right? Live a lie, and always worry about being found out."

"You're an idealist," Simon said softly. It seemed strange. Surely a whore should be realistic and jaded and hardened by life? "You want to live a truthful life, and you want to hold onto your friends even if they aren't good for you. You still think all of that is possible."

It was completely obvious what needed to happen. Tristan needed to grow up and accept reality. He needed to come down to Earth instead of floating around in the damn clouds. But for some reason, Simon really didn't want to see that happen. So he said, "Those are your goals. That's what we shoot for, then. We just need to figure out a way to make them possible."

Tristan had clearly been expecting a different reaction, probably one more in keeping with the way Simon knew he *should* have responded. "That's it? You're not going to call me a stupid duck and threaten to roast me, or something?"

"I don't think that would be productive." Simon leaned forward in his chair. He wished he had a pad of paper to scribble on. Ideas. He needed ideas. "You want to do something where you can be truthful about who you are and where you've been, and where you can stay friends with the people you're currently friends with." That part was easy enough, until he added in the second set of criteria. "You need to be doing something that will either keep you hidden from the Chens or that they won't object to you doing. Since you want to stay in touch with your friends, hiding won't work. So we need to find something you want to do, and that the Chens will allow you to do." He leaned back in his chair and squinted at the ceiling somewhere over Tristan's head.

"We need to make you less valuable to the Chens." It was so simple, now that he'd thought of it. "It's an equation. We need to find a different purpose that is equally or more valuable to them than your current purpose. Right now, you're quite valuable as a whore, so we'd need to find something quite valuable on the other side to balance that out." Maybe he was being a little petulant when he added, "I already came up with something valuable—not because of what you'd be doing, but because I'd agreed to give them some of my time in exchange for freeing you—but that opportunity is gone, and it was beneath your lofty ideals anyway."

"I didn't mean to insult you with that," Tristan said quickly. "Different people make different decisions, right? Doing what you do—maybe it's right for you. I can't say. I just know it wouldn't have been right for me."

It was childish to want to pursue that. Simon didn't need to seek Tristan's approval, or his understanding. That wasn't the purpose of this meeting. "The point is, I think we'll have trouble finding a way to find a non-whoring option that will make you as valuable to the Chens as you currently are as a whore. So if we can't do anything with that side of the equation, we need to work on making you less valuable." He cocked his head to the side. "Would you object to having acid thrown on your face? We could give you goggles to protect your vision."

Tristan stared at him, and Simon kept his face impassive. "I see that you would," he finally said, and then looked down quickly.

But not quickly enough to cover his smirk. "Did you just make a joke?" Tristan demanded. "A horrible joke about facial mutilation? Did that just happen? Were you being *funny*, Mr. Spock?"

"A momentary lapse." Simon looked back up. "But I think the underlying idea is still useful. If you're vetoing mutilation, we need to find another way to make you less valuable. What is it that makes you good at what you do?"

"Besides my smooth, unscarred face?"

"Unless you're willing to go back to my acid idea, yes. Besides your face."

"I don't know," Tristan said. He set the potato chip bag down on the bed and stared at it for a moment, then cast his eyes up toward Simon. "I guess there's just something—" He shrugged, and his hoodie slumped to the side, the too-big neck flopping down and exposing just a little of the tender skin of his neck. His expression was sincere, almost earnest. "Something that makes people want me." He caught himself, frowned a little, and leaned back, blinking hard. "Want to *fuck* me, at least. Not want me, for real. Not for *me*."

Simon wanted to take the little duck in his arms and comfort him. And *then* fuck him. "Shit. How do you do that?" he whispered.

Tristan's grin was wide and triumphant. "I don't know, dude! It just works. It's partly a protective thing, right? Or maybe just being *totally* non-threatening? I don't know the psychology behind it, I just know how to play it. Subtle differences for different guys—like, am I being sweet and innocent, or sweet and sulky, or sweet and mischievous. At the thing tonight, I guess I was going to end up sweet and tortured. Whatever. I just guessed which way to go for you, but it worked, right? Sweet and vulnerable?" His smile made it clear he didn't need a response, and he leaned back on the bed, smugly lacing his hands behind his head. "I've just got it, I guess."

"And the Chens *know* you've got it," Simon said, trying to ignore the signals his body was sending him. "That's our problem right now. You can obviously turn it off and on, but if you deliberately turn it off, they'll know what you're doing and punish you for it. You or your friends."

As expected, that reminder made Tristan serious again, which was just as well. As tempting as "sweet and vulnerable" had been, Simon had been just about as interested in all the other options Tristan had listed, and wasn't finding it easy to turn his excitement off just because he was being treated to the "sweet and cocky" version. He needed to keep his mind on the job at hand.

But apparently Tristan had other ideas. "Have you got a boyfriend?" he asked. "Or a husband, or something? What do Vulcans do? Have you mind-melded with anyone lately?"

"I'm not experienced with prostitutes, but surely this can't be part of your appeal? I can't imagine your clients would be turned on by discussing their regular partners?"

"You'd be surprised what turns some of them on. But, no, I wasn't actually being super-whore right then. I was just curious."

"I'm single," Simon said, which was already far more information than he should be sharing, and then he made it even worse by adding, "My employer wouldn't appreciate any public displays of my unfortunate tendencies."

"I thought you worked for your uncle?" Tristan said. Then, "Oh." A moment later, "My parents kicked me out when I told them I was gay and was going to stay that way, no matter what they did. It stung at the time, but looking back? Best thing that ever happened to me."

"Yes, it's clearly gotten you exactly where you want to be in your life," Simon said. "No negative repercussions from that situation whatsoever."

Tristan shrugged. "Still better than living with them."

"Well, as you know, I don't actually live with my uncle. I have a reasonable amount of independence. I just need to avoid public displays."

"And family displays," Tristan said. "Right? You're probably not bringing dates to family dinner or anything."

"Well, if there was someone I cared about enough to want to introduce them to my family, I'd care about them far too much to want to inflict my family upon them. So it all works out just fine. Let's focus on your challenge, please."

"My challenge?"

"Yes. How will we make you less valuable to the Chens without angering them or causing you permanent harm?"

"Let's do it without causing me temporary harm, too. Can we do that?"

"We can try." Simon frowned. "Don't do the 'Why I'm a good whore' demonstration again. Just—in words, without accompaniment, tell me what makes you valuable. Give me a list, and then we can look at which of the items on the list we could modify."

"Seriously?"

"Or we could do things your way, and sit around and pout for a long time before being dragged off to be a BDSM party favor."

"A list. Okay."

Tristan thought for a moment, and Simon tried to pretend he wasn't enjoying himself. He tried to pretend this wasn't the best night out he'd had in months, if not longer. The uncomfortable party, the hostility, the potential danger—and still, he couldn't think of anywhere he'd rather be.

Then he thought of being on a Caribbean beach, or at a London hotel, or a ski chalet in Aspen. No, none of them appealed, not until he made one small addition. Any of those places? Anywhere, really. It would all be fine, as long as Simon had Tristan Beck to talk to, and to look at, and spar with.

Damn it. He was really getting himself into trouble.

"Okay," Tristan said. "I'm good. Ready for the list?"

"Ready," Simon said. But really, he was anything but.

Lap Dog

Chapter Ten

"I COULD PUT ON weight and maybe rub grease on my face or something to get really pimply, but that would take longer than I'd like," Tristan said. He shouldn't have been enjoying himself quite as much as he was. It all seemed like a game, now. He was safe, in this distant motel room. Safe with Simon Yeung, which was weird, but really seemed to be true. And he'd always been pretty good at living in the moment, not worrying too much about what had happened in the past or was likely to happen in the future. So, yeah, he was having fun, even though his levity seemed to be driving Simon up the wall. Maybe he was having fun *because* he was driving Simon up the wall.

"The pimples would be faster than the fat," Simon said, "but I agree, neither would be instant. But stop thinking of ways to counteract your appeal. Just *explain* your appeal, and it'll be my job to find ways to lessen it."

"I seriously need to explain my appeal? I thought my demonstration took care of that." Was Tristan imagining the slight blush rising up from the clean white collar of Simon's carefully starched shirt? And if he was imagining that, wouldn't it be fun to

147

imagine a little more? Like what would happen if Tristan dragged himself to the foot of the bed and leaned over, loosened Simon's tie....

He caught himself. Where the hell had that come from? Sure, Simon had been—wait, Simon? No, *Yeung*. Yeung the evil corporate pawn! "I need to know why," he said quickly. "Why you're helping me. I mean, Shane came to see you, and you changed your whole approach? Shane's a good guy, and a good friend, but his main persuasion technique is violence, or threats of violence. And I don't think you're afraid of him. So—why?"

"I told you," Simon said. "I didn't realize how bad it would be. That thing tonight—I don't know what I expected, but it was nothing like that."

"No." There was no reason for Simon to give a better answer. His change of heart was a gift horse, and Tristan was asking to see its teeth. Still, Tristan was going to push a little. "You helped me before tonight, or you tried to. Like that job offer? That came before tonight, but after Shane came to see you. Why? What did he say?"

Simon squinted at him, then smiled. Damn, Tristan liked the man's smile, at least when it was a real one, not just a show of teeth. "You're jealous," he said smugly. "You think you're smart and Shane isn't, but you yipped away at me all you wanted and it didn't make a bit of difference. Then a five-minute conversation with Shane and, bam, I'm a new man. Is that pretty hard to take, Tristan?"

"Shane's smart," Tristan said defensively. "And I'm not jealous! There's nothing to be—" A sudden thought made his stomach twist. "He's really happy with Noah. If there was something—or if you're planning something—something that would get in the way of that? Please, don't. He's a good guy, and Noah's a good guy, and—"

"Slow down. Shane didn't seduce me into helping you." Simon sounded amused, but his face grew more thoughtful as he said, "Not with sex, at least. He just—he really cared. Does that make sense?"

"Does it make sense that Shane cares about me? I'd like to think so, yeah."

"Not that he cares, just that it mattered to me. All your friends, showing up like they did, breaking the law, and, honestly, being fairly stupid about it. They did it because they all care about you." He suddenly looked as if he felt he'd said too much. "I was intrigued, that's all. It started me thinking, and once I get started on a problem, I don't like to quit until it's solved. So—you were coming up with a list, weren't you? What have you got for me?"

"I'm tractable," Tristan said. He'd gotten all he was likely to out of Simon, at least for the moment, so he might as well cooperate. "I'm flexible—physically, I guess, but mostly mentally. Flexible enough so I can like what my clients like, or do a good job of faking it. Smart enough to have an okay conversation, on the rare occasion someone actually wants to talk to me. Punctual, discreet—I smell good—I don't know! And none of those are

149

going to do us any good anyway, right? If I start doing a shitty job, they're going to get mad, and if that happens, either I'm in trouble or my friends are in trouble. So—"

"Shhh," Simon said. He was frowning in the general direction of the bed side table, and then quickly looked back at Tristan and nodded. "I think maybe I can work with that. But only—are you okay doing a few jobs for them? I mean—you were a prostitute before, right? Are you able to keep doing that, for just a little while? It might take some time to set up what I'm thinking of."

Strange how hard it was to say yes. Just a little bit of talk about moving on and doing something different, and suddenly Tristan thought he was too good for his job? "Of course I can," he made himself say.

"But you don't want to." Simon ran a hand through his short black hair, ruffling it in frustration. "Maybe I can—I'm not sure. Maybe I can set something up fast. But I need to be careful, and be sure I'm doing it right. Do you understand that? Look, if you don't want to do it, I'll help you run. You can have the cash—shit, I shouldn't have left that in the car. But, whatever, I can go get it and you can have it, if you want to just go."

"That's really generous of you, to give *my* money to me."

"Is that what you want to be arguing about right now?"

"No, I don't want to be arguing about it. I just want you to give me the money. No argument needed."

"And since I already said I'd give you the money, why are we still talking about it?"

150

"Well, you gave me the money before, and then snatched it back as soon as I said something you didn't like."

"It's not my fault you're slow and naïve. And stubborn."

"I'm not slow. You're just really quick. Like a ninja."

"You know ninjas are Japanese, right? And I'm Chinese?"

"Dude, don't be so sensitive. I was just saying you were a quick person, not saying you were a quick Asian." Tristan paused before adding, "And if we're talking about stereotypes—you know Chinese people don't have to be totally obedient to their families, right? They don't have to be all cool and logical, either. And they absolutely don't have to be involved in organized crime. I know *lots* of people whose families came from China, and you are the first one I've met who was all Triad-y."

"I'm not Triad. And I'm definitely not Triad-*y*." Simon sounded like he wasn't sure whether to be flattered or insulted. "They're a whole different level. My uncle's business is mostly legit. He just likes to cut a few corners, and he likes to be connected to people who will help him with that."

"You know what happens when you cut a corner off something? You get a damn triad."

"No, you get a triangle. Don't overwork the imagery."

It was strangely enjoyable, sitting there with the man who should have been his enemy, bickering about rhetorical tools. Maybe just nice to pretend that overworked imagery was really all he had to worry about, but there was more to it than that. Simon was—fun? That didn't seem likely. Someone so stiff, so

151

controlled, and so damn corrupted. Fun couldn't be the right word. But it was the only one Tristan could think of.

He shifted around on the bed, suddenly aware that it *was* a bed, and that beds were really useful pieces of furniture. Not that his career hadn't involved pretty much every furnishing he could name, but in his personal life, he generally preferred the comfort of a bed.

"TV?" Simon said, and Tristan frowned. That had not been where his thoughts had been taking him. But Simon had stood up and moved closer, only to flop down on the other bed and reach for the remote control. "If there's anyone outside, watching the window, they'll see the light and know we're watching. But as long as we keep the volume low, they won't know what's on the screen. Could be porn, right?"

"What?"

"They could think we're watching porn. That seems like the sort of thing you might do with your clients sometimes, doesn't it?"

"But we wouldn't be?"

Simon looked as if he'd tasted something unpleasant. "No. I don't—no."

Tristan twisted around so he was sitting cross-legged, staring at Simon. "Seriously? No whores, okay, I can see that. But no porn, either? And you don't have a boyfriend. So you must be doing a lot of jerking off, but without any porn to inspire you. That's—"

"Personal?" Simon provided.

"How did your guys know where to look for my money?" Tristan demanded. "It was in my bedroom, under the damn floorboards. You knew about that, and you want to talk about me getting too personal?"

"Well, to clarify, I *don't* want to talk about you getting too personal. I just want you to stop doing it."

"How'd you know about the money?" Tristan made it sound like an offer; he'd stop getting personal if Simon confessed.

"I didn't know; I deduced. I had a fair idea of your income, and your expenses, so I knew you must have some extra money. You didn't seem sophisticated enough to have a money laundering system set up, so making bank deposits could be awkward. And you frequently leave people unattended in your apartment, including at least one drug addict and several drug users. So, you probably had money saved, you probably had it in cash, and you probably had it hidden somewhere your friends would be unlikely to find it. Your bedroom made sense. Finding it under the floorboards was just good work by the men who visited."

"And you weren't one of them? The money ended up with you, but you didn't actually go in and take it?"

"No. I've never been in your bedroom, Tristan. Is that what you're worried about?"

"Well, if we're talking about getting too personal...."

"You equate your musings about my masturbatory habits with the possibility that I've seen the furniture on which you sleep? Is there something unique about your bedroom, some telling detail that you're worried I might know about?"

"The pink unicorn wallpaper is my biggest secret in life."

Simon's lips barely moved when he smiled, but his eyes lightened, his chin lifted as if he were just about to laugh, and that was enough to make Tristan's own mouth curve in response.

"Well, now that I know about it," Simon said, "you have nothing left to hide. That must be refreshing."

"It's a great relief," Tristan agreed. "Confession is good for the soul. So if there's anything you want to tell me—about your masturbatory habits or anything else—please." He made a somewhat grandiose gesture toward the empty space in front of the television set. "The stage is yours."

"I have stage fright," Simon said calmly.

"You can just tell me from where you're sitting, then. Come on, Simon. Anything to share?"

It would have been easy to laugh it off, and Tristan was pretty sure he would have let it go if Simon had deflected one more time. Instead, Simon looked down at his hands, then over at Tristan, his expression serious, but somehow open. "I'm really not sure I'm going to be able to get you out of this," he said quietly.

Tristan sighed. The game was over, and they were back to reality. "I know," he replied. Strange that he felt as if he was the one doing the comforting. "But you got me out of tonight, and that's something. And you're trying to do more, and that's something, too. Although—" He frowned. It had been easy to let himself get sidetracked, but he shouldn't have allowed it to happen. "What is it, exactly, that you're trying? What's the plan, now?"

"I still need to work out the details."

"Yeah, okay, but—details of *what?*"

"I don't want to tell you."

"What? Why?"

Simon sighed. "Because you—well, *sometimes* you're a good actor. When you act seductive? That's very convincing. But I'm not sure you'd be all that good at acting innocent. And for this to work—for this to make things better for you, rather than worse? The Chens will absolutely have to believe you were innocent, and knew nothing about it."

"And you think the best way to ensure that is for me to *actually* know nothing about it."

"Yes," Simon agreed.

"That's a pretty huge leap of faith you're asking me to take."

"Yes." Simon waited a moment, then shrugged. "But also, no. I mean, if you don't feel you can trust me, then—don't trust me. The best option, by far, is still for you to take your money and get the hell out of town. So if you don't trust me, but you do want to be safe, then that's what you should do. And if you don't trust me, and you refuse to leave town, then you're going to be working for the Chens, right? So I'm not actually asking you to change your behavior at all. So no trust is required, really."

Tristan frowned thoughtfully. It made no sense, but he said it anyway. "But I do trust you."

"Really?" Simon gave him a long look. "That's not very smart, you know."

"Yeah," Tristan agreed. "I can see that. But I do things that aren't very smart pretty often. This is just one example."

"It's not smart, but it's also not wrong." Simon seemed to think whatever he was saying was significant. "You can't trust me to succeed—that's why it's still a much, much better idea for you to get out of town. But you can trust me to try."

"Okay. I do."

"And—were you trusting me earlier? The things you said about not wanting to live a lie, or to hide who you are—did you mean that, too? You wouldn't be upset if word of your profession reached the general public? Like, if your parents or grandparents or kindergarten teacher found out what you do for a living?"

Tristan had to think about that one, but he was finally able to shake his head. "The people I care about already know. The people who don't know? I don't care about."

"But you might change your mind, someday, about wanting a respectable career. You might decide you've been out of the game long enough, and maybe your friends will be more respectable by then, and you'll want to be able to leave it all behind. You've never been arrested, have you? There's really no lasting evidence of your activities at this point." He stopped talking and shook his head for a moment, then said, "No. Damn it, it won't work. My plan is terrible."

"You're still looking for the perfect solution," Tristan said quietly. "I appreciate the effort, but you need to understand—I don't need perfection. I've already thought about going in and talking to the cops, getting myself arrested and taking down anyone else I could name. And I'd totally make that sacrifice, if I thought it would get me out of this without getting my friends in trouble. But it wouldn't, right? They'd find a way to make me pay."

"Yes. If you did that yourself, they'd find a way to make you pay."

"So is that your plan? You're going to get me busted?" Tristan made himself stop and think it through, then nodded. "Okay, yeah. Honestly, the only thing I really care about is keeping me and my friends safe. That's the priority. So getting arrested would be worth it, if you can find a way to make it happen without getting them pissed off at me. But would it be enough to make them lose interest? I mean, people don't really care if whores have criminal records, do they?"

"I've already told you I don't want you to know my plan. You're not going to wheedle it out of me with guessing games."

"Maybe I could wheedle it out of you some other way?" Tristan already knew what Simon liked; he'd seen the heat in the man's eyes even as he looked away, seen the way his shoulders rose just a little as he applied his discipline to keep from responding. It was flattering, actually, that Simon seemed to have liked just about everything Tristan had tried so far. And also frustrating that he hadn't responded fully to any of it. "Remember how you said you didn't like to give up on a challenge?"

He slid off the bed onto his knees in the narrow aisle between his mattress and Simon's, and he looked up like a storybook child about to say his prayers, or like a totally different kind of person about to do a totally different kind of thing. "I don't like to give up, either."

For a moment, there, Tristan thought he'd won. He wasn't sure why he *wanted* to win, exactly; maybe as a point of pride, maybe to prove to this infuriatingly controlled man that he wasn't the only one who had a say in how their interactions would progress. Or maybe, at least a little, because Simon was handsome, and challenging and sexy, and possibly even kind. Maybe Tristan wanted Simon to respond to him because he was Tristan, and Simon was Simon.

But, of course, Simon *was* Simon, which meant he shook his head as if he were tired of Tristan's games. His eyes had heated and his shoulders tightened, but that hadn't been nearly enough to shake his self-control. "We should watch TV," he said firmly. "Not porn."

"You're no fun," Tristan groused, but he shifted back to his own bed and stared at the screen like a good little boy.

They sat there together, taking turns holding the remote, until the darkness outside began to turn to grey, and Simon looked over and said, "You ready to head back?"

Tristan wasn't. He wanted to stay in that dingy motel room for quite a while longer, and not just because leaving the room meant returning to the chaos of his life. But he nodded anyway. "Thanks for the rescue," he said.

Simon just shrugged. "Sorry I made it necessary in the first place."

And that was all. They drove back to the city in relative silence, Simon dropped Tristan off outside his apartment building with the envelope of cash, and Tristan went inside to face Shane and the rest of the crew. The escape from reality was over, and Tristan needed to get back to his everyday life.

Lap Dog

Chapter Eleven

IT WASN'T THE MOST complicated scheme Simon had ever set up, not by a long shot. But he found himself worrying about it anyway. He had a story figured out, a way to take all the blame on himself instead of letting Tristan get hurt, and it was close enough to the truth that he knew it would be believed. He'd become obsessed, he wanted Tristan for himself, he couldn't stand the thought of anyone else touching him, so he'd gone to great lengths. He'd betrayed the Chens, which meant he'd betrayed his own family, since his uncle wanted him to stay close with the Chens. It was all on him, all because of his selfish, unnatural desires. Tristan hadn't even known about it. That was what he'd say if he got caught.

So it was only his own life he was playing with, in a way. But in another way? If the plan didn't work, Tristan would be stuck with the Chens. And that clearly wasn't an acceptable situation.

Which meant Simon had to make things different. He called in favors, activated hidden contacts he'd spent years cultivating, and with every person he spoke to, he was aware that he was adding to the likelihood that he'd be caught. Every person who had a piece of the puzzle was one more person who might speak to the Chens.

If he'd been willing to take things a little slower, he could have been more careful. But he kept remembering Tristan's face when he'd said he could keep working if he had to. The determination, covering the reluctance. Tristan didn't want to work for the Chens, not even for one night. And that meant Simon didn't want him to, either.

His investigations told him the boys usually got at least one night off after working one of the parties, longer if they needed more healing time. He tried not to think about that second part, or about the tired, hopeless expression on the face of the whore who shared that information with him.

He learned that bookings were mostly handled online, and spent the better part of an afternoon pacing restlessly around the apartment of a hacker he'd kept out of jail with a few well-placed bribes a couple years earlier. The Chens' system wasn't that sophisticated and would be easy to shut down, but that wasn't what Simon wanted, and what he *did* want required a little subtlety. So he waited, and he paced. And when he saw the opportunity, he had the hacker make a little change in the scheduling.

It wasn't that hard to find the men with the firemen outfits, and the call to the press was completely simple. He just hoped Tristan had meant it when he'd said he wouldn't mind if his picture made it into the tabloids.

~*~*~*~

IT HAD BEEN STUPID to expect Simon to do anything in time for the first client contact. Stupid to hope for a miracle.

And stupid to build this up as any sort of a big deal. Tristan had been texted a room number at a prestigious hotel, told to dress conservatively, and to arrive exactly at ten thirty the night after his night off. He didn't know who his client was, but he couldn't be a princess about that. Sure, it had been a long time since he'd gone to a job without at least some idea of what to expect, but that wasn't something he could let bother him. He couldn't get caught up in how much more demeaning it was to do things this way, instead of getting to make his own decisions.

No, he couldn't think about any of that. So he arrived on time, his khakis and light jacket attracting no attention as he headed past the front desk, and he pushed the elevator button with a hand that only shook a little.

Don't be such a pussy. This is just work.

He stepped onto the elevator, smiled politely at the middle-aged couple riding with him, and tried not to imagine that he was being carried to his doom. Sealed in a metal box, its movement completely beyond his control. But it was just an elevator, not a damn metaphor. *Don't overwork the imagery*, he told himself, and that memory helped, at least a little.

The hallway was tastefully lit, tastefully decorated, and even smelled tasteful, a perfume so subtle it was barely there. Tristan tried to tell himself that nothing distasteful could ever happen in a setting like that one, but he knew better, and it was only his willpower that kept him walking.

Not too late. I have the money. I could just run. But he couldn't, of course. He couldn't live anywhere else knowing that he'd left his friends behind, in danger because of him. So he kept walking, and when he got to the right door, he lifted his hand and knocked.

Maybe he won't be here. But the door opened before the thought was fully formed.

The man was middle-aged, but fit and polished looking. His eyes scanned over Tristan, up and down, and then he shrugged and stepped aside. "Come in and get undressed."

Tristan was tempted to act outraged, maybe come up with some sort of line about having knocked on the door to see if the man was ready to accept Jesus as his personal savior. But he sensed that being a smart-ass wouldn't get him far, not with this client. Not with many others, either. So he stepped through the door and heard the man lock it behind him.

They were in a suite, not a regular room. Not palatial, but nice, with a wall of floor to ceiling windows, a gas fireplace, and two sofas facing each other in the middle of the room. "Here?" Tristan asked. "Or in the bedroom?"

There was a click behind him as the lights in the room flicked off. "Here," the man said. "Over by the window. Slowly."

Tristan could appreciate the aesthetic, he supposed. From the dark room, he'd be more-or-less silhouetted against the city lights through the window. Tasteful, almost artsy, and with someone else, probably pretty sexy. If Simon were the man behind him, the man settling into an armchair and reaching for his glass of scotch, preparing for the show? That would be something—something different.

But Tristan didn't want to imagine Simon as his audience. It seemed disrespectful, somehow, after Simon had made it clear he had nothing but distaste for Tristan's business.

No, there was no point in imagining.

Tristan shrugged out of his jacket and dropped it on the back of the sofa as he walked over to stand by the window. No music, at least—the guy wasn't looking for a dance number. He toed his shoes off—if there was a sexy way to get out of shoes, he had yet to find it—and bent over at the waist to get rid of his socks. Then he straightened and started on the buttons of his shirt.

"Slower," the man ordered from the shadows.

Slower. And despite his resolutions, he heard Simon's voice from two nights before, telling him to slow down and not leap to conclusions about how Shane had persuaded Simon to care. *I'm not slow*, Tristan could answer. *You're a ninja.* And then they could bicker about racial stereotypes for a while. Tristan undid a button and slid his hand inside his shirt, imagining it was Simon's, letting it play over his ribs, up to his nipple.

Another button undone with his free hand, and then the last one, and Tristan shrugged the shirt off his shoulders, caught it at his elbows, and tried to imagine how Simon would see him from his spot in the shadows. Was the light hitting his skin right? Maybe if he shifted around a little, like this—if he caught the moonlight right there on his chest, his nipple casting an actual shadow, then his hand caressing the illuminated skin. Maybe Simon would like that.

"Keep going. Drop the shirt." Not Simon's voice. Right.

Tristan let the shirt fall. He stood frozen for a moment, hopefully long enough for the client to appreciate the view, then brought his hands to the button of his khakis.

"Just the button," the man ordered. "Then reach inside."

Tristan turned his head toward the window as his hands followed the instructions. So many lights. So many lives being lived through the glass, far away from all this. He could see out to the water, could see the Ferris wheel spinning around down at the pier.

His hand was inside his underwear now, wrapped around his cock. Easier to get hard if he just allowed the physical to take care of itself, without letting his brain complicate things. His brain could think about the people on the Ferris wheel, wonder how many of them were on first dates, or, no, maybe it was more romantic if it *wasn't* a first date. Easy to do something special when you were first trying to impress someone, but more

166

meaningful if it wasn't about making an impression. Not an anniversary, not anything significant, just someone who loved someone, taking him out for dinner, then for a walk by the water, and then up in one of the cars, out over the water.

"Unzip and let your pants hang open," the client said, and when Tristan complied, "drop the pants. Push your underwear down." Tristan did as he was told.

He was aware of a different energy coming from the dark side of the room. A rustling sound, like the guy was unzipping his own pants, and that would certainly make this night a lot easier to take, if Tristan just had to put on a show while the client took care of himself.

But then the man said, "leave your clothes there, and get over here."

For a moment, Tristan's body almost rebelled. It would be so easy to pull his underwear back up, gather up the rest of his clothes and just walk out. He could get dressed in the damn hallway, or, hell, walk home in his undies. He didn't have to do this. Not with this guy, not on someone else's terms.

Except he did. So he hooked his thumbs under the waistband of his underwear.

That was when the alarm went off.

SIMON HAD WANTED to be on site for what he was coming to think of as "the extraction", but his common sense took over. It was an unnecessary risk, and Tristan might see him and react, and this was supposed to be about Tristan's freedom, not Simon's satisfaction. So he soothed himself with giving a few key actors earpieces he could speak into, and watching the whole thing through the remote cameras while sitting in the van below.

Now, with the sounds of the alarm coming through the camera microphones, he urged, "Go, go," into the earpiece of the already-moving fireman. Well, the man dressed as a fireman.

Simon braced himself as the fireman banged on the hotel room door and shouted, "Emergency evacuation! We need you out of there, now!"

This was the moment of truth. If the door didn't open, or if it opened too slowly—if they had a chance to get things tidied up in the room—then this was all a waste, and Simon really didn't know what his next step would be.

But just as he'd hoped, the alarm had done its job, and the man who yanked the hotel room door open looked flustered, almost afraid. "What's going on?" he demanded. And then he cast a worried look behind him.

Damn it, Tristan, get out of there. It's an evacuation—you need to be moving. Be visible!

The fireman said, "We've got an emergency situation, sir. Possible terrorist incident. We're evacuating, now! Move it!" And then, bless his heart, he took two steps into the room and bellowed

"Move it! Right now! Evacuate!" The camera on the fireman's helmet caught only a quick shot of Tristan, stripped down, looking startled but not terrified, and then it panned away as the fireman turned and herded the two men out the door into the hallway.

Where the second fireman, of course, was ready. The damn camera was mounted on the fireman's shoulder and the picture was too jerky, too off-to-the-side, for Simon to be sure what he was seeing. But he heard the bustling, then heard the bastard client's voice raised in angry alarm. "Hey! You! What the hell are you doing?" Sounds of scuffling, more swearing, and the camera jarred around. Simon was on his feet, half-crouched to keep from banging his head on the ceiling of the van, his fingers gripped tight around the shelf that held his laptop.

"Have you got the shots?" he demanded. He should be keeping his mouth shut and letting the others do their work, but he couldn't help himself. "If you've got the shots, get the hell out of there."

And whether in response to his urging or just because they were professionals with a sense of self-preservation, the fake firemen started moving, jogging down the hall toward the stairwell, just as they'd been instructed. They were heading for the emergency exit at the back of the building, and would emerge into the alley just a few feet away from Simon's van.

And that meant the important part of the job was done. The reporter dressed as a fireman had assured Simon that the photos would be sent out immediately over the hotel's wifi, with no need to get the actual camera out of the building. So even if the firemen were caught and their equipment confiscated, the photos would still be available. The images of Tristan, mostly naked, coming out of a hotel room beside an ultra-conservative congressman would make it to the tabloids.

If the firemen were caught? They'd talk, Simon was sure. They'd implicate him, and he'd be facing criminal charges as well as whatever the Chens and his uncle came up with. And he'd really rather not go through all of that. But still, even before the van door slid open and the fireman clambered inside, Simon was relaxing. The important part of the job was done. The rest was just details.

The driver pulled away, driving calmly and easily into the dark Seattle streets, and in the back of the van, Simon slumped into his seat. There would be repercussions, he was sure. But he'd done what he'd set out to do. Now he just had to hope it would work.

TRISTAN PULLED HIS clothes on while the client ranted into his phone. The alarm had stopped before the firemen had even disappeared down the back stairs, so clearly there was no real emergency. Or at least, there wasn't one that affected the hotel as a whole.

The client, though? This was pretty clearly a serious problem for him. Tristan hovered indecisively, waiting for his next instructions. Was he free to go? Did he need to stay and face the music right then, or could he put it off for a while?

Could he possibly take the chance of going to see Simon?

No. That wouldn't make sense. He had to act like this had nothing to do with Simon. Not anything to do with himself, either. It was just something unfortunate that happened because the client—who was apparently some sort of big shot—was involved.

His phone buzzed then, and he looked down to see the text. The address of the Chens' office, and then the word *IMMEDIATELY*.

Shit.

"Uh, sir?" he said. "I'm supposed to go—"

"Sit down and shut up," the man barked. "You can't walk out of here now, not after they took your picture!"

Well, he was going to have to walk out eventually. Unless the man thought he'd be leaving in a body bag, but, no, that wouldn't make sense. It was a high-end hotel, with lots of security, and honestly, if the client was caught with a whore and the whore subsequently disappeared under suspicious circumstances? That would be a sure way to turn a mid-sized scandal into a much larger one.

So Tristan texted back *Client wants me to stay here. Doesn't want me to be seen on the way out*. There was no immediate response.

But about ten minutes later, there was a knock on the door and the client almost ran to pull it open, then ushered in two men in business suits. "You'll leave now," one of them said. "Easy and casual, out the front doors." He glanced over at Tristan. "Not you. You'll stay here with me and answer some questions."

"I don't really have any answers," Tristan said. "I have no idea what the hell's going on."

But the other men all ignored him, focusing on getting the client into his overcoat, checking that his tie was straight, and giving him instructions on how to act appropriately calm.

"The pictures aren't out yet," one of the newcomers said, "and if we can figure out who took them and act fast, they won't get out. This isn't a crisis yet, sir."

The client nodded, looking almost dazed, and let himself be escorted out of the room. Tristan was left with the disapproving man, and then things got just a little worse when a knock on the door led to the younger Chen being escorted into the room.

There were some murmured apologies, some glowering, and then Chen stalked toward Tristan. "Who has the pictures?" the man demanded.

Tristan shook his head. "I have no idea. This is nothing to do with me!"

"You expect us to believe that? Your second job, after you had to be persuaded to work for us, and it goes wrong like this? You think we don't know you're behind it?"

"I don't even know what's happening. The guy was someone important—I get that! But you never told me who he was, not before I got here. I couldn't have told anyone about this because I didn't *know* about this." He had no idea how Simon had known, either.

"You know that our clients are *all* successful, important men. You know that none of them would relish having their photograph taken with a common whore."

"Yeah, sure, but—what would be in it for me? I mean, you and Yeung made it totally clear—I can't quit this job, or things won't be good for me. You really think I'm stupid enough to set something like this up? You think I don't know how important it is to maintain confidentiality?"

"I think you're about to *learn* how important it is," Chen said, and he stalked forward.

But the other man caught his arm before he got too close. "No marks," the man said. "We need to keep our options open, and one of those options may involve a statement from him. Some sort of story—" He took a step closer to Tristan. "You have a record? Any official notice that you're a whore?"

"No record." Tristan frowned. "But, you know, I've been doing this for a while. There are quite a few people out there who'd recognize my face. They might say something? I don't know how this works."

"No, you're completely innocent," Chen said, sarcasm making each word heavy. "You have no idea how any of this could have happened."

"I don't! I just did what you told me to do. I went to the address I was told to go to. That's all."

"Who else knew about the congressman's appointment?" the man asked Chen. "Within your organization. We need to go through every person involved. We need to track this, figure out who has the pictures and how to get them back. And if we can't get them back—" He looked over at Tristan again and glowered. "If we can't get them back, we need a cover story. And you will damn well be part of making it work."

Chapter Twelve

IT WAS EXCRUCIATING to pretend everything was normal. Luckily, Simon had a lot of experience pretending. So he went home that night and worked out, just as he normally did, went to bed and at least tried to sleep, and the next morning he shaved, showered, put on a suit, and drove over to his uncle's for breakfast just like any other day.

The façade of normalcy shattered when he heard his uncle's voice call out from his office. "Simon? Come in here, please."

He was caught. Busted. He knew it, and instead of the sick, sinking fear he'd expected, he felt only relief. It was over. Not just the business with Tristan, but all of it. Years and years of trying to be the man he was supposed to be, trying to be loyal and grateful and useful. It was over, now.

He crossed the marble-tiled foyer and entered his uncle's office. He was surprised to see David Chen sitting in one of the leather armchairs—of course the man would be involved in Simon's downfall, but it was unexpected for him to have come to the house. Simon's uncle might appreciate Chen as a business contact, but that didn't mean they'd ever socialize. Still, here Chen was, and Simon nodded respectfully to him.

"Mr. Chen has a problem," Frank Yeung said. "And he's hoping to enlist your help in solving it."

Simon nodded. This was the trap, the game. Again, surprising that Uncle Frank would play it in front of a stranger, odd that he'd let himself lose face with a public display of family disloyalty, but perhaps that was a sign of just how deep his anger ran. "I'd be pleased to be of service, of course."

"There's been a problem with my corporate security," Chen said. "A data breach, apparently. I don't know the first thing about computers, but my people tell me we were hacked, and important information was stolen."

Simon frowned. They were going to draw it out like this? His uncle and Chen were that committed to the game, and that much in synch? It seemed impossible, but— "What sort of information?" he asked, just because he couldn't think of what else to say.

"An appointment. Well, a series of appointments—*all* of our appointments, apparently, with—" Chen looked over at Frank, clearly trying to be discreet in the other man's home. "—with my son's arm of the business. You understand?"

Simon's nod was more like a jerk of his head. This was real. They didn't know he'd been involved. At least not yet. "I do. That information would be embarrassing to many if it were released. Do you know who has it?"

Chen raised his hands in frustration. "I don't know about technology. My people—I thought they were good, but I wonder now if they are. The problem is, I don't know how to find someone better, not someone who can be trusted with the sensitive information involved. Do you understand?"

"Of course." It wasn't like a standard IT company would want to help recover records of criminal activity, not without at least a chance they'd report things to the authorities. "I may have some contacts who would be helpful. But at best, they would be able to tell me who had the information." It would be the easiest job ever, really—his contacts would just tell him *they* had it. "It's much less likely they'd be able to actually retrieve it. That is—once the information is out there, it's out there. Were there names involved? Full names?"

Chen nodded despondently. "Unforgivably stupid," he muttered. "We thought we were safe."

Simon was tempted to tell him how difficult it had been for his hackers to break through the Chens' security; maybe that would make the old man feel better. Instead, he said, "When did all this happen?"

"My people say the breach occurred the day before yesterday."

What would Simon be asking, assuming Simon didn't know exactly what was going on? "And nobody has contacted you yet? Is it possible this is someone who doesn't know what they've got? Or has there already been a—well, a ransom demand?"

"They haven't contacted us. But they've used the information. One of our most respected clients—a man who has a great deal to lose—he was photographed last night. A clear set-up, with very incriminating pictures. He was with—" Chen paused as if the idea had come to him for the first time "—with Tristan Beck."

And there it was, the first suggestion that Chen was finally getting a clue. Simon couldn't say why it had taken the old man so long to catch on, but now that he was beginning to, Simon's professional pride drove him to obfuscate as well as he could. "Do you suspect Beck?" he asked. "He didn't strike me as someone with significant technological abilities. And I can't immediately see a motive—but did he do anything incriminating? Did the pictures look posed?"

Chen frowned thoughtfully, then shook his head. "We haven't seen the pictures. But from the way the client described it, no. The client was out in the hall, but Beck stayed in the room. The photographer's assistant had to practically force him out into the hallway, as I understand it."

"Possibly just a coincidence, then, that a reluctant employee would be involved. But I can look into it." Which gave him an excuse to see Tristan again.

Chen's phone buzzed, then, and he looked down, then back up, even paler than before. "The pictures have been released," he said, and for a moment he looked as if he might slump right over and pass out in his chair. "The—the client—damn it, everyone who gets a morning paper will know—the client is Congressman

Tarenson. He's—very conservative—this will—oh, this is not good."

"Not good for *him*," Simon said quickly. It had been a gift, finding Tarenson's name in the appointment listing, and even luckier to realize that he liked a new whore every visit, so it wouldn't be suspicious to assign Tristan to him. "But his people will have a way they want to spin it. And if you can cooperate— does he know the breach came from your side? Have you admitted that to him yet?"

"No," Chen said, and for the first time he seemed to be regaining his sharpness. "No, we've admitted nothing. And you're right—there are other ways this liaison could have been discovered by the press."

"The reporter shouldn't disclose his sources," Simon said. He'd damn well better not—that had been part of the deal. "So if you can deny involvement, and if you cooperate—if you make sure Beck cooperates—with whatever the cover-up is, this might not be terrible for you. Not as long as it's an isolated incident. The other names, the other appointments—all the bookings need to be cancelled, or rescheduled or moved or something. The information in the bookings can't be valid anymore. So then the thieves will still have the list of names, but they'll have no proof, not without photos or other evidence. This might not be too bad."

"What sort of cover-up could they use?" Chen wondered. "The pictures—" He turned to Frank. "May we look at the pictures on your computer? The ones the newspaper has printed? Just to see how bad they are."

Frank clearly wanted to refuse, but he'd already allowed Chen into his home, and once the man was a guest, certain courtesies were required. So he stood up and allowed Simon to sit at his computer, where a quick search brought the images on screen.

Tristan. He looked confused, mostly. That was good. And just as angelic as always, despite his state of undress and the generally incriminating situation. "If you keep him out of sight," Simon said, wondering how far he dared push this, "keep him completely away from your business? There's nothing to say he's a prostitute. No criminal record, no previous photographs. I couldn't even find a record of him doing business on the internet, back when I was investigating him. Honestly, if this had to happen with one of your employees, it's good that it was him. He's clean."

Chen was frowning again, but Simon didn't think it was a problem. Yes, Simon was going to get what he wanted from all this; Tristan was going to be out of the business. But Chen didn't seem capable of drawing any of the necessary lines to prove that Simon had been involved, and without clear proof, Simon was protected by his family connections. Even if Chen's suspicions grew, he couldn't afford to throw around accusations against Frank Yeung's nephew, not without something to back him up.

"So I can have some people look into the data breach," Simon said. "Very quietly. And if they find something—well, perhaps you should think about this and get back to me. If they find something, it's possible that the best thing for them to do would be to hide it better, so no one from the congressman's camp would ever find out about it. That would give you continued deniability."

They talked a little longer, and then Simon showed Chen to the door before returning to his uncle's office.

"You didn't want to get involved with the Chens in the first place," Frank said thoughtfully.

Simon was surprised his uncle had heard his concerns, let alone remembered them. "It seemed like an unnecessary complication. But you were right: there is money to be made. They have good connections."

"But there's always a chance of something like this flaring up, and making everyone involved look bad."

"Yes," Simon agreed. "There's always a chance." He didn't bother to point out that the center of this scandal was a congressman, someone Frank would have been pleased to do business with ordinarily. It was silly to pretend that respectability was more than skin deep, but there was no benefit in bringing that up.

"You'll help them with this situation," his uncle said. "And you'll collect as much information as you can. If Chen manages to cover up his involvement in all this, but *we* still know about it? That will be useful leverage."

Simon was suddenly exhausted by it all. Leverage, secrets, collecting information. That was his role, his life. Not because he'd chosen it but because someone had to do it, and he was smart enough to get by. And he wasn't free.

But Tristan was, he told himself as he followed his uncle to the dining room for breakfast. The plan was working, and Tristan was going to be free. The congressman would figure out a cover-up, and he'd insist that Tristan be retired from active service, because any further evidence of prostitution would blow the congressman's cover-up out of the water.

Simon had met his goal, and Tristan could live his life now, free of the corruption that tainted Simon and everything he touched. It was good. It was a victory. And it was pure selfishness for Simon to not be happier about it.

"WE'D LIKE TO OFFER you a scholarship," Mr. Smith said with an oily smile. That was how he'd introduced himself, as Mr. Smith. Then he'd made a general, vaguely annoyed wave in Simon's direction and said, "I believe you already know Mr. Yeung."

Somehow, it was the dismissiveness toward Simon that got Tristan's back up. "A scholarship?" Tristan frowned at the suited man who was standing in his apartment and waited for the words to make sense. "You want to give me a scholarship?" It was late afternoon and he hadn't slept since the mess the night before—maybe his brain wasn't working right, but he truly didn't

Kate Sherwood

understand the plan. He let himself take a quick look in Simon's direction; if they'd been alone, they could have talked it through, but as it was, Simon was just watching, waiting for Tristan to figure it out on his own.

"That was why the congressman took an interest in you in the first place, Tristan," Mr. Smith prompted. "He used to know your parents, years ago, and when he heard you were living in Seattle, having a rough time—not prostitution, of course, but general poverty and a lack of direction in your life—he got in touch with you. He invited you to his hotel, you were sopping wet and chilled from the rain, so he offered you some dry clothes. You were changing into them when the fire alarm went off."

"You really think people are going to believe that?" Tristan asked.

"Why wouldn't they? We can't be cynical, Tristan. The people who are seeing something sleazy in those photographs are reflecting their own souls, not the reality of the situation. People with pure hearts, people who believe in the congressman? They'll be pleased to understand how innocent it really all was. And when they hear that he's supporting you in higher education, when they see you making a life for yourself, with no hint of anything illegal or illicit? They'll believe."

Tristan shook his head. He was so tired of all this. He'd told Simon he didn't want to live a lie, and now he was being asked to do just that. But, really, he'd said the most important thing was that he and his friends were safe—that was clearly the part Simon had

183

focused on when he came up with this plan. "I don't want your money," he said, and he made sure to keep his attention on Mr. Smith, because he was pretty sure Simon wouldn't approve of that decision. "The scholarship, or whatever? I don't want that. I'm not—I'm not blackmailing anyone. I'm sorry the guy got busted— I mean, I've been reading about him, and honestly, it sounds like he kind of deserved it, with all the mean shit he's said about gay people—but it's not my place to judge other people like that. I'll keep my mouth shut because of me, because of what I believe in. I don't need money to reinforce that."

"*We* need you to take the money, Tristan," Mr. Armstrong said. "Because as sweet as 'what I believe in' is as a motivator, it's just not quite enough for our peace of mind. So you'll take the money, and you'll sign contracts that make it crystal clear that any breach of confidentiality at any point in the future will result in the forfeiture of all sums paid to that date, with interest at a punitive rate."

"And what if I just turn around and give all the money to charity or something?"

"That would be your choice, although it would not be a wise one." The man turned and walked over to the patio doors that led to the balcony, cluttered with folded up lawn chairs, chunks of bicycles waiting for repairs, and other evidence of Tristan's limited outdoor life. "It's very important that you take advantage of the congressman's interest and generosity. Your life, from now on, must be—not crystal clean, I suppose. A few youthful mistakes can be accepted. But they can't be tied in to anything that would make this ridiculous rumor seem true. You can *not* engage in any sort of prostitution. Nothing close to it—stripping, or porn, or whatever else. If you're arrested for running naked down the street, it had better be because you were drunk and accepted a dare, not because you were engaged in some kinky sexual activity. Do you understand what I'm saying, Tristan?"

Tristan snorted. "Yeah, I get it, John."

"John? My first name isn't John."

"No, but you didn't bother to tell me what your first name is, and since we're apparently on a first name basis, I thought I'd guess. Want me to guess again?"

"I want you to stay focused on the current discussion—Mr. Beck." Tristan was pretty sure he saw a bit of reaction from Simon on that one, just a tiny little nod of his head, an acknowledgement that Tristan had won at least one point in all this. And that was enough to make the whole conversation worthwhile. Unfortunately, Mr. Smith didn't seem to be through. "Do you understand what I'm saying about the nature of any future misbehaviour?"

Tristan smiled sweetly. "You want me to be a bro. A good ol' boy. If I use the money to go to school, you'd really like it if I joined a fraternity. Maybe a little date rape would get past your moral filters, as long as it was heterosexual?"

"I'd like it best if I never heard your name again," the man said. "I'd like it if you went on to lead a quiet, ordinary life, just

185

like the vast majority of the population. And the terms of the contract you're going to sign will reinforce my wishes."

Tristan glanced over at Simon, who was back to looking carefully neutral. It would probably be best to go along with all this, for Simon's sake, but Tristan wasn't quite ready to roll over. Not yet. "What if I don't sign it? You think all I care about is money, so what if I decide I could make more money from selling my story to the highest bidder and then selling my services to anyone who wants to know what it feels like to fuck the whore who brought down a congressman? What was that list of stuff I couldn't do with your contract? Stripping? What if I decide I could make more as a celebrity stripper, or doing porn? What happens then?"

"I believe at that point this would become an issue between yourself and your current employer," Mr. Smith said. He glanced over at Simon. "I believe there have already been discussions about this sort of non-cooperation?" No threat, not really. Not in the words themselves. But the tone? The ice in his gaze? And, of course, Tristan's ability to imagine just how the Chens would react if Tristan refused to go along.

He shook his head. "Wouldn't this all be simpler if we just—agreed to let it go away? If we went back to the 'I'll keep my mouth shut because that's who I am' idea?"

"Simpler? Maybe. But not more effective." The man stepped away from the patio doors. "I don't suppose you have a lawyer?"

"No."

"Fine. I'll be back in a few hours, and I'll bring a lawyer with me—she can explain the contract terms to you. And when she's done, you'll sign, and this will all be over with."

Once again, Tristan was just a pawn, on the sidelines for a decision that affected his whole life. Once again, Simon Yeung was the one in control, even if he wasn't technically the one in charge. Even if all he was doing was standing there and watching, he was the one who'd set all this in motion.

Of course it was harder to be angry at him now that Simon was using his scheming as a way to help Tristan rather than hurt him. But Tristan still wished—well. Maybe that was why Simon was the one making things happen. He didn't waste his time on wishing, he just made decisions and then followed through.

"I'm interested in the plan," he said. He thought about insisting on getting his own lawyer; it was the smart thing to do, and he knew it. But how the hell was he supposed to find someone good, someone he could trust? Someone who'd be interested in helping a gay whore deal with a homophobic gay congressman? He had no idea where to begin, and was too tired to deal with it. Still, Simon had gone to a lot of trouble for this—Tristan needed to follow through on his end. "Look—I'll agree in principle, right now, so there doesn't have to be such a rush to get things signed. I'm not going to sign anything tonight. I need to take my time and make sure it makes sense."

"I'm afraid that's unacceptable. Time is of the essence—we need to have the congressman make a statement before this malicious gossip spreads any further. And we can't have him make that statement until we're absolutely sure you're on board."

"And you won't believe I'm on board until you have something to hold over my head, something to threaten me with. That's your problem, not mine."

Armstrong narrowed his eyes, then said, "I'm going to go arrange for the contract. I'm also going to speak to Mr. Yeung and the Chens about your lack of cooperation."

Tristan felt old. He should have been afraid, and he probably would have been if he weren't so damn tired, but as it was he just said, "Do what you gotta do. But do it somewhere else, okay? I need some sleep."

"You aren't taking this nearly as seriously as you should be."

"I promise to have a better attitude when I wake up."

"I hope so," the man said, and then, right on cue, "for your sake."

Tristan closed his eyes. If it were just him and Simon, this conversation would be way more fun. More frustrating, of course, if Simon were on the other side of things, but, still, at least Tristan's brain would be engaged. As it was?

"You can show yourself out, okay?" He didn't bother to stifle his yawn. He shouldn't sleep, really. He needed to get a lawyer, needed to make a plan.

He needed to try to be a bit more like Simon Yeung. The idea wasn't nearly as repulsive as it would have been only a few days earlier.

THE CLINIC WAS CLEANER than Simon had expected. He didn't know much about animals, but he definitely had the impression that they were dirty. Smelly. But the front room of the clinic was spotless, and Simon was pretty sure that the faint odor he detected was human in origin, almost certainly coming from the man in the corner with the little dog on his lap.

And the woman behind the counter looked clean and professional, as well. Simon waited for her attention, then said, "You have someone who works here, someone named Shane? I hate to interrupt, but would it be possible for me to speak to him, just for a moment?"

The woman gave him a long, assessing look, then said, "He's not here. Do you want Noah?"

"Actually, yes." The college student seemed much more civilized, much less likely to make a wild, emotional decision. Much less likely to attack. "If he's available, I'd really appreciate that."

"I'll go find him," the woman said, and she left Simon at the counter, staring behind the desk at a grey and black, long-haired cat that seemed about twice the size of a typical domestic feline. Not that Simon was an expert on cats, but surely they weren't all that large?

The cat was clearly aware of Simon's attention and leaped from the ground to the desk, landing with a thud that, again, challenged Simon's preconceptions. Weren't cats supposed to be light and graceful?

The cat stood on its hind legs and balanced the front two on the raised counter by Simon's elbow. It leaned forward, its orange eyes intent on Simon's, and Simon gingerly raised a hand toward the animal's head.

It was more like a tackle than a head-rub, and Simon had to actually brace his arm to keep the animal's broad, heavy skull from pushing his hand away. The rumble that emerged from the cat was probably a purr, but could just as well have been a growl. When Simon curled his fingers in and scratched a little, the animal added a few little chirping sounds to its repertoire. Hopefully they weren't the warning signal for an impending attack.

"Making friends?" Noah asked from the hallway behind the desk.

Simon jerked his hand back, feeling almost guilty. "I need to talk to you," he said. He was there on business. The place wasn't a petting zoo. "Is it possible for you to get a message to Shane? Or to Tristan?"

"Last I heard, there was no reason to believe either Shane or Tristan would be interested in hearing from you." Noah glanced at the man in the corner, and then stepped aside so the woman could return to her post behind the desk. "Can we talk outside?" he asked.

"Absolutely. Thank you."

Simon stepped aside and let Noah precede him out onto the concrete steps, then down the walkway to the street. It was cold out, and Noah didn't have a coat, but he just hugged his arms around himself and said, "Whatever your message is, will Shane want to hear it? Will Tristan?"

"I think so. I don't know for sure."

"Is there a reason you can't just go to the apartment, or give them a call?"

"There is." Getting a congressman involved had raised the stakes all around, and it was much better to be safe than sorry. "And whoever gives Tristan the message—it shouldn't be on Tristan's phone, or in his apartment."

Noah frowned at him. "That sounds like you think—you think—Jesus, you think they've got his place bugged?" He looked around as if suddenly worried *he* might be under surveillance. "This is for real? He told Shane about the picture in the paper, and I looked it up online. But—seriously? This is actually happening?"

"It's all going to go away very soon. But right now? It's happening. Can you get a message to Shane or Tristan?"

"Uh, yeah, sure. Shane's phone is still okay, right? Assuming he answers it. And then he could go over to Tristan's and they could go up on the roof to talk? Would that work?"

"That'd be perfect." Disappointing to not have an excuse to talk to Tristan himself, but it was probably better this way. Simon would keep his mind on business, or at least what he was calling business these days. No distractions from the task at hand. "I can't be there tonight, but tell him the contract's okay as long as he strikes clauses seven and nine. He can't take responsibility for the story leaking from some *other* source. And he gets the forty thousand a year for five years, even if he's not in school. They can call it a scholarship if they want, but he should make it clear that it isn't, really. And he needs to modify clause seventeen to allow him to discuss the issues with lawyers, medical professionals, or other people sworn to confidentiality."

Noah looked a little taken aback; probably he'd been expecting a slightly less complicated message. "Uh—can you say that again? And is it okay if I write it down?"

"As long as you're careful with what you write. It's important no one knows this came from me."

Noah frowned. "Except Tristan. Because I'm going to tell Shane, and Shane's *definitely* going to tell Tristan. He needs to know who it's coming from so he can decide whether to trust it or not."

Strange how confident Simon had become that Tristan would trust him. But, of course, Tristan's friends weren't likely to do the same, and that was good. It was good Tristan had people looking out for him. "That's fine. Of course Tristan can know. But no one else. It could ruin the deal for him, and make things very difficult for me."

"Okay," Noah said again, and he pulled out his phone and tapped the screen a few times. "I'll delete it as soon as I tell Shane about it. And I'll make sure Shane and Tristan know it's secret. What was the first thing, again?"

So Simon gave him the list of changes. And that was it. That was all, and if Simon had even a tiny bit of common sense left, he'd be hoping it stayed that way. Because being involved with Tristan in any way was dangerous. That was what he needed to remember, while he tried hard to forget everything else.

~*~*~*~

IT SHOULD HAVE BEEN a relief. More than a relief, it should have been a celebration. And it clearly was, for Shane, and even for Noah and Micah. They were the only people Tristan had told about the settlement, so they were the only ones who *could* celebrate after Tristan had insisted on the changes and then signed the contract. There were only the four of them who knew what had happened.

Except for Simon.

And that was the damn problem. This was Simon's victory. Tristan had been swept along for the ride while Simon did all the work, and now Tristan had gotten what he wanted and Simon was—well, who knew where Simon was? Certainly not at their little impromptu party on the roof.

"Best Christmas present ever," Micah announced, tossing Dodger's stuffed badger for the dog to retrieve. Micah had popped a few pills as they'd climbed the stairs, but they didn't seem to

193

have taken effect yet, so Micah was just at his typical low-level stonedness. "It's like a sugar daddy, but you get to keep all your sugar!"

"It'd be a pretty damn cheap sugar daddy," Tristan retorted. "Forty grand's nice, considering I don't have to do anything for it, but it's less than I've been making, and I'm not allowed to work anymore."

"You're not allowed to—to do *that* work," Noah cut in. He was always a bit delicate about Tristan's whoring. Maybe he'd find something new to be embarrassed by now. "But you could get a regular job. Or go to school. You could do whatever you wanted."

Whatever he wanted. Tristan stood there on the roof and looked out at the city, and when Shane passed a joint to him he took a drag and tried to think. *Whatever he wanted.* What did that even mean?

"You can take it slow," Shane said. He sounded gentle, almost like the way he spoke to Dodger when the pup was scared about something. Of course, Dodger got scared of some pretty strange things—pigeons, most recently—so Tristan wasn't really sure he wanted to be treated the same way as the little dog. Then again, it was pretty comforting to hear Shane's words, and his tone. "Take a few weeks off—maybe even go somewhere warm, away from all the fucking rain. Then you could come back, and, I don't know, take some classes or something. Just try shit out and see if you like it." Shane edged a little closer, and then lifted his heavy arm and rested it on Tristan's shoulders. "You know it doesn't matter, right? To us? You can buy a million games for the Xbox and sit around in your underwear and play them for five years straight, and that'd be cool with us."

"Not underwear," Micah said firmly. "The lazy fucker can get dressed, at least."

"Showering," Noah chipped in. "I vote for mandatory showers."

Shane shook his head in mock disbelief, then grinned at Tristan. "They're fucking oppressive, right? You get a bit of cash, and all of a sudden you have to conform to social rules. You've probably got a theory about that? Marx or Chomsky or that French guy?"

"Foucault," Tristan said softly. Then he grinned back. "What the hell do you know about Marx or Chomsky or Foucault?"

"Not much. But you and Micah never shut up about them. I picked up a little." Shane raised his eyebrows. "Hey, you could study them in school, right? You'd already be, like, an expert! You could show the teacher how it's done."

"I'd probably have to shower and get dressed if I was going to go to school."

"Oh." Shane crouched down to greet Dodger and lift the little dog up. "That sucks."

"Maybe basic hygiene isn't that much of a chore." Tristan took the joint back and sucked a lungful of smoke. "Maybe I could go to school." Or do anything else, and still have the support of his friends. He reached out and rumpled Dodger's ears. "Thanks," he said, then realized it probably looked like he was thanking the dog. He looked up and smiled. "For everything, guys. For helping me out with all of it."

"No problem," Shane said.

"You'd do the same for us," Micah added.

And it was true. These were his friends, and they made a point of supporting each other.

Simon Yeung, on the other hand? Simon had been a stranger, and he'd gone far out of his way to help Tristan out. And Tristan wasn't sure he'd ever shown his gratitude at all, back when he'd had the chance.

Chapter Thirteen

IT WASN'T EASY FOR Simon to go back to the mundane tasks of his life. Well, the tasks themselves were easy. Too easy. But paying attention to them? Pretending he cared whether the head accountant in the Jakarta plant was skimming off the company profits? Not easy at all.

Still. Simon did as was expected. He showed up to the house for breakfast, discussed his day's work, and gave his compliments to his aunt and uncle. He ignored his aunt's questioning looks and appreciated his uncle's obliviousness. He was Simon, the family robot, and if that's all he was, at least he'd try to be a *good* robot.

Christmas came, and as usual, Simon was expected to stay at the house after breakfast for the gift exchange. Cufflinks from his uncle for the fourth year in a row, and as always the man looked vaguely interested in discovering what his assistant had purchased for everyone on his behalf. Other impersonal items from his cousins, and then Aunt May's gift.

"It's a little delicate," she said as she handed it to him. "Keep it right side up."

He did as he was told and carefully tore the paper away to reveal a small potted plant. He checked the tag. An African violet. He was pretty sure he'd seen them for sale at corner stores, probably in the same plastic pots as this one.

He schooled his face into a calm smile. "Thank you," he said. "I've got a windowsill in the apartment that could use a little color."

"I want you to look after it," she replied. "This is an easy plant; it won't take much work. But I want you to think about it. What it needs, and how you can help it grow."

The emotion was unpleasant, and unwelcome. She thought he was selfish? She thought he needed to learn how to care for others? The one person in his life—the one person left—but he shut that thought off quickly and forced himself to nod. "I will. Thank you for the opportunity."

She smiled as she stepped closer. His cousins were distracted, admiring each others' gifts, and his uncle seemed to be asleep in his chair. "I want you to look after it," she said quietly. "And I want you to decide if you like it. If it adds to your life, or takes away from your life. And then, if you decide you don't like it? If it takes more than it gives?" She held his gaze as she said, "I want you to drop it out of your window and let it smash into a million pieces on the sidewalk."

"My windows don't open," he said numbly. "And it would be dangerous to drop something from that height."

"Then maybe you need to move," she suggested. "Maybe you need to make some changes so you're able to drop things more easily."

It suddenly occurred to him that he'd like her to meet Tristan. He'd like to listen to them talk to each other, bouncing hidden meanings around like tennis balls. He'd like them to like each other, and trust each other.

But that was a dream he was better off forgetting. "Thank you for the plant," he said. "And for all your kindness."

She frowned. "Alternatively, you might at some point want to yell at me for buying you a gift from the grocery store when I'm showering riches on the others."

"But you don't normally go to the grocery store yourself," he replied. "I'm flattered that you made a special trip for me."

Her quirked eyebrow was the victory for his day. He'd managed to be more enigmatic than his enigmatic aunt. But she recovered quickly. "You deserve more than that. You deserve to have someone who goes out of their way for you every day, not just for Christmas."

And that was a little too close to the bone. He stepped backward, holding his plant in front of him like a shield. "Thank you for the gift." He raised his voice enough to be heard by the others. "Thank you all. I have some things to do, but I'll see you all for dinner." As was expected. "Merry Christmas."

"Merry Christmas," Mitchell said with a smile that seemed genuine. "See you later."

And that was all. He escaped from the family home, drove to his apartment, entered the parking garage, and then slammed on the brakes when someone stepped in front of his car. Someone large, wearing a hoodie and carrying some sort of box with a handle.

Simon cautiously stepped out of the car. "Shane?"

"Yeah. Merry Christmas or whatever."

"Uh, yeah, okay." Simon tried not to let his stomach twist in excitement, tried not to let himself turn his head to scan the parking garage, looking for someone who really shouldn't be there. "What's up?" he asked as casually as he could manage.

Shane raised the plastic box. It had perforations on the sides, a metal screen in front—"Noah said you liked him," Shane said. "But you can't have him unless you want him."

"What? I'm sorry, Shane, I don't—" Simon stepped around his open door and moved closer, peering into the box. Oh. "The cat? The big one from the clinic?"

"Having a pet is a big responsibility. If you're going to get pissed off if he—I don't know, if he scratches your furniture or something—'cause, seriously, he's probably going to scratch your furniture a bit—cats are bastards that way, and declawing them is really cutting off their toes, so you can't declaw him, you just have to accept that he's a bastard and get past it—but if you can't get past it, or whatever else he does, you shouldn't take him. And if you don't want him, I can take him back. I told them this was just a try-out. But I thought you might want him." Shane frowned. "Your apartment's really clean. Tidy. But it seemed like—I don't know. It seemed like maybe it's just kind of that way by accident. It seemed like maybe you wouldn't mind if it was a bit less perfect, if there was—you know. If it was something you cared about doing the messing it up."

Jesus Christ. Was Simon going to have to introduce Tristan *and* Shane to his aunt? "You want to give me a cat?"

"Only if you'll take care of it." Otherwise…" Shane reached into the pocket of his hoodie and pulled out a small rectangular box. "Chocolates."

"You got me a Christmas present? I mean, cat or chocolate— you got me a present?"

Shane shifted uncomfortably. "Not if you don't want them. But, also—" and he dug back into his hoodie pouch, leaving the chocolate behind and pulling out a sheet of bright yellow paper. "I thought you might be interested in this. It's a band. A bar. A band playing at a bar. Tomorrow. They play the same bar, the day after Christmas, every year. A tradition or whatever. And a bunch of us are going."

"A bunch of you," Simon said. He wouldn't let himself dig, wouldn't let himself beg. "You've come to give me a cat or some chocolates and to invite me to a bar to listen to a band with a bunch of you. It's kind of alphabetically synchronous."

Shane frowned. "I don't know about that last part. But, yeah. Cat or chocolate, and then bar, if you want. That's why I'm here."

Simon knew the smart choices. Chocolate, which he could throw out upstairs, no flyer, and get on with his life. Instead, he asked, "Does the cat have a name?"

"They've been calling him Sparkles," Shane said, "But that's just because there's way too many chicks in that clinic. I think it'd be fine if you gave him a different name. A better one. It's not like most cats give a shit what you call them—they're going to ignore you anyway."

"That's strangely comforting." Against his better judgement, Simon stepped forward and peered into the cage.

The cat was as huge as he remembered, crouched down in the carrier as if he might explode at any moment, sending chunks of plastic flying as he made his bid for freedom. It wouldn't be good if that happened; wouldn't be safe for the cat, and Shane would feel bad, and—"Okay. I'll take him. But he needs stuff, right? Like—?"

"Food, and a litter box and litter," Shane said, and jerked his head toward a little pile of containers leaned against the wall. "He's had his shots, but you'll need a vet by next fall. The clinic can give you his records, if you don't want to take him back there."

"Okay." It was all happening far too quickly, and for a nearly hysterical moment Simon wondered what would happen if the cat shredded his new plant, or if the plant was poison and the cat ate it. There was suddenly quite a bit of life invading his apartment, and he wasn't at all sure how to deal with it on a practical or symbolic level. "Thank you."

"Can you carry it all?" Shane asked. "I could help, but your building security—I'm guessing you gave them shit for letting me in last time? So if I show up again, *with* you, that's going to make you look a bit flakey, right?"

"There are cameras in the parking garage," Simon said. "They've already seen you."

"Nah." Shane pointed. "There's a camera there, and there, and one right down by the door, but I dodged around it when another car was coming in. I'm clean, so far. Seriously, dude, you should probably complain about the security here, for real."

"But that might interfere with our lovely visits."

Shane grinned, quick and easy, and his threatening face was transformed into something—well, still not something Simon could easily imagine introducing to his aunt, but something pleasant and friendly anyway. Then Shane grew more serious and thrust the flyer at Simon. "I'm not going to tell him I gave that to you. I'm not going to—I mean, I'm just guessing. He might not care at all, or he might be kind of pissed if you show up. No guarantees here, you know. But—I'm not going to tell him I gave it to you, because I don't want him to be disappointed if you don't show."

It wasn't much, but it was so much more than Simon had expected. "Okay," he managed. "Thanks."

Shane handed the flyer over, then the cat. "The present's just the cat and the other stuff, not the carrier. I borrowed that from the clinic. If you can bring it back, that'd be great. Or if you need it, you could send them twenty bucks or something. They take credit card payments over the phone, if you don't want to come by. Or just leave it somewhere and tell me where to come pick it up. Or bring it to the bar tomorrow, if you're going, but—probably a bit weird to bring it to a bar?"

"I'll figure something out," Simon promised. "And, thank you. For the flyer, and for—General Meow? Is that a stupid name? I don't know how to name cats. He might end up just staying Sparkles."

"General Meow is really stupid, but it's still way the fuck better than Sparkles." Shane shrugged. "Get to know him, then name him. Like I said, there's no rush—he's never going to answer to it anyway."

Simon's cat would answer to his name, Simon decided as he waved goodbye to Shane and then loaded everything into his car for the short ride to his parking spot. "You're going to come when you're called, right, Fluffy? Snowball? Gravelly Snowball? Prince? Meow Tse Tung?"

The cat gazed at him with its orange eyes and showed no reaction. Possibly not a great start to their relationship.

Simon parked and carefully loaded himself up with his new belongings. Food and litter balanced in the litter box, with the African violet wedged into a corner, all carried under one arm while the other hefted Sir Fur. Sir Purr. Fur and Purr. Was there something in that? Damn it.

"I can't really handle this level of responsibility," Simon told the cat carrier as they stepped into the elevator. "Business deals and quasi-criminal behavior, fine. But how the hell am I supposed to name a cat?"

The cat didn't answer. He just sat quietly in his carrier as Simon staggered into his apartment, made sure the door was closed tightly, and then opened the cage door.

He'd been expecting a mad dash for cover, or a refusal to leave the carrier until the time was right, or some other fear-based reaction. Instead, the cat strutted out of his carrier like it had been a litter carried by his most trusted slaves. He surveyed his new surroundings with a regal gaze, then calmly stalked toward the bedroom.

Simon followed at a respectful distance, and by the time he reached the doorway, the cat was springing up onto the bed. A few sniffs, a glance around the room, and then the animal collapsed with a nearly audible flop, lying on his side in the very middle of the bed, gazing back at Simon as if daring him to object.

It wasn't a perfect match. The cat was huge and fluffy, and, well, a cat. But there was still something in his gaze, a calm insouciance that made Simon smile. "I know you," he said. "You're a little duck. Aren't you?"

And the cat meowed, then rolled over on his back and began to purr, his eyes shut.

Simon approached cautiously. Was he allowed to touch?

He reached out a tentative hand and glided it just along the cat's fur, barely brushing the surface. The cat opened one eye. Then, so quickly Simon had no time to respond, it reached up and grabbed Simon's hand in its front paws. No claws dug into Simon's skin, and he remembered Shane's lecture about declawing. So the cat could be shredding him, but wasn't.

Simon relaxed his arm and let the cat drag his hand closer. A furry snout, still much larger than Simon could really accept, sniffed each of his fingertips in turn, a careful inspection searching for something Simon couldn't imagine. Then the cat turned his head and drove his entire body upward, butting his ears into Simon's hand with force.

"You aren't subtle, are you?" Simon murmured, his fingers curving instinctively to caress the animal. "I think cats are supposed to be creatures of great mystery. Do you think you're doing that right?"

The cat clearly thought he was doing everything perfectly and arched into Simon's hand with sensuous abandon.

"I have a cat," Simon told his cat.

Then he looked out toward the front entry, the pile of cat belongings he needed to unpack—and the bright yellow flyer.

He had a plant. He had a cat.

Surely that was enough. Surely he couldn't be greedy enough, reckless enough, to try for more. Especially when the *more* he wanted was dangerous in so many ways.

And yet his eyes returned to the yellow flyer, and he let himself wonder just how far he could push the universe's generosity before it decided to push him back.

~*~*~*~

"DODGER WOULDN'T BE happy at a bar," Noah was saying as Tristan left the bathroom after his shower, towel wrapped around his waist.

"How do we know that? He's been to bars before, and he's had fun."

Tristan paused in the hallway to see how the argument resolved. Shane had his stubborn face on, and once that happened, negotiations didn't generally go too far. But he was wrapped around Noah's little finger in most ways, so this was an interesting struggle between his two strongest instincts. Do his own thing against do whatever Noah wanted.

"Has he had fun, or has he just hung out in your hoodie?"

"You think he doesn't have fun in my hoodie?"

"Well, not, like, *fun*, no. I think he mostly sleeps, doesn't he? He's not in there play-fighting or chasing toys around or anything. He's just kind of neutral." Noah stepped closer and looked up at Shane with his best puppy-dog eyes. They weren't in Dodger's class, but they were pretty damn good. "*You* should get to have some fun tonight. If Dodger's there, you'll just be taking care of him. Don't you want to relax a little?" He edged even closer and ran his fingers up the front Shane's jeans, then tucked them under his shirt.

Tristan's own skin tightened, thinking about cool fingers on warm abs, but Shane seemed unmoved. "If you think it's not fun inside my hoodie," he said primly, "maybe you should pull your hands out of there and go chase a toy or something."

"Dude, *I* have fun inside your hoodie—lots of fun! But I sincerely hope Dodger has different tastes than I do. More chew toys, less—" Noah stopped as if suddenly aware that he had an audience. Not just Tristan, but Micah and Trey and Rebecca and a few others, all watching, wondering if they were about to witness the first big fight between the new couple. "Less human-style fun," Noah finished lamely.

Shane looked down at the puppy, currently snuggled on the couch between Rebecca and Trey, contendedly chewing on a chunk of wood. "He'd be lonely," Shane said.

Well, this was getting a bit too sad. "I can babysit him," Tristan volunteered. "I wasn't really looking forward to tonight anyway. I'm kind of tired, or something." He got a firmer grip on his towel and then brushed past Noah, heading for the couch. "What do you say, Dodge? You want to hang out with Uncle Tristan tonight? We can order take-out. Do you like Thai?"

"No," Shane said quickly. Far too quickly.

Tristan squinted at him. "What? Do you not trust me with your dog? You think I can't babysit? I mean, he wasn't going to get *lots* of Thai, you know. Just a taste."

Shane frowned in consternation, then reluctantly said, "Noah's right. Dodger should learn to spend some time on his own. That's why we got him the crate, right?"

"And he likes the crate," Noah said supportively. "He thinks it's fun."

Shane was still frowning. "He thinks it's fun when he's in there for a few minutes. He might not feel the same way if he's in it for a few hours."

"He'll just go to sleep," Noah said.

"We could Skype him, to be sure," Rebecca said. She was staring into space, as usual, but also paying attention to her surroundings, as usual. "We could set up Tristan's tablet here, propped up so it's looking at the crate. And then we could watch on our phones and be sure he's okay."

"Seriously?" Trey said. He looked from one person to the next. "Shit. You're serious. The Legend Wreckers are playing tonight and you're going to be watching a sleeping puppy instead of the damn show?"

Tristan grinned at him. "We're getting old, man. Can't keep up the pace anymore."

"Only half of us are even old enough to get in without fake ID, and we're already too old to really party?" Trey scoffed.

"You show us how it's done," Micah suggested. "Lead us down the paths of debauchery and excess." He looked over at Tristan. The junkie and the whore, daring Trey to teach them something new about rule-breaking. Tristan grinned back. Micah was a pain in the ass, intent on self-destructing and not too concerned about who he took down with him, but damn, he could be fun to talk to.

And that, of course, made Tristan think of someone else who was fun to talk to. "I'm going to get dressed," he said, standing abruptly. "My tablet's charging in the kitchen. But let's have dinner here instead of going out for food—that'll mean Dodger's just alone for bar time, not bar-and-dinner time."

"Fucking spoiled little mutt," Trey grumbled as Tristan headed for the bedroom.

It was true, of course. The band of them, Shane especially, spent way too much time babying the little dog. But sometimes it was just nice to take care of something. Nice to feel powerful enough to offer protection instead of having to take it.

And, of course, thinking about being protected brought *more* thoughts of Simon Yeung. It was pathetic, probably.

Self-indulgent, definitely.

But it just all felt so pointless. Of all the people in the world, there were so few who Tristan truly felt connected to. The people in his apartment were his friends, and he cared about them. But Micah and Shane were the only two he was really close to, and Micah was busy drugging himself into oblivion while Shane was so wrapped up in Dodger and Noah that he barely seemed to remember Tristan was alive.

Not true, of course. Just self-pitying bullshit.

Tristan just—he felt like he'd lost something. And it was easier to pretend that he'd lost Shane than admit who he was really feeling cut off from.

What a mess.

It was good that he was going out, he decided as he pulled on a pair of jeans. He'd drink and dance and hell, maybe he'd flirt a little. Maybe he'd fuck a stranger in the back alley, just because he wanted to, not because he was getting paid for it.

And the fantasy washed over him with such power he could almost feel it. Simon's strong, lean body pressed up behind Tristan, the softness of his skin contrasting with the rough bricks Tristan was being driven into. The muttered words, the moans, the perfection of being there when the infuriating control was finally lost, when Simon let himself go, let himself take what he wanted. When he wanted Tristan, not as a whore, not as a problem, but as himself.

Tristan drew a deep, shaky breath. "Fuck," he muttered. He was getting worse, not better.

He needed to get over it.

So he *would* drink and dance and flirt and maybe fuck. He'd get on with his damn life and leave the old one behind. Simon had given him his freedom; now he needed to find the guts to take advantage of it.

Lap Dog

Chapter Fourteen

SIMON'S RECKLESSNESS HAD apparently become so overwhelming that his common sense had completely surrendered and was now lying, exhausted and silent, deep in his subconscious mind. It was a truly beautiful feeling, possibly augmented by the two double-vodkas he'd consumed since he got to the bar.

When he'd first arrived he'd felt overdressed, the slacks and dress-shirt that made up his casual uniform setting him apart from the jeans-and-t-shirt wearing crowd. But a few girls had come up to talk to him and he'd bought them a round and flirted a little before making his confession.

"I'm actually hoping to meet someone here tonight," he'd said. "A guy I sort of know, but would like to know better."

He was pretty sure it was the first time he'd admitted to being gay, at least in words, to people who didn't need to know. Obviously he'd made his preferences clear to various men in the past, and the Chens and others like them had clearly seen something in him that he wasn't hiding too well, but to just come out and say it, to strangers?

He liked it. He wondered if there was any way to get access to the club's sound system so he could announce it to the world, and then wondered if there'd been something a little stronger than vodka in his drinks.

But, no. He recognized the energy thrumming under his skin and he knew it wasn't artificially induced, not unless the thought of seeing Tristan counted as artificial. And he didn't think it did, not when wanting to be with him felt like the most natural thing in the world.

He smiled at himself as he finished the last of his drink. Maybe he was a *little* drunk, if he was getting that sappy.

His eyes scanned the room for about the fifth time in the last minute, but this time, he saw something—someone—that caught his attention. He took a few sideways steps through the crowd at the bar, trying to get a better look, and then froze.

Vinnie Dean, one of the few non-Chinese people to work for his uncle, was across the bar, talking to a blond.

Maybe just a coincidence. Dean was pretty slick, and this didn't really seem like his kind of place; he was just as overdressed as Simon was. But still, maybe a coincidence.

Or maybe something else.

Simon wanted to run. He hadn't done anything wrong, not yet. If his uncle asked about this, he could just say—it didn't matter. His uncle didn't care what he did with his free time, didn't care if he went to see a band.

But something was going on. Something Simon needed to know about. He'd thought his job was done, but if Dean was here? Things weren't over, not yet.

He worked his way through the crowd and was relieved to see Dean's expression of mild surprise as he neared. So it wasn't Simon being spied on. Good.

"He thought I needed backup?" Dean said when Simon was close enough to hear.

He forced a smile. "No. I'm here independently. I didn't realize my uncle had already taken care of it."

"Your—" Dean frowned. "No, I'm on loan, just like you were. I'm working for the Chens tonight."

Of course he was. Why would the Yeung family be interested in Tristan's behaviour? The Chens, on the other hand? "Just making sure he's following the contract? It doesn't say anything about not going to bars, does it?"

"Just a general sort of surveillance." Dean peered around, suddenly alert. "So you'd better head off. If he sees you, he'll know he's being watched. And if he sees you talking to me, my cover's blown."

"But what are you watching *for*?" Simon was pushing too hard and he knew it. But Dean was a talker, and not that bright.

After another quick scan of the room, Dean said, "I'm just supposed to be watching him. They didn't really say why. I think they thought it was a bit too easy for him, you know?" He looked around, then back at Simon. "He didn't want to work for them,

215

right? That's how you got involved? And then things shook out and he suddenly *wasn't* working for them. So he got just what he wanted from all this, plus a pretty sizeable cash bonus, and the Chens have to pay half of that. So, they're pissed. They know they can't off him, or mess him up too bad without drawing attention they can't afford. But if they see any sign that he planned all this? They'll find a way to make him pay."

Simon wished he hadn't finished his drink. His mind raced, fogged only a little by the alcohol. Had he been too damn clever? No, he'd been too damned desperate. He'd known it was risky, but he'd taken the chance because it had been important to Tristan that he not work for the Chens. Or because it had been important to *Simon* that Tristan not work for the Chens. Because he'd gotten possessive, stupidly, pointlessly territorial over a man he had no claim on.

"What the hell do they think they're going to find?" he asked. "I mean—you think he—" He frowned, exaggerating the effort of thinking it through, but only by a little. "You think he set up the reporter? I saw no sign of him having those kind of contacts. He's just a small time whore—he doesn't know anybody. He couldn't have planned this."

Dean shrugged. "Not my call, man. And they're not just watching him, they're digging all over the place. I don't know what they've got, but they're not giving up. But if you aren't here for that, what are *you* looking for?"

Excellent question. "I just wanted to be sure he was keeping at least a bit of a low profile. The press don't have his name yet, so he should be fine, but I want to be sure it stays that way."

Dean nodded. "But he'll recognize you, right?"

"I don't care if he does. I *want* him to know he's being watched. Hopefully that'll keep him in line."

Another nod. "Makes sense. But it's just about the opposite of my job, so—we'd better not be seen together, okay?"

"Sure, right," Simon said. Then as if as an afterthought, he turned and said, "You found out about this the same way I did? About him coming here tonight?"

"The junkie friend? How much did he milk you for?"

Simon's stomach churned. Tristan's friends, the people he'd been willing to sacrifice so much for. One of them had betrayed him. "Too much," he said, and made himself smile. "I paid him too much."

Then he turned and headed for the door. He couldn't stand around in there, in the heat and the noise and the flashing damn lights. He needed to get out, needed to think. He needed to fix it all, and he needed to do it permanently this time.

~*~*~*~

"HEY."

It was one word, hissed from an alleyway, and it should have been beneath Tristan's notice. It certainly shouldn't have made him jerk to a halt, his friends charging on without him until Shane stopped, and then Noah. The rest kept going.

"Simon?" Tristan said. It made no sense, but he was sure he'd recognized the voice, and the lean body standing in the shadows.

"Get in here," Simon hissed.

Tristan did as he was told, vaguely aware that Shane and Noah were following.

"What's going on?" Shane demanded. "What are you doing out here?"

The second question was a bit strange, maybe, but the first one was pretty solid. Tristan would like an answer to it, but first he let himself just look for a moment. Simon in the shadows was Simon at his dark, mysterious best.

But the mood was pretty much blown when he said, "There's a guy in the club, a guy working for the Chens. It shouldn't be a problem, but—you need to watch yourself. You need to watch what you do, and—" He stopped, then said, "I'm sorry, Tristan, but you need to watch what you say. Around you friends. Shane and Noah are okay, but the others—" He stopped, and Tristan got the feeling he could have said more, but wasn't sure if he should. "The Chens found out you'd be here tonight," he finally said. "If you say other things, the Chens might find out about that, too. You need to keep your mouth shut, okay? Only Shane or Noah. And you guys will stay quiet too, right?"

"What the hell is going on?" Tristan demanded. "You can't come here and feed me all this cryptic shit, Simon! Not after everything!" He wasn't quite sure what he meant by that, but he meant *something*. He needed *something*. "I trusted you, and I did what you said, and now what? You're accusing my friends of something? Is that what's going on?"

"I'm trying *not* to accuse your friends," Simon said. "But Chen's man is inside and knows you're coming here, so clearly there's been a leak somewhere. And—shit, Tristan, I'm sorry. But he said it was one of your friends who told him."

"It could have been you who passed it along," Shane said in his flattest, most threatening tone. He glanced at Tristan and said, "Sorry. I told him we'd be here. I thought—whatever. But if the news got out? If we have to decide who to not trust, this asshole or one of us? I know which one I'd choose."

Tristan wanted to sit down. He wanted to have never left the apartment, or maybe to have never been born. It was all just too damn much. "I thought this was over," he whispered. He'd thought he was free of the confusion. Sure, there was still the disappointment, the sense of loss when he thought about never seeing Simon again, but if having Simon in his life also meant having all this chaos? God, was the trade worth it?

"Tristan!" Trey yelled from the mouth of the alley. "Shit man, look at this!" He jogged forward, holding a phone out in front of him. "Becks was going to Skype with the dog—but look! There are people in your apartment!"

Tristan's mind spun. "People?" He reached out for the phone. "Who?"

He didn't want to know the answer. He didn't want it to be the same people who'd stolen his money last time, didn't want to know that Simon had changed his mind, changed his loyalty, recovered from whatever insane notion had allowed him to help Tristan in the first place.

"The stupid camera's pointed at the dog," Trey said. "All we can see is their legs."

Shane burst into action then, sprinting down the alley and spinning right, running toward the apartment. Home was twenty blocks away, at least, but he was on his way. Protecting his dog.

"Call the police," Noah urged, staring desperately after Shane. "If he gets there and they're still inside—"

"Don't," Simon said. There was something in his voice that made everyone stop and pay attention to him. He seemed to have an authority they responded to, which was strange. He was a bit older, a bit better dressed, but Tristan and his friends had been ignoring older, better dressed authority figures for most of their lives. So what was it about Simon that made them all shut up?

"Why?" Tristan demanded. "Why shouldn't we call the cops? Who are you trying to protect?"

"I'm trying to protect *you*," Simon said, his voice low and intent. "They've got no reason to hurt the dog, and they'll be long gone before Shane gets there—he won't get hurt. And once the police are involved, everything is under their control. Once you've called them, you can't *un*call them. But if you've got these guys?

Even just their legs, on tape? You've got another weapon. You've got something we can—"

"*We?*" Trey interjected. "Where the hell is this 'we' shit coming from?" He stepped forward, clearly ready to take on Shanc's role and try to solve the problem with a little violence.

But Tristan stepped between them, his gaze fixed on Simon's face.

"What did you mean," Tristan asked, "earlier? When you said—" He wished he could have this conversation somewhere more private.

"About keeping your mouth shut?" Simon supplied. Yes, that was a more discreet way to refer to it. Simon pressed his lips together, looked up at the sky, then hissed, "Shit." He looked back at Tristan. "If it was safe to let you blame me, I'd let you blame me. Do you understand that? If I *could*, I would, just so you wouldn't have to know. But—if you blame this on me, then you won't be as careful as you should be. I'm sorry."

"What are you saying?" Tristan demanded.

Simon didn't respond, not directly. Instead, he looked over Tristan's shoulder and said, "Somebody told one of Chen's workers where Tristan would be tonight. Maybe he didn't think it was a big deal; just a chance to get some cash for some unimportant information. Maybe someone should say something about that, now."

Tristan spun around to find a cluster of confused faces staring at him, denial clear on each one. Each one except—"Micah?" Micah, standing closer to the street, his gaze locked on his feet.

Fuck. Of course, Micah. The drugs made him weak, and he wouldn't give up the drugs. "Shit, Micah, what did you tell them?"

"Not much," he said, jerking his head up so he could look at Tristan with desperate intensity. "And like he said, I didn't think it was a big deal. Somebody wanted to know where you'd be tonight? That's not a big secret, is it? Is it?"

"What else did you tell them?" Simon asked. He laid his hand gently on Tristan's shoulder—no weight, just warmth. "It's important that we know."

"Nothing else! Just where we were going, what time we'd be here—that's all. It's not a big deal, right?"

Tristan felt like crying. Just flopping down there in the dirty alley, drawing his knees up to his face, and bawling like a little kid. Instead he echoed, "Not a big deal."

"I'm sorry," Simon said, so quietly only Tristan could hear. "I wish it had been me, but it wasn't."

"Yeah," Tristan said. It was weak, but he let himself lean back, just for a moment, just long enough to feel Simon's strong chest behind him, ready to hold him up. But he wouldn't let himself need the support.

"Hey, assholes!" Trey yelled, and Tristan jerked away from Simon only to see Trey yelling into a phone. "Fuckers in the apartment! We can see you! We're filming you, and we called the cops! You better get the fuck out before they get there!"

"You have the sound turned on?" Simon asked.

Trey grinned as if he'd solved all the world's problems. "Yeah, you'd better run!" he yelled into the phone. Then he turned toward Tristan and said, "We had it muted, but just on our end. Becks remembered, and we turned it off." Another look at the phone. "Yeah, they're running, the shitheads."

"Why were they there in the first place?" Tristan asked. He made himself stand straight and turn to look at Simon, but the cautioning expression on the man's face reminded Tristan of the larger problem. "Shit." He could see Micah from the corner of his eye, fumbling with a plastic baggie and fishing out a pill. "Micah!"

Micah jerked his head around. He stared at Tristan, and Tristan stared back. It wasn't how things should end—Tristan didn't want them to end at all. But—

Micah looked down at the pill in his palm, then back up at Tristan. "I'm sorry," he said.

"You have to stop, Micah. If you stop now, we can—I don't know. We can figure something out. But no more drugs." Tristan felt as if he was fighting the tide, trying to hold the water back with just his words. He spoke more quickly, more desperately. "We can get you help. I have some money—you could go to rehab. A good one. And when you get out, if you stay clean, we'll just forget about this shit, okay? We'll make it work."

Micah, of course, was already high. Already flying away from Tristan and everyone else stuck back on Earth. Still close enough to see them, though. Close enough to raise his hand into something like a wave, right before he tossed the pill into his mouth and crunched down, chewing to get the drugs into his system faster.

Tristan turned away and found himself looking straight at Simon Yeung. And Simon was looking back at him with an expression that seemed very much like sorrow. "Sometimes people can't be as strong as we want them to be," he said quietly. "I'm sorry."

Tristan blinked hard, and then again. He wasn't going to break down. He wasn't. "So, what do we have to do?" he asked, proud that his voice wasn't shaky.

Simon nodded, clearly appreciating the return to a less emotional topic. "I'll take care of it. Just keep a low—"

"No," Tristan said. He hadn't exactly planned to interrupt, but he was glad he had. "Not again. We did this last time, you being the white knight rescuing the poor helpless maiden. But I'm not a maiden—pretty far from it in all ways, as far as I understand the term—and I'm not looking to get rescued."

Simon raised an eyebrow.

"Okay, yes, I could use a little *help*," Tristan admitted. "But mostly just because I don't know exactly what you did last time, and it'll be a lot easier to get myself out of trouble if I know exactly what you got me into." He didn't want to do it, but he made himself look back over his shoulder to find Micah, leaning against the wall of the alley, eyes closed as he surfed through whatever galaxy he was visiting. Such an asshole.

Still, Tristan couldn't abandon him entirely. "I don't want him in my apartment," he told Trey and Becks. "If you guys—I don't know. Can you take care of him, a little? Is that okay? Get him somewhere safe?"

"He's a junkie," Trey said. "Where's safe?"

It was an excellent question, but not one Tristan wanted to think about too much. "Maybe just take him to the bar with you? I have to sort some stuff out."

"And you're okay with him, alone?" Trey asked, sending a suspicious look in Simon's direction.

"Yeah, I'll be fine." Tristan turned to Noah, who was on the phone, clearly recounting the yelling-over-the-phone strategy to Shane. "Tell him to keep his phone handy in case I need him, okay? Tell him to actually listen for it, and answer it if it rings?"

Noah nodded, then cast his own suspicious look in Simon's direction. "Do you have somewhere to go?" he asked Tristan.

"Yes," Simon answered on his behalf. He turned to Tristan. "My car's around the corner. We can go somewhere, and I'll tell you the mess I got you into."

Tristan nodded, then said, "And I won't forget the mess you got me out of."

A flicker of a smile, and then Simon nodded toward the alley entrance. Tristan started walking. He was vaguely aware of Simon carefully interposing himself between Tristan and Micah, which was a bit strange, as if he thought one of them was going to get violent.

Or maybe he was just doing what he could to shield Tristan from having to confront reality. And while that wasn't a good long-term plan, wasn't a luxury Tristan could afford to enjoy for long, it was kind of nice, at least right then. So Tristan let himself be herded to Simon's car, and he refused to look back toward the alley.

~*~*~*~

IT HAD FELT GOOD to have Tristan back in the car, and Simon had been tempted to just keep driving. Maybe right out of town, right out of state. They could start over together, somewhere else, without having to deal with any of the crap they were leaving behind.

But of course, Tristan had a life in Seattle, friends he cared about and wanted to stay with. One betrayal didn't ruin all that.

So Simon drove them to the same motel he'd taken them the day of the Doggie Display or whatever the hell it had been called. Not that long ago, but it felt like forever.

They didn't talk as they drove. Simon concentrated on the road, and Tristan gazed out the side window, lost in a world where Simon wasn't welcome. But as they climbed out of the car at the motel, Tristan looked across at Simon and said, "He's ashamed of himself. That makes it worse. He's ashamed of himself, and the drugs are the only thing that takes that away, and then to get more drugs he does things that make him ashamed of himself."

Simon nodded. "I'm not suggesting that you start hating him. You just need to recognize that you can't trust him, not right now."

"Because he's not as strong as I want him to be," Tristan said. "Yeah." His smile was a little forced, but at least he was trying. "So. What's our plan now?"

"Come inside."

"Is it okay that we're here?" Tristan asked. "I thought this was some sort of business place. Are you going to get in trouble for hanging out with me?"

"New plan. None of the rest of that really matters anymore."

"I don't think I like the sound of that."

"I think you'll be okay. I really do."

"You need to explain this to me." Tristan stood expectantly by the door and Simon dutifully unlocked it and followed Tristan inside.

Tristan looked around. "You know, I don't think I've ever spent this much time in motel rooms with someone I wasn't fucking."

"That's not a train of thought that's going to help us achieve our goals," Simon replied. Did he sound like an uptight spinster? Too damn bad. "So, let me give you the details from what happened before. And then I'll tell you what I want to do next."

Tristan walked to the far corner of the queen-sized bed and sat down cross-legged just beside the pillow. Simon thought about taking a seat himself, but decided he'd rather pace.

So he walked, he talked, he explained, and he defended, because Tristan really didn't like the revised plan.

"That's taking too much on yourself," Tristan protested. "This was my problem, and the way you've got things set up, I'm going to get off with five years of free living and you're going to get totally shit on!"

"No, it's okay," Simon said. "It's time for me to—well, not to get shit on. That's a fairly distasteful image. But, it's time for me to stop taking the easy way out."

Tristan frowned at him. "From what you've said, I don't see too much easy about the way you've been living."

"I've been a caged bird. I'm fed, so I sing on command. Easy."

"Only with a really limited definition of the word." Another frown, and then Tristan scooted forward across the bed until he was sitting on the edge closest to Simon. "Look, if you want to break out of the cage for your own reasons, that's great. I mean it. It's *great*." He twisted his face up into possibly the first expression he'd ever made that Simon didn't find appealing. "But it's not just a coincidence that you're doing it now. That you're doing it to help me out."

"That's not something you need to worry about."

"As if anyone in the history of the world, ever, has stopped worrying about something because they were told they didn't need to worry about it."

Simon smiled. "Come on. In the history of the world? *Ever*? I bet someone, somewhere, sometime, has stopped worrying because they were told they didn't have to."

"Do you really think you're going to distract me with this? I mean, you think I'm going to start arguing with you about whether anyone has ever changed their mind about what to worry about?" Tristan pushed himself off the bed; apparently it was his turn to pace. "Shit, Simon. This doesn't feel right to me. Maybe it isn't necessary. I mean, they're watching me—big deal. I'm doing what I'm supposed to do, so what are they going to complain about? And Micah? He doesn't know much. If he talks more, is it really that big of a deal?"

"It's not just you, and it's not just Micah. They're digging. It's not surprising—honestly, I didn't really expect us to get away with it as long as we did. And it was the plan all along for me to confess if things got too hot. So this is just following the plan. With a slight modification."

"It feels like you're taking too much of the pain, and you're not getting any gain."

"It's my call," Simon said. And then he just stood there.

Tristan frowned at him, and then, in the space of one step between the bathroom and the bed, he transformed. The creases in his brow smoothed away, the fierceness in his eyes softened, and his movements slowed. "But you could get *some* gain," he said, his voice lower than it had been only a moment before.

Shit. Simon hadn't prepared himself for this. He took a step backward. "I don't think that's a good idea."

"Why not? We both know you want me. Hell, the *Chens* could see you wanted me. And I like you, Simon. I truly do. I'm grateful—"

And that was the magic word that let Simon break the spell. "No," he said firmly. "What I want short term can't be more important than what I want long term."

The seduction machine ground to a halt, and real Tristan peeked out long enough to say, "Huh?"

"You're right," Simon said. It felt like he was exposing a part of his soul to admit it, but he gathered his courage and said, "I do want you. But that would be short term, right? And if I let it happen like this—with you thinking you owed me something, trying to pay off a debt—that would cost me something, long term. It would cost me a lot." He turned away and was tempted to just leave. There was no point trying to explain this. No point trying to make Tristan understand something he didn't truly understand himself. But something kept his feet anchored to the ground and he heard himself say, "I would like it if one thing in my life was pure. I don't mean sex is unpure, I mean—" What the hell did he mean? "I would like it if my motives, for once, weren't practical. I'd like it if I did something because I thought it was right, not because I thought I could get something out of it."

He turned, thought once more about bolting, then said, "Do you know how humiliating it is to sell your soul for a handful of beans? To—to subjugate yourself and be rewarded with hardly anything?"

And then he heard a completely unexpected sound. He whirled to be sure he was hearing correctly, and stared at Tristan as he—as he *laughed* at Simon. The little bastard was sitting on the bed, rocking back and forth, and *laughing*. "Yeah, you emo bastard," Tristan gasped out between his cackles. "I think maybe I have some fucking idea about that!"

"Well—" Simon started, and then he stopped. Was he really going to try to out-compete Tristan in the soul-selling Olympics? "So, okay," he managed. "So you understand, right? About doing something for its own sake, not because you expected a reward?"

Tristan's laughing subsided, and after a moment's thought, he nodded. "Me and Shane used to fuck sometimes. Well, quite a bit. And he's not—he's not really into sex, for its own sake. But he's a good friend, and he just—it was important to me. It was like I didn't want to *just* be a whore, you know? Like it was important that I sometimes had sex because I wanted to, because I cared about someone...." He fell silent, then looked up at Simon. "So, yeah, okay. You've been whoring out your brain, and now you want to use it just for itself. No payment, no reward. I get that. But for what it's worth, that wasn't really what I was offering."

"Yeah?" Simon challenged. "Because that whole sex kitten act? You're saying that was how you came on to Shane when you just wanted to have sex with someone you care about?"

Another frown, and then Tristan flopped back on the bed. "Can you never just turn your brain off and not analyze everything? Can't you just be *stupid* sometimes?"

Simon snorted. He was gearing up to be stupid to a completely unprecedented degree, but he didn't think Tristan wanted to be reminded of that. So he just said, "We have work to do. If you're okay with the plan?"

Tristan nodded slowly. "I don't like it. But I don't have a better idea, and I respect your decision."

"Good." Simon dug in his pocket for his keys. "So you stay here and I'll go pick up some gear."

"No." Tristan slid off the bed and crossed the floor in two big steps. "I'll come with you. We're a team, right? I don't want to sit here going crazy and worrying about every time I hear someone moving outside the door."

"Okay," Simon agreed. He was acutely aware of how close Tristan was standing to him. If either of them shifted just a little, they'd be touching, their shoulders first, then maybe their chests, and then if they rolled a little, if they pressed in—

"Hey," Tristan said, and Simon jerked his head up guiltily. Had he been staring down? Where had he been looking? But Tristan's smile wasn't accusatory; it was sweet. "I know it's been kind of weird, and a bit too intense, but—I'm glad I've gotten to know you, Simon. I really am."

And then he stretched forward, not far, just enough for his lips to find Simon's. And thank god, Simon had the presence of mind to stay still, and then to let his lips press back, and then—then they were kissing. Not hungry, not desperate, just calm and somehow friendly.

Simon knew he could take things further. He could wrap his arms around Tristan and pull him closer, or else push him backward, toss him down on the bed and fall on top. His body ached for it, roared for it, but his self-control held. He stood still, kept one hand on his keys, and left the other hanging at his side until Tristan reached for it and entwined their fingers.

The kiss didn't last much longer, but when Tristan pulled away it felt like the warmth of his lips was transferred to his eyes. "In case you were wondering," he said, "that wasn't for you. That was for me."

"Okay," Simon managed, and Tristan grinned at him.

"Better than okay," Tristan said. Then he started for the door, still holding Simon's hand. "Now, stop distracting me. We've got work to do."

Lap Dog

Chapter Fifteen

THEY SPENT THE NIGHT sorting it all out. The second night Tristan had spent with Simon in a motel room, the second night with Simon treating him like—well, Tristan really wasn't sure how to classify the way Simon was treating him. Like a friend? Sort of, but there was an undercurrent of something else. Like a problem to be solved, a challenge to be met? A bit of that, sure, but Simon made it clear that this was *their* problem, now, the two of them together. Mostly, he treated Tristan like someone deserving of respect. It wasn't an approach Tristan was used to, not from anyone but his closest friends.

Shit. He'd done pretty well through the night, not thinking about his friends, but now the sun was up and Simon was driving him home and Tristan couldn't just forget about it anymore. Micah wouldn't be at the apartment. At least, he'd damn well better not be. But that didn't mean his presence wouldn't be felt, didn't mean Tristan wouldn't be fighting to balance his anger and his concern, his frustration and his fear.

And he had more than just Micah to worry about, of course. "You're sure there's not more I can do? Sure I shouldn't come with you?"

Simon shook his head. "This will only work if I can allow them to save face. Having a *gwai lo* standing there watching it all will just make that more difficult."

"And if it doesn't work?"

Simon sighed. "It should work. For you, at least. I don't think you need to worry."

"You don't think I should worry about *you*?" Tristan demanded.

"No." They pulled up in front of Tristan's apartment building and Simon turned to look at him. "You shouldn't. You should be fine with all this—I'm pretty sure after this morning you'll just be a footnote, if that. They have no reason to take the chance of messing with you, or your friends. I'll make that clear to them."

"You're talking about me again. I'm still talking about *you*."

"It'll either work for me or it won't. Either way, worrying won't help."

"But if it doesn't work—they might kill you. Right? I mean, that's what it means when you say 'doesn't work', because your version of 'works' still involves you losing everything you've worked for, losing your—"

Simon held up his hand. "This isn't actually helping me get in the right mindset. I need to be calm and confident, Tristan. Please don't try to shake that."

Shit. Was that what Tristan had been doing? He stopped talking and knew that he should be getting out of the car. It was time to get on with the next step. But he hated the thought of Simon driving away and never coming back, all because he'd gotten into a mess trying to help someone he barely knew. Tristan took a deep breath, then said, "We could leave. If you want. I'd go with you, if you wanted. You don't have to take this chance. My friends are important to me, sure. But like you said before, I could stay in touch with them even if I lived somewhere else." Tristan knew he was speaking too quickly, sounding too desperate, but he didn't seem to be able to calm himself. "We could go down to LA, if you wanted. I've never been there, but it'd be big enough to get lost in, right? And far enough away that they wouldn't worry about you too much? Wouldn't that be okay?"

Simon's smile was genuine, which made it just a little bit more heartbreaking. "Thank you for offering," he said. "And it is tempting. But, no. It's not as likely to work as the current plan. This is a better option, for both of us."

"A better option for *me*, you mean. Safer for *me*."

"Shhh," was all Simon said.

Tristan wasn't crying, not quite. But it had been a long, difficult night; a long, difficult couple weeks. He was tired of being afraid, he was tired of being confused, and he really, really didn't want to lose Simon before he even had the chance to get to know him properly. So possibly he was a little less graceful than he usually would be as he reached across the center console, grabbed Simon's jacket, and pulled him in for a kiss.

Deeper, this time. Tristan didn't have to worry about scaring Simon off, not when Simon was already determined to leave. So he pulled their faces closer and wrapped their tongues together, hoping his mouth could be more persuasive with touch than it had been with words.

But apparently it wasn't, because Simon pulled away far too soon. "It'll be okay," he said gently.

"Define your terms."

"The sun will still set tonight and still rise tomorrow. Shane will still be obsessed with his dog. I'll still—oh, shit, did I tell you I got a cat? And a plant." Simon banged his head back against the seat. "He's okay overnight—the internet told me that. He's got food and water and a litterbox. But if—you know. If things don't work out for me, can you go get him? I guess he should go back to the shelter—"

"Jesus Christ, Simon, if what you're doing is that dangerous, forget it! If you don't want to run away, we can call the cops, or— we can do something!"

"The police can't protect you, me, and all your friends—not to mention my cat, who really needs to be considered in all these things, now that I've remembered he exists—not forever. They're only useful as a threat, not as an actual tool."

"We should figure something else out, then," Tristan said. It wasn't acceptable that Simon was taking any risks at all, not on his behalf.

But Simon nodded his head toward a car parked on the far side of the street and said, "Too late."

"What?"

"Vinnie Dean, the guy I told you about last night? He's been parked over there since we arrived. He just saw us drive up together, saw us kissing, and I'm sure he'll be sending that intel to the Chens, or maybe straight to my uncle. Either way, cat's out of the bag. If I try to leave town now, he'll follow me, and if I don't leave? Either the Chens or my uncle—probably both—will send someone to pick me up. I need to go head them off at the pass. I need to show them that level of respect."

Tristan felt cold. "He saw—oh, God, Simon, I'm so sorry—"

But Simon shook his head. "Never apologize for kissing me, Tristan. I knew he was there; I could have stopped you. But my mind was already made up, so it didn't matter. And I wanted the kiss."

Okay. It was going to happen. And Simon needed Tristan to be brave about it. So he smiled and said, "You're really not a very good evil genius, you know that?"

"I'm beginning to realize it. Might be time to get out of the field."

Tristan nodded, took a deep breath, and put his hand on the door handle. "Call me when it's over."

Simon looked like he was about to say something, and Tristan shook his head vigorously. "No. Call me when it's over. That's an order." He pushed the door open. "And at some point you're going to have to tell me where you got a cat."

Then he shut the door. He didn't want to hear any more warnings, any more preparations for approaching doom. But he didn't want to go into the apartment, either. So he stood on the sidewalk and watched as Simon pulled away. Then he watched as the man in the car across the street set down his cell phone and made a u-turn, following Simon. Following instructions. Making sure Simon was going where he was supposed to. Making sure he didn't escape.

Tristan couldn't go inside. He couldn't be comfortable in his apartment, safe and secure, while Simon was heading into a dangerous situation.

So he stood on the curb, and he watched the cars disappear. And when he heard the front door of his building open and saw two people coming out, he didn't bother trying to smile at them.

"Didn't go too well?" Shane asked. He stood beside Tristan and looked in the same direction. Maybe interested in the view, or maybe giving Tristan the gift of avoiding eye contact.

"He's going to confess to his uncle. And maybe to the Chens, if they're there. He's going to tell them he was behind it all."

"Wow."

Noah sidled up on the side of Tristan that Shane wasn't covering. It made him feel surrounded, in a good way. "They might—" Tristan didn't want to say the words. "They might *kill* him. Not his uncle, he doesn't think. But the Chens might. And he doesn't think his uncle would try to stop them."

"So why the hell is he telling them?" Shane demanded.

"He has a plan. *We*. We have a plan. And it should work. It's just—what if it doesn't?"

"Can we do something?" Noah asked quietly.

"I can't think of anything," Tristan replied. "He said if I was there, it would make it worse."

"There's got to be something," Noah insisted.

"Sometimes—" Shane tried. Then he shrugged. "Sometimes all you can do is be there."

Tristan wanted to scream at him. Simon had made it clear he *couldn't* be there. Was there something about that Shane didn't understand? But then the idea sank in a little deeper. All he could do—he could just be there. "Did you drive?" he asked Noah. "Last night. Do you have still have your mom's car?"

"Yeah," Noah said cautiously. "Why?"

"Can you drive me somewhere?"

"Us," Shane said quickly. He looked at Noah, some unspoken communication flashing between them, then turned to Tristan. "He can drive *us* somewhere. Whatever you're doing, it sounds like it's probably stupid. And if you're doing something stupid? You're not going to do it alone."

~*~*~*~

IT FELT STRANGE to let himself into the family home, and then felt odd to feel strange. He'd lived in the house for a decade and a half, come back for breakfast on a daily basis for years, and now? Now Simon felt like an outsider, even before any official proclamation.

He toyed with the idea of going to the dining room for breakfast and drawing it all out a little, but he wanted it to be over. So he went straight to his uncle's office, knocked, and heard an angry grunt to bring him into the room.

Both Chens were there, William and David. It made sense— they'd have gotten the call when Simon was leaving Tristan's apartment, and they lived only five or ten minutes from the Yeung estate, while Simon had driven the better part of an hour. They'd come right over to complain, probably, and then sat there, stewing, as Simon drove. Now William was red in the face, clearly on the edge of an explosion. His father looked calmer, but that wasn't necessarily a good thing.

Simon made a short bow to each of them, a deeper one to his uncle. Then he stood and waited. He was subservient, here; he wouldn't be the one to run the meeting.

William took a deep, snarling breath, clearly intending to speak, but his father grabbed his arm. It was Frank Yeung's office, and Frank Yeung was in charge.

Simon's uncle kept his gaze on Simon's face, angry but controlled. "So?" he demanded.

So. It was time. "I have dishonored my family," Simon said. He could argue right and wrong, maybe, but he couldn't argue about dishonor. "I have abused your trust, and the trust of those you asked me to serve."

His uncle didn't answer right away. Instead, he stood up and stalked around the desk, coming to stand in front of Simon. "You did all that." The old man shook his head. "Because you were infatuated with a whore. A *male* whore."

"Only partly, Uncle." Stupid to dig the hole deeper, but it felt good to speak the truth. "Also because I wanted to do what was right. Not right for the family, just—right."

"You care so little for the family who raised you? Who provided for you, when your own parents abandoned you?"

Simon thought about mentioning the truths his aunt had revealed, but there was no point. Instead, he said, "It was a difficult decision."

The blow wasn't unexpected. It had been some time since his uncle had struck him, but only because it had been some time since Simon had given any reason for it. Now, his uncle flailed at him, too uncontrolled to be truly dangerous. A slap to the face, a punch that landed somewhere around Simon's ear, a kick to the shin, and then one to the thigh. Painful, but not dangerous.

"You challenge me?" his uncle snarled, and then it came, the elbow to the face that Simon had only seen used before, not felt. It felt as if his cheekbone had been driven back into his skull. An explosion of fiery pain, then dizziness, and Simon stumbled backward. He wasn't trying to escape the punishment, just hoping to keep his feet. That was all he wanted from this meeting; he just wanted to stay on his feet.

He managed it, at least for the time being, and made himself straighten. His uncle stared at him, probing for weakness as Simon had seen him do to others so many times before. "So," the older man finally said, "what did you do? You set it all up? The reporter, the congressman? The whore couldn't have done that, but you? You could have."

"I did. Tristan knew nothing about it. It was just me."

"So noble," his uncle said. "Taking all the blame."

"I want to tell you the truth. I owe you the truth."

"You owe me much more than that!"

For a moment, it seemed as if another attack was on its way, but then his uncle shook his head in disgust. "So. You want to be independent? Fine. You can be independent." He turned to the Chens. "I'll give him to you, and you can do as you see fit."

"That wouldn't be what I'd advise," Simon said. He could taste blood and his cheek was swelling so much it was starting to push his eye shut on that side. "There are elements you aren't aware of."

"Like what?"

"I'm sorry, Uncle. But I've taken steps to protect myself. And to protect—the whore." No. Damn it, no. He wasn't playing the game according to his uncle's rules anymore. "To protect Tristan."

His uncle squinted at him. "What does that mean?"

The moment of truth.

"Apologies, Uncle, but—I was willing to throw myself on your mercies. I would have taken any punishment you wanted to deliver." Easy to say it, at least. "But I couldn't subjugate myself to outsiders like that. I know I'm not your son, but I'm still a Yeung, and I wouldn't insult the name by giving another family power over me."

Manipulative? Absolutely. Simon swallowed some blood and then said, "I made recordings. Video recordings. I made Tristan describe his treatment at my hands, and at the hands of the Chens. And, I'm sorry, uncle, but I recorded my own business dealings with the Chens. And also those I engaged in on your behalf. I spoke about every detail I could remember—and I have a good memory—from every deal I've been part of over the last years. Everything that was illegal, or even immoral. I recorded my testimony." He turned to the Chens and said, "My apologies."

"You recorded it," Frank Yeung growled. "And did what with it?"

"I've set up a variety of systems," Simon said. It felt wrong to keep saying "I" when Tristan had been with him every step of the way, but this wasn't the sort of project where it was a kindness to share credit. "An out-of-town lawyer, an e-mail account set up to auto-send the files to a variety of sources—journalists, government officials, business associates in your more legitimate ventures—unless I go in each month and postpone the message." He paused to let the information sink in. "It's a sort of dead-man's switch. If

I'm dead—or otherwise unable to cancel the message—or if anything happens to Tristan, then the messages are sent. The information is shared."

His uncle was staring at him, and Simon kept his gaze carefully neutral, directed somewhere near the older man's feet. He could almost feel the battling factions in his uncle's mind: pride versus practicality, anger versus awareness. "You betrayed your family like that?" For a moment, the old man sounded almost hurt, and Simon wanted to beg forgiveness.

Instead, he nodded. "I'm sorry, Uncle. I know I've disappointed you."

"Disappointed?" The voice was quiet, but there was depth to it. "Oh, no. I was *disappointed* when you acted against the family to protect the whore. I was *disappointed*, but you were still family. I would have punished you, and I might have threatened, but I wouldn't have actually given you to the Chens." His uncle paused as if daring Simon to dispute this, but he didn't bother. It was too late to ever know, now. "But this? This—this is more than a betrayal! I cannot—" He shook his head. "No. I cannot tolerate this."

Simon let his mind fly to Tristan, just for a moment. Just a second of warmth. Then he said, "I understand."

"I can weather the consequences," his uncle said. "The unsubstantiated ravings of a disaffected employee! That's all it would be. There is no proof of anything. And *you*." He stared at Simon, his lip lifting in a snarl. "You won't be around to testify."

Simon nodded. "It isn't necessary, Uncle." He felt strangely light. "I anticipated your reaction, and I've arranged an alternate plan." After all, Tristan hadn't been looking over his shoulder every single second. It had only required a slight change to the e-mail he'd sent to the lawyer. "Tristan has the information to stop the e-mails from being sent. And the lawyer knows to only distribute the information if he receives news of *Tristan's* death, not of mine. As long as Tristan stays safe, the videos will not be distributed. And you have no reason to be angry with him. He knew nothing about this. He's only a whore, Uncle. Beneath your notice."

"You would sacrifice yourself?" his uncle asked. "For—?" He stopped, then shook his head. He turned to the Chens. "Is that adequate restitution for the insult? I give you my neph—"

That was when the knock sounded on the door, and then it opened. Aunt May swept into the room, her pearls and vintage Chanel as quiet and calming as her expression. "Good morning," she said sweetly.

Everyone stared at her. "We're in the middle of a meeting," Simon's uncle said, his voice clipped.

Aunt May looked Simon over, clearly noting his battered face, then raised an eyebrow at her husband. "Yes," she said, "I see that. I was waiting to speak to the Chens on their way out." She looked over her shoulder and smiled warmly at the two visitors. "But then I was contacted by a security guard who was concerned about something happening on the street."

"The street?" Simon's uncle said. He turned to his computer and punched a few buttons, bringing an image from one of the security cameras onto his screen. "What? Who are they?"

Simon took two cautious steps, then stared at the screen. There were people on the far side of the quiet residential street, standing calmly, staring at the house. They seemed to be waiting. And even over the grainy security footage, Simon knew who they were. Tristan. Beautiful, reckless Tristan. Shane, and Noah, and the big friend who was even goonier than Shane, and the girl with too much eye makeup who hung around with them. And two other women, one wearing scrubs, the other Chinese, wearing cowboy boots. Probably the vet from the clinic and her partner; Tristan had mentioned them the night before.

"I could be wrong," his aunt said, "but I believe they may be waiting for Simon." She smiled at her husband. "Just as I was waiting for the Chens. Did you know David's wife is interested in art of the Tang Dynasty, just as I am? I was thinking we should invite them to our gathering next month, when we'll hear from Dr. Seun about the lacquerware."

Everything hung frozen in time. Sound travelled well from the office to the library; Simon had overheard more than his share of conversations by lurking outside the door. If his aunt had been out there, she'd heard what was going on in the office.

And knowing what she did, she'd come inside with a proposal to save her idiot nephew's life. An invitation to a Yeung gathering? She was offering respectability, an entrée for Chen's family into the elevated ranks of Chinese-American society. It was a valuable commodity. But was it valuable enough?

"This is a business meeting," Simon's uncle said, fighting for control. "Please go back to the dining room."

His aunt nodded calmly. "Of course. Simon, you've hurt yourself somehow. Come with me and we'll put some ice on it."

"Thank you," Simon said. He tried to put enough warmth in his words to let her know he really meant it. "But I should stay here and finish this, I think."

Her smile became only a little more forced as she turned to her husband to say, "Please remember there are people outside waiting for Simon. We don't want to disappoint them." Then she turned to the Chens and added, "He's like a son to me. I value him very highly, and would do anything for him."

Simon realized he was holding his breath. He'd been prepared for the worst; disappointed, mostly at the thought of not seeing more of Tristan, but resigned despite it all. But now this flash of hope? It was almost cruel.

He gave himself a quick look toward the Chens. William wasn't red in the face anymore, and David seemed almost pleased. "Your wife is a charming woman," he said to Frank Yeung. "I know my wife would be honoured to make her acquaintance."

There it was. The offer. The Chens would take the deal. They'd trade their rights to punish Simon in exchange for social climbing. But how angry was Simon's uncle? Would he allow the trade?

The older man seemed almost deflated. He frowned at Simon, then looked down at the image from the camera. "Who are these people?" he mused aloud.

They're my friends, Simon wanted to say. But his uncle wouldn't understand that. "One's a social worker. Another's a vet." Respectable members of the community who couldn't be threatened without repercussions. "The others are—" *my friends! My friends!* "They're nobody to worry about. I think they're just here to give me a ride. Because my car belongs to you, of course."

Was that enough of an invitation? Over the years, Simon had gotten fairly good at subtly directing his uncle. And, sure enough, the older man said, "The car stays here. And you leave. If the Chens are willing to be merciful—with your aunt speaking on your behalf—then this can be over. But you will be gone. No more apartment, no more free food. You are no longer my nephew. Understood?"

Simon nodded. It was the best outcome he'd imagined before he'd come to the house. Frightening, but still. The best he could have hoped for.

"You have disgraced yourself; if I allowed you to stay in my family, you would disgrace us all. But by casting you out, I make it clear the shame is all yours." Wishful thinking, maybe, but the Chens didn't seem inclined to argue. And that was because of Simon's aunt, of course; her offer to help the Chens rise in society would only be valuable if the Yeungs maintained their place.

"I'm sorry, Uncle," Simon said, and then he turned to the Chens. "I apologize to you as well. My behavior was unforgiveable."

William Chen puffed up, clearly ready to elaborate on Simon's sins, but he was again restrained by his father, whose expression was a little too thoughtful for Simon's taste. "You'll start over," David Chen said slowly. "You will not be part of your family anymore."

Simon tried to breathe normally, tried to show only regret and shame, not apprehension. There were three people in the room who knew that it wouldn't be a terrible thing for Simon to escape from his family. Simon and his aunt had no reason to share that information. But Mr. Chen?

"Has your wife seen the Anderson's collection?" Aunt May asked David Chen with a bright smile. "Liam Anderson does a great deal of work in China, and while he doesn't specialize in Tang artifacts, he's certainly added some to his collection since his wife and I began educating him. I'm sure she'd be happy to make a new friend, if your wife would be interested in seeing the art?"

Another offer. An even higher level of social access in exchange for silence. After only a moment, Mr. Chen smiled and nodded. "I'm sure she would," he said calmly. Then he looked at Simon. "You may not have appreciated how much of a gift it was to have a supportive family. But now you will know."

"He will," Uncle Frank said ominously. "Simon. Your car belongs to me. Leave it here. Your apartment is in my name.

251

Everything you own was purchased by me, so there's no need for you to pick any of it up."

"I have a cat," Simon said. "And a plant. I'll need to go to the apartment to pick them up."

"A cat. And a plant." Uncle Frank looked disgusted by both, then waved a dismissive hand. "I'll call building security and tell them you are permitted to remove a cat and a plant. That's all."

"Thank you, Uncle." Another general sort of nod-bow around the room, and then Simon got the hell out before anyone could change their minds.

He was almost out the door when his aunt called to him, "You should repot the plant, Simon. It needs space to thrive."

He wasn't sure if it was another damned metaphor or just an oddly timed gardening tip, but he nodded his understanding.

He would have liked the chance to say a proper goodbye to his aunt, and to his cousins. He would have liked it if so many things were different. But they weren't. So he went straight to the front door, stepped into the cool air, and shut the door carefully behind him. Then he started down the driveway toward the gate. Toward freedom, toward people he might be able to call friends. Toward Tristan.

Chapter Sixteen

CALLING TORI AND LENA had been a brilliant move on Noah's part; in addition to adding some respectability to the gathering, they were excellent in a crisis, calm and thoughtful. Shane had been the one to find the security camera and positioned everyone in just the right spot for maximum coverage. And Becks had her phone out, filming everything in case something important happened.

Tristan, though? He was useless. Just standing there, staring at the house, wondering if he was making things better or much, much worse.

"Maybe we should call the cops and just make something up," he said. Lena had already been in touch with some of her contacts on the police force, but without any real proof that Simon was in danger or that he was even in the house, they'd said all they'd be able to do would be to knock on the door and make general inquiries. Tristan had decided that might end up making things worse rather than better. But, damn, it was hard to just stand there and wait.

Now, Lena frowned in Tristan's direction and said, "This is not the sort of street pimps live on. I'm not saying the wealthy never commit crimes, but—are we even in the right place?"

"Yeah, we are," Shane drawled.

"How do you know?" Lena asked.

Shane just nodded his head toward the house.

The gate was opening, and there Simon was, walking through it, unhurt—

Not unhurt! Tristan jogged across the street, then skidded to a stop, suddenly awkward. Was he allowed to touch? "What happened?" he demanded, then softened his voice. "Are you okay?"

"Thanks to you," Simon said. "They saw you out here. Whatever you were doing? It slowed them down. Told them they couldn't do whatever they wanted, not without it being noticed."

"Really?" That had been the idea, certainly, but since when had Tristan's ideas ever worked?

"It was stupid and dangerous," Simon said. "You shouldn't have done it. But I think—" He looked over at the crowd, then quietly told Tristan, "I think it's over for good. For real this time. They know everything, and I think they're going to let it go."

"Really?" Tristan wanted to be relieved. He wanted to just let it go and trust Simon's judgment and never think about it again. But this was his life; he needed to understand what was going on in it. "Why?"

"Mostly because of my aunt. It's a long story, but—I really don't think my uncle will cross her. Not unless something changes."

"Like what?" Tristan let himself be guided across the road back to the crowd, but that didn't mean he was going to let his questions be brushed off.

"Like a bunch of strangers holding a protest on the street in front his house," Simon shot back. Then he shook his head and addressed the group. "It helped. A lot—really. Thank you. But we need to get out of here now." He frowned. "That is—can I get a lift from someone?"

"Where's your car?" Tristan asked. He supposed he knew the answer, but he didn't really believe it.

Simon's smile was a little sad. "I don't have a car. It belongs to my uncle."

This had really happened. Simon had told him it was what would happen; he'd said it wasn't Tristan's fault, said it *needed* to happen, said it was the only way to get free. But, still, somehow, Tristan couldn't believe it.

"Where can we take you?" Noah asked, nodding toward the Corolla parked just down the street. He turned to the women and said, "If you guys could take Becks and Trey back with you, we'd have room."

"No problem," Lena said calmly. She'd been watching Simon almost as closely as Tristan had, and now stepped a little closer and said, "If you need a hand with anything—getting back on your feet—let me know. There are programs to help."

Simon nodded, but Tristan could tell he was just being polite. Simon Yeung was always in control of things, always in charge— he wouldn't allow himself to show weakness by taking charity, even if it was well disguised.

They all piled into the cars, Tristan and Simon in the backseat of the Corolla with Noah and Shane in the front, and drove off. "You want to go home?" Noah asked.

Simon nodded, still subdued, then leaned forward. "I don't think I can keep the cat. I've been a terrible owner so far, and I don't think I'm going to be any better for a while. I like him very much and I appreciate the thought, truly. If the situation were different, I'd keep him. But is it too late to return him to the clinic?"

Shane frowned. "Seems like you're gearing up to be a pretty good owner, aren't you? I mean, you don't have a job anymore— can't you just hang out with him for a while?"

"Uh, no," Simon said. "I—I'll have to concentrate on finding work. That sort of thing. I won't have time for a pet."

But that wasn't quite right, Tristan realized. "You won't have a *home*," he exclaimed. "That bastard is kicking you out of your apartment? He owns that, too?"

Simon closed his eyes as if gathering patience, then said, "I told you this last night. He owns everything."

"Okay, but—how long have you got? Like, don't landlords have to give you time before they evict you?"

"He's not my landlord. I never paid rent. And it's really, really not a good idea for me to antagonize him right now."

"Because of me. You were doing *fine*. You had a car and a family and an apartment and everything was going well, and then you tried to help me out even though I wouldn't do basic stuff to help myself—wouldn't leave town even though I could afford it, wouldn't compromise at all—and now you're totally fucked. Because of me."

"I'm fine, and I will continue to be fine. I just don't think this is a good time for me to take on a pet. If he can't go back to the clinic, I'll try to find somewhere else for him to—"

"The clinic's fine," Shane said. "They always have a few cats in the place, just waiting to get adopted. Having another one there isn't a big deal. And he's only been gone a couple days, so there won't even be an adjustment. It'll be fine."

"I'm not worried about the damn cat!" Tristan said, earning a frown from Shane and a tired head shake from Simon. "This is serious—what are you going to do? Stay with friends? Get a hotel? Shit, no, you can't right? Because any friends you have would be connected to your damn uncle. And he's probably already cancelled your credit cards, so you can't even—Oh, shit, Simon, I am so—"

"It's fine." Simon smiled. "I still have marketable skills. I just need to find someone who's interested in paying for them. This isn't a serious problem, Tristan."

"Yeah, but it's—"

"Tristan," Shane said, turning to frown at him. "Let it be. For now, at least. We'll go get Simon's stuff and the cat and take it from there."

Tristan wanted to argue with the plan, but he was pretty sure it was a good idea. Simon was probably still in shock. He'd just gone through something pretty horrible with his family, and—Tristan let himself turn in his seat and lifted gentle, tentative fingers to the bruise on the side of Simon's face. "Is this okay? Are you hurt? I mean, obviously you're hurt. But do you need a doctor or anything?"

Simon caught his hand before it connected with his skin. "I'm fine, Tristan. I appreciate the rescue. I really do. And obviously I needed the ride, and I need to give the cat back. But this—it's over now. You understand that? When I left you this morning I didn't expect to see you again. That was the plan. And, really, it was probably a good plan, wasn't it?"

"I'm so sick of your goddamn plans."

Simon laid his head back against the seat and closed his eyes. "So it'll be good to get rid of me. No more goddamn plans."

Well, that wasn't what Tristan had meant at all, but nothing he was saying was coming out right, or at least it wasn't being heard right. So he bit back his retort and turned to look out the window as they drove downtown to Simon's apartment.

"Is there guest parking anywhere?" Noah asked.

It was Shane who answered, "There's a spot around the corner. Turn here."

"You did some serious scouting of the scene, huh?" Simon asked. He sounded a bit more relaxed, maybe even amused.

"I believe in being prepared," Shane replied.

They parked, and Simon said, "If you guys just wait here, I can come back down with the cat."

"We can help you get packed up," Tristan said, undoing his seatbelt.

But Simon quickly said, "No, there's no need. Thanks—I really appreciate everything you've already done."

"I'll come help with Sparkles," Shane said.

"I don't really think that's his name," Simon replied, but there was no other objection. Apparently it was okay for Shane to go upstairs, but not Tristan. Damn it. Simon *was* blaming Tristan for this whole mess, which was completely fair, but—damn it.

So Noah and Tristan sat in the car, one in the front and the other in the back, and watched the other two head for the building. "You okay?" Noah asked.

"I have no idea," Tristan replied.

"Shane'll take care of things," Noah said.

"What? Shane? What's he going to take care of? I mean—we don't need Simon beat up, do we?"

Noah frowned, clearly not impressed with that comment. And maybe it had been—well, no, definitely it had been snarky. "Shit, sorry. I didn't mean Shane isn't smart or capable or whatever. I just don't really know what the problem is, so I don't really know how Shane, or anyone else, is going to fix it."

"That's the best thing about Shane," Noah said. Then he blushed a little, shrugged and amended, "One of the best things. He doesn't always have to *know* stuff. He just fixes it anyway."

"What, just with the glory of his Shane-osity? I think maybe that works mostly for you, Noah."

But Noah wasn't to be dissuaded. "No. Maybe it doesn't work for everyone, but I think it'll work this time. At work, Shane's specialty is stray animals. When they're that horrible mix of scared but hopeful? Like, they really want to come closer and be friends, but they're too afraid to do it? Shane just—I don't know, it's like he casts a spell on them. Lures them right in and makes them trust him."

"You think Shane will fix things with Simon because Shane is good with stray animals?" Tristan frowned. "You think Simon is like a stray animal?"

Noah looked over the back of his seat and gave Tristan a quizzical look. "Well, yeah, kind of. Don't you?"

~*~*~*~

SIMON WAS PRETTY sure he was being handled, but he wasn't at all sure why. What outcome was Shane hoping for from all this?

"You didn't name him?" Shane asked as they gathered the cat's belongings into a pile in the middle of the living room. "Like, not even a maybe-name?"

"I called him Duck a few times," Simon admitted.

Shane nodded approvingly. "That's a pretty stupid name for a cat. But it's still way the hell better than Sparkles."

The cat—Duck?—had been watching their activities with interest, but when he saw Simon bring the carrier from its temporary home by the front door, he arched his back and stepped away on stiff legs.

"He likes it here," Shane said. "You must have been doing something right."

"I abandoned him in a strange place with no company."

"With food and water and a litter box and lots of warm, soft places to sleep? That's really not a bad thing for some cats."

"Well, hopefully he can find a new owner to abandon him in a strange place really soon."

"Where are you gonna be?"

Simon didn't answer right away, and Shane looked toward him and smiled. "We're being cool. You and me and Duck. There's no big thing going on, we're just hanging out, talking. Nobody's about to grab anybody and stuff him into a little box or anything. We're just friends. All three of us. And it'd probably be a bit friendlier if it wasn't just one of us doing all the talking."

"Duck isn't saying much."

And with perfect timing, the little bastard let out a plaintive meow.

Simon sighed and crossed the room to pick the African violet off his windowsill. "I don't have a plan yet. I don't know where I'm going to be. That's why I can't have a cat."

"Noah and me are getting our own place," Shane said. "We just found it, and it's available right away, even though we wouldn't start paying rent until next month. Kind of a shit-hole, because it's all we can afford, but still. It's closer to school for him, and we'll have, like, our own bathroom and a little mini-kitchen and everything. It's kinda scary, but it's going to be great, I think."

"Congratulations. Tristan didn't mention that to me." Not that Tristan was in the habit of keeping Simon updated about his friends' living arrangements.

"Tristan doesn't know yet. We just found out last night that we got it, and he's been a bit preoccupied."

"Oh. Well, yeah, congratulations." Simon cast a look toward the cat. "We can't just pick him up now?"

Shane shook his head. "You ever tried to catch a cat in a room with this much furniture? He's onto us, and if we make a wrong move he'll be behind the couch or through your legs into the bedroom and under the bed, or who the hell knows where. Cat-catching is not the way to go. Cat-luring is the secret."

"You're kind of an expert on all this, huh?"

"I've been literally living in a veterinary clinic for a couple months now." He stopped talking, frowned in thought, then looked at Simon. "Hey, are you straight-up homeless? Like, you don't know where you're going to sleep tonight?"

He made it sound like an opportunity rather than an ordeal. "That's the current situation," Simon admitted.

"You wouldn't want to—" He stopped, frowned again, then said, "Nah. It's not a great place, to be honest. I mean, it was good for me, but for you? But if you had the time, and you wanted to stay with Duck, and, you know, kind of help me out...."

"Are you going to start making sense soon, or should Duck and I go in the other room and let you babble to yourself in peace?"

Shane had the grace to look bashful. Maybe—maybe a bit too bashful? Where was the tough, bold punk who'd pushed his way into Simon's apartment only days earlier? "It's just—" Shane made a face. "The apartment with Noah came up kind of last minute. So I want to take it, obviously—want to move in as soon as I can! But I live at the clinic for a reason. I'm the night watchman. I don't have to do much, just sort of *be* there, and turn lights on and off sometimes so people know I'm there. It's not great—just a little room with a bed and not much else, and a shared bathroom and kitchen. Not much, but I said I'd do it and I can't just ditch the job, you know? Not until they can find a replacement." He cast a look in Simon's direction. Hopeful, a little shy—and, again, something underneath it all.

263

"Are you luring me?" Simon demanded. "Am I the goddamn cat, being lured instead of chased?"

Shane didn't even drop his gaze. "What if you are?" He shrugged. "What if you aren't? Do you want to turn down a good offer, something that would help you and Duck out until you get back on your feet, just because of a *maybe* insult to your pride? Do you want to look that hard for a reason to be miserable?"

Simon fought for equanimity. "It's not an offer you can actually make, of course."

"I can offer to ask Dr. Anderson about it, and offer to move out a bit early, which would, straight up honest, be really cool for me. If Noah and I could spend New Year's Eve in our own place? That'd be—" He stopped as if remembering his own pride, and finished with a less gushing, more dignified, "It'd be good. So, should I give Dr. Anderson a call?"

"You understand that it's been about an hour since I exited my last relationship of servitude and dependence. You really think it's a good idea for me to be taking on a new patron so quickly? I shouldn't even *try* to live an independent life?"

Shane looked almost shocked. "Independent? Like, completely? Fuck, no, I don't think you should try that. No friends, nobody helping you out? I mean, taking a place to stay in exchange for being a night watchman? That's not servitude, dude, that's just a job. Doing something useful, getting something useful in return? You don't want to do that? What are you thinking, you're going to go off and live in the wild somewhere, no help from anyone?"

Shane gave Simon a quick once over, then grinned and said, "I really don't think you have the wardrobe for that lifestyle."

Simon began to sympathize with Duck. Whether the cat knew it or not, he was going to be climbing into the damn carrying crate pretty damn quick, with Shane on the job. "I honestly had no idea you were so manipulative," he said.

And he earned another one of Shane's brilliant smiles. "I didn't either, until Noah pointed it out. It's pretty excellent, huh?"

"I'm really not sure it is."

"Well, are you sure about helping me out, at least? Will you stay at the clinic until you and Dr. Anderson figure something else out?"

"Stop talking like it's a done deal. You have no reason to believe she's going to agree to this."

"Okay, okay," Shane held up his hands in surrender. "So we'll leave it up to her. If she's in, you're in?"

"I—" It was too fast, and too much, and Simon really didn't want to rush into anything. But he didn't want to sleep on the streets that night, either. "Okay. It's up to her."

Shane grinned, punched a number on his phone, and waited only a moment before saying, "He's in. We'll get his stuff and come over now to get him settled, okay?" A pause, and then, "Yeah, I can give him my keys, and show him around. Thanks, Dr. Anderson." He punched the screen to end the call, then grinned at Simon's expression. "Did I forget to mention that I texted her about it while we were driving here? She thought it was a great idea."

He stood up, then headed casually toward the window, stopping along the way to pet Duck. As soon as the cat arched into his caress, Shane slid his hand under the cat's belly, lifted him in one gentle swoop, and guided him into the crate, with Duck too surprised to protest. Simon latched the door shut, turned to Simon, and gave him a smirk absolutely oozing with smugness. "I'm a manipulative son-of-a-bitch," he said proudly. "Don't even try to resist my powers."

"Shit," Simon managed. "I—" He knew better. A clean break was the only hope. He needed to start his new life completely fresh, needed to put this entire group of people—*friends*—out of his mind, needed to not think about Tristan—*more than friends*—anymore, needed to smarten up and use his brain. That was all important, and he knew it. But instead of doing the smart thing, he nodded, and said, "Thank you. I appreciate your efforts."

"Not a thing," Shane said. "So, what else do we need to pack up?"

"Not a thing," Simon echoed. "I've got my cat and I've got my plant. What else could I need?"

"Well, I've got an idea about that," Shane said slyly. "But for now? Cat and plant. You're good to go."

~*~*~*~

TRISTAN DIDN'T THINK he was imagining the triumphant swagger in Shane's step as he stepped out of the apartment building, cat carrier in his hand, Simon in his wake. And he didn't think he was imagining the increased lightness in Simon's step, either.

"Shit, did he really fix it?" Tristan whispered to Noah, but then the doors were opening and Shane and Simon were climbing in and there was no time for discussion.

"Simon's gonna help us out," Shane told Noah. "He's going to cover for me so I can move in to the new place sooner."

"What new place?" Tristan asked. "Cover how?"

But Noah was turning to give Simon an excited look. "Seriously? You don't mind? That'd be awesome! It's part of that whole 'start the new year the way you plan to live it' thing, you know? We want to start the new year together."

"Together where?" Tristan asked.

"I don't mind," Simon said. Maybe sarcastically? It would be a hell of a lot easier to pick up on subtleties like that if Tristan had any idea what was going on. "And Duck will probably be okay there."

"Duck? Who's Duck?" Tristan asked.

"He won't stay there forever, obviously," Shane told Noah. "But long enough for Dr. Anderson to find someone else."

"Hey," Tristan said. And then, when nobody turned to look at him, he said, "Hey! Hey! Over here!"

And all three of them turned to look at him with identical overly innocent looks plastered on their faces. Had they somehow—were they conspiring? Were they teaming up to make him crazy?

"Tristan?" Simon said. "What's up?"

"What's up?" Tristan held up his fist, then lifted his thumb. "One. Who's Duck?" He lifted his index finger. "Two. How are you helping Shane out?" He turned his attention to the front seat as he added his middle finger to the queue. "And where are you going to be starting the new year together?" He looked at his hand and threw all the fingers open. "What the hell is going on?"

"That was very dramatic," Shane said. "But I think you can probably figure this all out for yourself, can't you?"

Simon was a little more helpful. "Noah and Shane are getting a place together and it's available immediately. Which means I can move into Shane's room at the clinic. Just temporarily."

Tristan blinked hard. Okay, that mostly made sense. "The room at the clinic's not—it's not what you're used to. You get that, right?"

And there was Simon's sad smile back again. "I do. Not what I'm used to, but what I should get used to. At least for a little while."

"It's clean," Noah said defensively. "And safe and warm and dry and everything."

"I'm not complaining," Simon said. "I'm grateful. And so are my cat and my plant."

Tristan tried to catch up to it all. "So we're driving you over there now?" he said. "But where's your stuff?"

"I'm starting fresh."

Tristan frowned. "Because you want to, or because that's what your uncle decided? Did he buy all your stuff for you, and now he's saying it's his? Seriously, Simon?"

"Sorry," Simon said.

It was a strange response, strange enough to silence whatever rant Tristan had been about to embark on. Simon's uncle was being petty and cruel, and Simon was apologizing to *Tristan*? What kind of sense did that make?

"Congratulations on the new apartment," Simon said, apparently to Noah, and the conversation shifted in that direction. Tristan was no more a part of it than he'd been when he had no idea what they were talking about, because now his mind was racing in a different direction, trying to figure out a different puzzle.

When they pulled up at the clinic, he bounced out of the car before anyone said he should do otherwise. But of course that wasn't enough for Simon, who said, "They can probably drop you off at your place," and waited expectantly for Tristan to climb back into the car like a good little boy. Like an obedient fucking whore.

"No," he said. "I want to talk to you."

Shane, burdened with cat supplies, knocked into Tristan's shoulder and nodded at him with a grin. Congratulations disguised as clumsiness, and it was enough to make at least half of Tristan's nerves fade away. He was doing the right thing. Shane thought so, and Shane was, apparently, becoming some sort of authority on these things.

"I'm not sure what you want to talk about," Simon said cautiously.

"Well the best way to find out what someone wants to talk about is to talk to them," Tristan replied. "So let's take your cat— and, honestly, I still don't really understand how you have a cat— inside, and we can go for a walk or something while Shane packs up his shit and makes space for you. Okay?"

"Perfect," Shane said, and apparently that was enough to steamroll over whatever objections Simon was coming up with. Tristan was going to have to look into that dynamic a little more closely at some point. But for just then, he followed the others into the clinic, stood through the introductions and Shane's explanations of Simon's new duties, and watched as the cat, apparently named Duck, stalked out of his carrier and looked around his new-old domain with interest.

"I can keep an eye on him," Shane said. "You guys should go for your walk. You have the keys, Simon?"

Simon nodded, and let Tristan herd him out onto the street.

And after all that, once he finally had Simon alone, Tristan had no idea what to say.

After about a block, Simon said, "You don't have any obligation to me, you know. You don't owe me anything."

Tristan didn't really agree with that, but he didn't object. If he had the right idea of what was going on, it wouldn't be a good idea. Instead he said, "And you don't owe me anything either. Right?"

Simon frowned. "I guess not. I mean, I hope you're in a pretty good place, now? So, no, I don't think I have a debt to pay. I think we're—I think we're done. Aren't we?"

"Yeah," Tristan said quietly. Then in a stronger voice he said, "We're done with all the old shit. But are we *done,* done? Do we have to be? If we wanted to get to know each other, now, as—just as people? No power dynamics, no threats or rebellion or whatever other bullshit, just you and me. We could do that, couldn't we?" He took two more steps, then stopped and whirled toward Simon. "And I will tell you right fucking now—if any part of your answer to that question is going to involve you not being fucking *rich* anymore? Like, if you're going to act like I'm still a whore and that's all I can ever be, and all I could possibly care about is how much money or power a guy has and whether he can afford me? If that's any part of your answer, then our new relationship, whatever it's going to be, is going to start with me telling you the fuck off, because you're an asshole if you think that about me and you can go fuck yourself right now, if you let your self-pity spill over so you're thinking less of *me* just because you're in the middle of feeling sorry for yourself! And if you aren't interested in me because of how I used to make money—because I used to be a whore—then you can fuck yourself *again,* because nothing you were doing was so damn pure either, and what I did was a lot less likely to hurt anybody. So, yeah, if you've got a problem with me being a whore, fuck you."

Simon said nothing. He blinked once, then again.

"Possibly that came out a little stronger than what I meant it to," Tristan said. "Do you think you could rewrite it a little? Like, make it say the same stuff, mostly, but with a bit less of the calling-you-an-asshole part? Maybe a little less 'fuck you'?"

Finally, Simon said, "I'm not bothered by you having been a prostitute. And I don't think you still think that way, necessarily. But, yes, I think I have less to offer you than I used to. Aside from that, I'm not sure what you're suggesting. I don't know what you mean by getting to know each other."

Because they didn't teach him that at robot school? Tristan took a deep breath. Simon had risked his life for Tristan that morning; the least Tristan could do in return was risk his pride. "I like you," he said. "I mean, you're sexy and mysterious, and if you think I only think that because you had money and connections then we're back to the 'fuck you' part of our conversation, because, yeah, your power is part of the sexiness, but the power comes from your brain, not your family. And on top of all that, you're physically—" He wasn't sure what the right word was. "Excellent? You're good looking? Is that what you want to hear? But the thing is, Simon, you're also really funny, and fun to talk to, and I don't know—I just *like you*. I like spending time with you, and I'd like to do more of it. Maybe we'll end up as friends, maybe

272

something more or something less. I don't know, but I'd like to find out. You know?"

They were on a side street a couple blocks from the clinic. It was raining a little, and the cars driving by hissed as they cut through the puddles. Tristan was wearing a rain jacket but there was a trickle of cool water working its way down from the collar onto his back.

All of that disappeared when Simon said, "I know. Yes."

Tristan gathered his courage. "'Yes' you understand what I'm saying, or 'yes' you also want to see what we can be?"

And then Simon, the bastard, turned away. He didn't *walk* away, and Tristan tried to take at least a little comfort from that. So he waited, and was rewarded when, finally, Simon turned back around. "There's a lot of history between us. Not a lot of time, but still a lot of history. And today has been—dramatic. Well, the past couple weeks have been dramatic, really. I think it might be good to make a—well, I'd call it an agreement in principle. We could agree that, right now, we'd both like to pursue—something. We'd like to see more of each other. But I think we should give ourselves some time to adjust. I'm quite sure the Chens are done with you— they can't afford to have your name in the papers anytime soon for anything negative. And I *think* they're done with me, thanks to my aunt's intervention. And I think my uncle is willing to let me go, thanks to my aunt but also, really, to your intervention. You reminded him that people are watching, and it's very important to him that he be seen in a certain light. So." He paused, shrugged, then said, "The drama should be over. We should have time to calm down and let the adrenaline leach out of our systems. And once that happens?" Another shrug. "The things we feel now may not be the things we feel then."

The only part of that speech Tristan liked was the part about the trouble being over with. The rest, though? "That sounds like you're saying 'no'. Like you want to walk away."

"Want?" The word came out in a tone of disbelief, and Tristan felt frozen in place as Simon turned to face him head on. "Want?" he repeated. "What I *want* is—" He drew a deep breath, one with a quaver in the middle, and Tristan knew—he *knew*—that Simon's self-control was at the breaking point. One move from Tristan, one more invitation, one touch, and Simon's resistance would crumble.

Which meant it was Tristan's turn to show some self-control. Because as much as he wanted Simon, he wanted him on terms that would be mutually agreeable. Terms that wouldn't make Simon hate himself. So he waited, again, and he didn't make any of the moves he wanted to.

When Simon finally spoke, his voice was under control, but more subdued than usual. "I'm starting over. My whole life is starting over. And I want to start it *right*. Does that make sense? If I have to be alone, I should be alone, not clinging on to someone else who doesn't really want me and just feels a sense of pity, or whatever."

"And I can tell you that I like you for you, but that's not enough?"

"I guess not." Simon made a face. "I'm not really in my area of expertise, here. I don't have a lot of experience with this sort of thing. But—no. I guess you telling me that isn't enough, even though I know it should be and I'm sure I should go fuck myself for not taking your word for it. I just—there's just been too much going on."

It wasn't quite as satisfying to tell someone off when he'd anticipated the response so well, so Tristan said only, "So what's the plan? We just walk away and never see each other again?"

"I hope not. But—could we take some time? A week, maybe, just to give us time to calm down? And then, if we both still want what we want now, we could do—something?"

"That's a bit too vague for me," Tristan said. Surely he had a right to at least a little input into this decision. "How about New Year's Eve? It's a bit less than a week, but I feel like we're both pretty quick—we'll be calm by then. And it's a good time for a fresh start, right?"

"New Year's Eve," Simon said quietly. "Okay. We should meet somewhere?"

"My place?"

"No. If you decide you don't want to do this, you won't want me at your place."

Tristan sighed. "It's New Year's Eve. Anywhere public is going to be a zoo and we'll have trouble finding each other, or having a conversation if we *do* find each other. Come to my place, but not before, say, eleven. It's okay if you take a night off from the clinic, right? It was for Shane—they said as long as he's there *most* nights, people will assume he's there all nights. So if I decide I don't want to start something with you, I'll go out before eleven. I can leave a note on the door telling you where to meet me if you just want to be friends. And then you can decide if that's worth it to you."

"This is elaborate," Simon said.

"Dude, you had someone hack into a pimp's website to change an appointment, got people to dress up as firemen and take photos, sent me a message about a confidentiality contract through a secret intermediary—me leaving you a note is pretty damn simple, really."

Simon didn't look completely convinced, but he finally nodded. "After eleven on New Year's Eve, I'll come to your apartment. If you're home, we'll talk. If you're not home, you'll leave a note."

"And you don't have to come," Tristan said quickly. "If you decide it's a bad idea and you'd prefer a fresher start, that's fair. You don't have to come."

"Maybe it would be better if we did this a different night. One with less pressure."

"No. New Year's Eve. It *should* be an important night. This is important to me."

And Simon didn't argue with him. Instead, he turned to look back toward the clinic. "Okay, then. We'll take some time, and we'll figure things out on New Year's." He nodded a sort of goodbye and clearly thought they were finished.

But Tristan caught his hand before he walked away. "Wait," he said quietly. And he stepped forward, into Simon's space, and he felt welcome there. He felt at home, comfortable enough that he was tempted to go back to his seduction plan and leave this whole New Year's Eve nonsense alone. But Simon wanted to do things right. So Tristan needed to control himself.

He settled for a fairly chaste kiss. But he tried to make it different from their other kisses; those had always tasted too much like goodbye, and Tristan wanted this one to be new, full of hope and reaching for the future.

For the first time, it was Simon who intensified things, one strong hand catching the small of Tristan's back and pulling him closer, his other hand cradling his jaw, claiming and cherishing him in a single gesture. Tristan grabbed hold of Simon's jacket mostly for balance, trying to find something stable in the suddenly swirling universe, but once he had a grip he didn't want to let go. He didn't want to let Simon slip away one more time, didn't want him to be dragged back into his old world where Tristan couldn't follow.

When they finally broke for air, Tristan was dizzy in the best possible way, his body pressed against Simon's as if they were trying to melt into each other. "I'm not sorry," Simon murmured, and that was enough to catch at least a little of Tristan's attention.

"Not sorry for what?"

"For meeting you. For everything that happened. No matter what happens after this, I'm *glad* it happened. You need to know that. Even if I never see you again, I'm glad I met you."

"And if you come to my place on New Year's I'll make you even gladder," Tristan promised. A quick peck, then, trying to keep it casual, trying to show confidence he didn't really feel. Then he turned and made himself walk away, because that was what Simon wanted.

Chapter Seventeen

SIMON'S WALLET HAD contained a few hundred dollars when he left his uncle's house, and while his pride told him he should have returned it, his practicality dictated otherwise. So he'd had enough money to buy basic toiletries and groceries along with a few changes of clothes, although nothing name brand or high quality.

He saved his one good set of clothes, the ones he'd been wearing when he'd left his old life, for New Year's Eve. And then, after dressing, he paced through the abandoned clinic, worrying. About his clothes. Practically—were they too dressy? And symbolically—was it a good idea to start a new life wearing remnants of the old? And about the bottle of champagne he'd bought in a moment of desperate optimism—presumptuous, surely, to arrive assuming there'd be something to celebrate? But mostly, he worried about showing up at Tristan's and finding a note on the door, because his feelings, his wants, his damn needs hadn't changed in the slightest, and of course Tristan would have come to his senses now that he'd been given a little time.

He'd gotten pretty good at riding Seattle's public transit in the last few days, so there was really no need for him to leave the clinic quite as early as he did. He ended up down the street from Tristan's by ten thirty and had to do a little more pacing down there, trying to stay warm in the unusually frosty air, waiting for the time he was allowed to discover his fate.

He was staring at his phone when the alarm he'd set for eleven o'clock went off. For a brief moment, he thought about running. Not back to the clinic, but somewhere further, somewhere he might actually have a chance of forgetting the brief glimpse he'd gotten of a better world. Surely it was better to not know than to have his hopes crushed without doubt?

But he couldn't be that much of a coward, and, no, it wouldn't be better not to know, not in the long term. So he made his way down Tristan's street, almost deserted at this hour, but with lights shining brightly from many of the windows. New Year's Eve. The start of something new. But that also meant that something had to end, didn't it?

The lock on the front door of the building was still broken, as it had been for the entire time Simon had been aware of Tristan's existence. So there was no excuse for buzzing up, and he really wasn't sure the intercom worked anyway. He had to go right upstairs.

His legs felt heavy as he climbed. He was walking to the scaffold, and he wanted to run, wanted to beg for mercy or a second chance, but there was no one to hear his pleas. So he just kept climbing, and when he reached Tristan's floor, he kept his eyes on the battered, ragged carpet of the hallway for as long as he could before forcing his gaze up to look at—

The apartment door. Just the door. No note.

Had Simon misunderstood the system?

He fought back the excitement, refused to acknowledge the hope suddenly burning in his chest. There was no guarantee. It could be a glitch. An annoying neighbor had ripped the page away, Tristan had forgotten all about it, it was all an elaborate prank.

Then the door swung open, a blur of movement, and someone—someone blond, someone lithe and lean and beautiful—was hurtling toward him.

It was more of a tackle than a kiss, Tristan's mouth landing somewhere on Simon's chin before they both tried to adjust, overshot and missed again, and then finally, *finally* joined. Tristan's legs were still driving and they both staggered backward, their arms locked around each other, both refusing to let go even to break their fall. Luckily Simon's back caught the corner of the wall and he twisted, found his balance, and let himself be crushed against the faded wallpaper. The bag he'd been carrying, with its bottle of champagne, thudded to the floor, and Simon didn't care in the least.

But then Tristan pulled away. "Fuck. You didn't knock. I was watching through the peephole, and I ran out of patience, but you didn't knock. Were you still thinking about it?"

It was Simon's turn to push, then. He spun them around, pinned Tristan's hands with his own, shoved his thigh between Tristan's, leaned in, and kissed him hard. It was the only answer he had, and apparently the only one Tristan needed.

Simon let go of his doubt. This was real. It was Tristan's lips crushed to his, Tristan's fingers holding on so tight, Tristan's breath filling Simon's lungs, his mind, his whole body. This was *Tristan*.

He let his mouth wander, just a little, kissing his way down Tristan's jaw, then his neck.

"We should go inside," Tristan gasped. "Too many clothes, too many laws against public nudity."

Simon wasn't that much bigger than Tristan, but he was big enough to lift him, strong enough to stand while Tristan locked his legs around Simon's hips, and balanced enough to stagger into the apartment and turn to let Tristan kick the door shut behind them.

And standing there in the dimly lit hallway that led to Tristan's living room, his bedroom—things slowed down.

"I wasn't sure you'd come," Tristan said, and the kiss that followed those words was less desperate, more languorous. "Sometimes I was sure you would, but sometimes I was sure you wouldn't. But you did."

"I almost didn't," Simon admitted, then quickly added, "Not because I didn't want to. I was just scared you wouldn't be here."

"So we were both sure, right from the start," Tristan said. "Makes it seem kind of stupid that we had to suffer through those days of doubt, huh?"

Well, he wouldn't be Tristan if he was afraid of giving Simon shit. "I wanted to be sure," Simon said. "Sorry."

Tristan arched an eyebrow. Their bodies were still glued together, their faces only pulled away far enough so they could see each other without going cross-eyed. "You *say* you're sorry. But why should I believe you?"

"I brought some apology champagne. It's in the hallway."

"That's a start," Tristan said. "Go get it before my neighbors scavenge it."

And it was okay to do that. Okay to leave Tristan, for just a moment, because he'd still be there when Simon got back.

Tristan met him in the living room with two crystal champagne glasses, and Simon didn't ask where they'd come from, who'd given them to Tristan. He didn't need to know.

"You may pour," Tristan said regally, and Simon popped the cork and then filled the glasses Tristan held. He set the bottle on the battered coffee table and looked back at Tristan, who handed Simon a glass, raised his own and said, "To new beginnings?"

"For both of us," Simon agreed, and they drank.

Tristan wrinkled his nose almost immediately. "I always pretend I like it, but, honestly I'm not sure I do." He took another experimental sip. "I know I'm supposed to."

"No," Simon said. He had the feeling this was somehow important. "Let's not do that. You and me? Let's not do what we're supposed to, not for something like this. If you don't like champagne, don't drink champagne. That's fine."

"But it's your apology champagne," Tristan said, and it was only then Simon noticed the wicked gleam in his eyes. "If I don't drink it, have you really apologized? You put us both through several days of unnecessary pain. There should be some sort of consequence for that, don't you think?"

At some point Simon was going to work it all through and decide if the delay really had been unnecessary, or if the added peace of mind made up for the pain. But he didn't think this was the right time for that. "A consequence?" he said. "I'm not sure— what did you have in mind?"

"I have a few ideas," Tristan said, and he reached out for Simon's glass, then turned to set them both down on the coffee table. When he straightened back up, his bold, seductive face was firmly in place, and Simon felt it tug at his body in all the right places.

"So, what are these ideas, exactly?" As if Simon cared. But the playful atmosphere was important, somehow. He'd had too much drama, and was ready for a little comedy.

Tristan gave him an over-the-top sultry look, then broke character to laugh. "You know," he said, "I really have no idea. I mean, I don't really know what I like. I've been really busy doing what everyone *else* liked—I'm honestly not sure about myself."

"Well, you emo bastard, I think I have some idea about that myself," Simon said, and his good memory was rewarded with a smile of recognition.

"So we can figure it out together?" Tristan suggested.

"Absolutely," Simon said.

"In the bedroom?" Tristan suggested.

"That seems appropriate," Simon managed. "If you think the pink unicorn wallpaper won't spoil the mood."

"I think this mood is unspoilable." Tristan took Simon's hand and led them down the short hallway to the bedroom door, then inside. The room wasn't that big, and when Tristan turned them around, then shoved Simon hard enough to have him stumbling backward, it was only two steps until his legs hit the mattress and he fell down onto the bed. Tristan followed right behind him, pressing down, straddling Simon, and leaning forward to pin Simon's arms above his head against the comforter. Then a grin. "What do you think so far?" Tristan asked.

"This is a terrible, terrible punishment. I'm very sorry for my misbehaviour."

Tristan shifted, keeping Simon's hands pinned with one of his own while the other started on the buttons of Simon's shirt. "I'm in charge," Tristan growled. Then another smile. "Okay?"

Simon laughed. It started deep in his belly and rose through his chest like warmth from a fire he thought had been extinguished. "Yes," he said, "it's okay. But I want my hands free. I want to be able to touch you."

Tristan leaned back, his ass putting some intriguing pressure on Simon's filling cock. Almost certainly deliberate, but Tristan did a good job of pretending to be oblivious. "Okay," he said. "Hands free, but only because *I* want you to touch me. Not because of what you want. Got it?"

"Is this a permanent thing?" Simon asked, bringing his hands forward to Tristan's hips, then up along his ribs. "Your little power trip."

"Maybe," Tristan said. He leaned a little closer, pressed a kiss to the corner of Simon's mouth, and whispered, "Probably not, though. Just experimenting."

"Okay," Simon said. "Either way, probably." And he meant it. So he let himself relax, let Tristan undress them both, let himself be re-arranged and explored and admired. And when he got the chance, he did his own exploring and admiring, and he and Tristan smiled at each other, and kissed each other, and it was all exactly what Simon needed. More than he deserved, he was sure, but he managed to shut that part of his brain up, mostly.

He wasn't sure how long they hovered around each other, aroused but not desperate, excited but not yet frenzied, before Tristan pulled away and put his serious face on. "Do you have strong feelings about fucking?" he asked. "I mean—do you like it? And, if so—do you have a preferred—?"

"Are you being coy all of a sudden? The vague language is adorable, but a bit out of character, isn't it?"

"Do you want my dick up your ass, or yours up mine?" Tristan asked, and then he let himself be pulled down for a sloppy kiss.

"I don't care," Simon said when they came up for air. "You're the boss, remember?"

"Yeah? So—I mean, I don't get to top that much. Like, hardly ever. I'm not saying there's no johns who want to be fucked by pretty little twinks, but I haven't met many of them. So, just in the name of variety...."

"Okay," Simon agreed. "Seriously, it's not a big deal for me. I just—" He shook his head. This was what it had come to; the honesty virus had infected him and turned him into an enormous sap. "*You're* the important part. The rest is details."

Tristan's smile made Simon's self-consciousness completely worthwhile, and that just made it even clearer that he was a sap. Damn it.

"Stay on your back," Tristan ordered as he fumbled for supplies in the nightstand. "I want to see you."

So Simon gave in to Tristan's arrangements once more, made himself relax, and tried to allow the invasion into his body. It was too intimate, too intense, too damn much after everything else— and then he looked up to see Tristan's look of concern. "We don't have to—" Tristan started, and Simon let go of the tension.

"I want to," he said, and he meant it.

The pressure came again, and this time Simon welcomed it. He *wanted* Tristan inside him, wanted to adapt and change and— oh. Hell, yeah. The pressure turned into a slick, easy slide, and

Simon's whole torso arched, apparently of its own volition. Now that it had accepted a little, it wanted so much more.

"You're perfect," Tristan told him, his voice strained but happy. "God, Simon, so perfect."

It wasn't true, of course. But for a few moments, there in the dingy apartment? There, with Tristan Beck. For just a few moments, Simon let himself believe. He wasn't perfect. And Tristan wasn't perfect. But the two of them together?

The two of them together seemed to create something pretty damn close.

Shelter series – Interlude – 2.5

Shane and Noah

NOAH STRETCHED LUXURIOUSLY, feeling his body complain in all the right places. Well, almost all the right places; he was pretty sure that the bruised feeling on his ribs was from the lumpy mattress, not from any of the fun he and Shane had managed the night before. Still, he wasn't going to complain about the mattress, not after its heroic service the night before.

And he wasn't going to complain about the lack of walls in their studio apartment, not when sleeping in the same room they cooked in meant he got to wake up to not just the smells of breakfast but also the sight of his gorgeous boyfriend, wearing a low-slung pair of jeans and no shirt, puttering around the kitchen. Dodger, of course, was at Shane's feet, looking up at him in clear anticipation of a treat.

Shane glanced over, saw that Noah was awake, and smiled. "Happy New Year," he said, and pulled a mug from the cupboard.

By the time Shane had poured the coffee and added the milk, Noah was sitting up in bed, waiting to be served. They were still working out how they'd share their housekeeping responsibilities, but at least so far in their cohabiting lives Shane seemed to get a kick out of taking care of Noah, and Noah really couldn't bring himself to object.

"Is it too early to call Tristan and see how things went?" Noah asked.

"Too early and too nosy." Shane handed the coffee over and eased onto the bottom end of the mattress, turning to sit cross-legged with his knees nudging against Noah's bent legs. Dodger jumped up to give Noah's face a quick lick, then snuggled in under his arm. It felt familiar and cozy and perfect. "Besides," Shane said, "do you really think we need to call? You think for a second that Simon wasn't going to show up?"

"I don't have the deep connection with Simon that you do," Noah said, letting just a little primness and jealousy into his voice. He wasn't really mad at Shane, but it didn't hurt to offer a warning. "So I guess I'm not really sure what he's thinking."

"I bet right now he's thinking 'Oh, yeah, just like that. That's—oh, that's good.'"

Shane's porn soundtrack made blood rush to Noah's cheeks *and* to lower areas, so maybe he had an excuse for not answering too quickly. But the sounds also made him think about other topics, things he'd been thinking about but hadn't brought up. He wanted to talk about them, but everything always seemed so perfect, and he didn't want to ruin the perfection. Still—maybe it would actually make things *better*, if Noah didn't have the nagging worry running around the back of his head.

"I've been doing some reading," he started.

Shane snorted. "No shit. You study too hard."

"Not reading for school. Reading for—us."

Shane's suspicious look was completely justified, but still not reassuring. "What does that mean?"

That was when Shane's phone rang. He ignored it, as usual, but Noah almost spilled his coffee, bouncing with excitement, instantly distracted. "Get it! Get it! It'll be Tristan! Tell him we can meet them for brunch, if they want!"

"It won't be Tristan," Shane said. "He's busy." But he leaned over and grabbed his phone from the bedside table anyway, frowned at the screen, then tapped it and lifted the phone to his ear. "Hello?"

He listened, and within seconds, Noah knew something was wrong. Shane hadn't said anything, but there was just something about his posture, his expression, the intensity with which he was listening while trying to seem calm—none of it was good.

And that impression was reinforced when Shane said, "Sorry—what hospital, again?" He listened to the answer, then nodded slowly. "Okay. Thanks." And then he hung up.

Noah swallowed hard, and waited.

Shane looked down at his phone and Noah could actually *see* the impulse Shane was resisting. Hurl the phone against the wall, watch it shatter, punish it for conveying bad news. But they didn't have money to replace that, so Noah reached both of his hands out, using one to take the phone, the other to hold Shane's. "What happened?"

"Fucking—" Shane stopped, clearly hearing the same out-of-control edge to his voice that Noah heard. A deep breath, then a little more calmly, "Fucking Micah. He ODed. He did it before, once, but it wasn't that bad. We got him to a hospital and it was okay."

"This time?" Noah asked. He wasn't sure he wanted to hear the answer. He liked Micah well enough, but really didn't know him well. Shane, on the other hand? The two were much closer friends, *plus* Shane had the damn compulsion to look after everybody, to be the perpetual den mother. He wouldn't take this well. "How bad?" Noah asked gently.

"Worse than last time. I guess they don't know yet—he's still unconscious. Somebody found him in a park this morning. They figure he was there all night, and—shit, Noah, it was fucking *cold* last night."

"Maybe that's not bad," Noah tried. He felt desperate, and completely unprepared. "There are those stories about kids drowning but being okay because the water was cold. Maybe—I don't know, maybe if they've got him now, if they're warming him up—maybe it'll be okay."

"Until the next time," Shane said. His voice was dull, and for a moment Noah *hated* Micah. Hated him for being so selfish, for making Shane unhappy, for ruining Noah's perfect New Year's morning.

"Should we go see him?" Noah asked.

Shane nodded. "I guess. Stupid fucking *junkie*." His body was regaining its energy, its vibrant anger. "What's the fucking point, though? We go see him, we get him out of there and clean him up, and then what? I mean, assuming he's not brain damaged or something, and they said he wasn't conscious yet so they don't know how bad he's fucked himself up. But even if he isn't fucked *now*, he's just going to go do the same fucking thing again!" He pushed himself off the bed, pacing around the apartment that had seemed cozy only moments before and that was now clearly too small to contain Shane's energy.

"I don't know enough about it," Noah said, trying to sound calm. "I think there's a theory that addicts have to hit rock bottom before they start getting better."

"Rock bottom? Like, say, getting kicked out of your house? Micah's not like the rest of us—he has good parents, aunts and uncles and everything. When he got bad, his parents tried to get him to go to rehab by saying he couldn't live at home unless he got clean, and he just walked. His aunt used to come down and see him once a week or so, bring him clean clothes and take him out for a good meal. She'd take all of us out, sometimes. But he pissed all that away. He'd rather shoot up than have people love him. And he stole from Tristan, stole from me, he ratted Tristan out so people could break into the apartment and so the guy could follow

Tristan—fuck, Noah, he let me leave Dodger in Tristan's apartment, *knowing* those assholes were going to break in! What's more rock bottom than that?"

"Overdosing," Noah suggested.

"He's done that before, though."

"Maybe—" Noah stopped. Did he really want to suggest this? Was he stepping over a line? He looked at Shane who was frowning in concern, waiting patiently for Noah to speak. "Not a suggestion, exactly," Noah waffled. "But maybe a—a possibility. One to be discarded if it doesn't make sense."

"Okay...."

"Maybe rock bottom comes when he wakes up from an OD and nobody's there."

Shane didn't look shocked, but he didn't look like he loved the idea, either. "It seems—I don't know. It seems wrong. That's not the way the story's supposed to go, is it? He should wake up and see us all there and see how worried we are and that should be what makes him turn it around. He should—he should change because people care about him, not because we don't."

"I'm not sure there's a 'should' when it comes to junkies."

Shane sighed and flopped back down on the bed. Dodger had been watching him with confusion that bordered on alarm; the little dog didn't like it when Shane was upset. Now, Dodger trotted down the side of Noah's legs and climbed into Shane's lap, then sat up, resting his front paws on Shane's chest, and peered at him in concern. Shane's hand, so large, so strong, cradled the little dog's body in reassurance. "It's okay, buddy," Shane said. "Uncle Micah's just—he's just an asshole."

He looked over at Noah. "I should talk to the gang, I guess. See what they say."

"If you want, I can call Lena. She doesn't specialize in addiction stuff, but she definitely deals with it. She might have some insight."

Shane snorted. "Do you think they knew what they were getting into when they let me stay at the clinic? I mean, we've started kind of sucking them into our drama."

"I think they like it. They like helping. No kids of their own, so—I think they like feeling needed."

Shane didn't look convinced, but he said, "Sure, if you think it's a good idea. We should meet somewhere, probably? I'll call Tristan and see if we can all meet up over there?"

"Sounds good," Noah said.

It didn't sound good. What sounded good was crawling back into bed with his boyfriend, pulling the covers up over their heads, and letting the world take care of itself for a while. But Shane wasn't going to relax any time soon, not with something like this hanging over his head. So Noah stumbled out of bed, looking for his phone. The day wasn't going to get better until he did something to make it better.

~*~*~*~

BY THE TIME HE and Noah made it back to their apartment, Shane was exhausted. It had been a good meeting, he was pretty sure, but emotional. Everyone had been there, and they'd all been—upset. It was a weak word, but it was about all Shane could think of that would cover all the emotions. Anger, fear, frustration, sorrow, and maybe, just maybe, a tiny trace of hopefulness when Lena stepped in, introduced her friend, an addictions counsellor, and started trying to figure out a plan.

"I don't like thinking about him," Shane confessed as he flopped onto one of their two dining chairs and unclipped Dodger's leash. "He's met Lena, what, twice in his life? And now she's going to be the one sitting by him when he wakes up?"

Noah didn't say anything, just sat in the other chair and reached out for Shane's hand.

Shane gripped tight. What would all this have been like without Noah? Well, it would have been just another OD, with no solution in sight. Just another attempt to manage an unmanageable situation. "It might not work," he said. "If Micah doesn't want to change, it won't work."

Noah nodded. "Yeah." He looked down at his watch. "It's not even one, yet, and the hospital said they wouldn't be waking him up until mid-afternoon. Then they'll have to do tests, and Lena and her friend will have to talk to Micah, and he'll have to think about it—we're not going to hear any news until after dinner at the earliest."

"He's such an asshole," Shane muttered, and Noah didn't argue.

Shane stood up, restless. Maybe he should go out, but he loved the apartment, loved being in it with Noah. It was his home, his refuge, and he kind of needed that right then. "We should do something. Like—we could clean? I could make soup—that takes a lot of chopping. That'd be good." Anything to distract him from Micah.

He looked over at Noah, and something about his expression made Shane's restlessness stutter to a stop. Noah looked sad? Was that the expression?

"This hasn't been a great New Years for you," Shane said. The more he thought about it, the worse he felt. "I was worrying about all the times we've dragged *Lena* into our shit, but I've been dragging you into all of it, too, haven't I? The stuff with the poison, and then Tristan, and now this—it's—" He winced. "It's way more than you signed up for, right? Your life was a lot easier before you met me."

"Easier?" Noah stood up, moved right in front of Shane, and caught both of his hands, holding them tight. "Yeah, I guess. It was easier. But, Shane?" His smile was sweet and pure. "That's not really my goal for life. I don't want to be lying on my death bed and look back and say, well, that wasn't too hard. I want—I mean, I don't like it when you get hurt. I wish things weren't so hard for you. But I want to be with you, I want to feel what you feel, and I want to try to help you get through it all. I don't care if it's not easy." He stretched up and kissed Shane, then dropped back onto his heels and smiled again. "Easy is over-rated. I'm ready for the challenges."

"Yeah?" Shane thought about Tristan and Simon. They were still new, still fresh, but watching Simon as he watched Tristan that morning, going over the options for Micah? Seeing the genuine concern Simon was feeling, and realizing it was born from tenderness, from protectiveness, from caring—it had been something special. They were becoming a team, just like Shane and Noah already were. "Okay," he said. "Thank you." Then he tugged Noah's hands and nodded toward the bed. "We were talking, this morning, before the phone rang. You said you'd been reading something?"

"Yeah," Noah said. He let Shane lead him over to the bed, and they sat on the mattress, both cross-legged, facing each other. "I was just—well, yeah, reading. I guess it's like I said, I want to help you get through stuff. I want to feel what you feel, and understand it all. So—reading. And I was reading about asexuality."

Noah seemed to think the word was some sort of time bomb, but Shane wasn't sure what the big deal was. "Yeah? Okay. I've heard of it."

"And—do you think it applies? Is it how you think of yourself?"

"No. It's not how I think of myself." Shane leaned back and waited, because he was pretty damn sure Noah wasn't going to give up that easily.

"It's not," Noah said. "Okay. But—it kind of seemed to fit. Like—you're not that into sex, right?"

"Dude, if you want to fuck more often, you can just say so. I'm fine with that."

"What?" Noah looked genuinely startled, maybe even alarmed, and for a moment Shane was tempted to take pity on him. But only for a moment. "No, this isn't about me! It's about you. I want to be sure I'm not taking advantage, or pushing you to do anything you don't want to do."

"So if I said I didn't like sex, and didn't want to have sex any more, ever—you'd be okay with that?" Shane tried to look serious.

"I—I mean—I'd—" Noah looked like he was being asked to castrate himself with a rusty garden trowel, and it was enough.

Shane let himself smile. "Relax, Noah. I'm not going to say that. You're making too big a deal out of this."

"Really? Am I? Because if you're asexual, then—"

"Noah. I'm not asexual, I'm Shane. Right here. That's all. I don't need some label in order to understand how I feel—I *know* how I feel. And I like having sex with you. I mean, seriously, do I seem like I'm unhappy when we're messing around?"

"No," Noah said reluctantly.

"So. I'm Shane, you're Noah. Stop reading so much."

"But sometimes it helps to understand things if you get an outside perspective. There are experts who've spent their entire careers studying—"

"Studying how I feel about sex? That's kind of creepy, Noah. Tell them to stop spying on me."

Noah rolled his eyes, which was a good sign. "Being able to label something can help you understand things better."

"Nope. Not me. That doesn't work for me." Shane paused, raised an eyebrow, and said, "But this isn't really about me, right? It's about you. We're not trying to help *me* understand, we're trying to help *you* understand. So, come on, Noah. Instead of reading stuff some strangers wrote about some other strangers, why don't you just ask *me*?"

"Because you'll tell me what I want to hear, not what I *should* hear!"

"There's no big secret here, dude. I'll tell you the truth. Ask me what you want."

Noah paused, thinking it over, then said, "Do you like having sex with me?"

"Yup."

A frown. "Always? Like, do you sometimes feel like I'm— chasing you around, or something? I had an aquarium when I was younger and there are some species of fish where you need, like, six females for every male, because otherwise the male will harass the females for sex so much that the females can actually *die* from the stress. You need lots of females so the male will spread his horny annoyingness around."

"Is this your way of saying you want an open relationship?" Shane asked, and he was rewarded by the shocked expression on Noah's face.

"No! No, I just—I don't want to be that male fish! He's not an asshole because he doesn't know any better, but I know better, so I need to—"

"You need to calm down. You're not a horny fish. You're fine. We're fine. I am absolutely fine with the amount of sex we're having. I'd also be fine if we were having more, or less. It's all good."

"Because you don't really care?" Noah asked, and for the first time Shane felt as if Noah was the one setting traps instead of Shane.

"I care about *you*. And it's not like I'm not getting off when we fuck. But—" Shane shrugged. "I don't really care about cooking, you know? Like, I don't think about it all the time, or have dreams about it, or read books and watch shows and whatever about it. But I like cooking *for you*, because—I don't know, because I'm thinking of you when I do it. And I guess because I like eating—I'm not sure if that fits into the sex thing, unless eating is like coming? I don't know, I got a bit lost there, but the point is—you're worrying about stuff you don't need to worry about."

"I'm not a horny asshole fish?"

"No, you're not. And I'm not a wimpy female fish, running away or giving in instead of telling you to fuck off. I'm way bigger than you, and I'm pretty stubborn, too. If I don't want to have sex with you, we won't have sex. It's that simple."

"So we're okay," Noah said. He wasn't asking, but he wasn't exactly telling, either. It was like he was talking to himself, trying the words out to see if he could believe them.

"Well, *I'm* okay. You? You're wound a little tight, in general. But that's cool—I don't mind."

Noah smiled. "That's very generous of you."

"True," Shane said. "So, are we done? You're done?"

"For now, at least. I can't guarantee I won't want to talk about it some more, some time."

"Okay. So, what are we going to do this afternoon? How the hell am I going to distract myself from worrying about that asshole junkie?"

And just as Shane had anticipated, Noah raised his eyebrows, his eyes dancing, and said, "Well, now that we've cleared things up…." He edged a little closer to Shane. "I can think of a pretty good way to spend some time."

Shane waited until Noah's face was inches from his own, then raised both hands and braced them against Noah's shoulders. "No, thanks," he said. "I don't really feel like having sex right now. I think I'm going to make some soup. Want to help me?"

Noah stared at him. Then, slowly, a smile blossomed on his face. He nodded, still beaming, and said, "Yeah, okay. Let's make some soup."

And together, they crossed the room to the kitchen.

Coming Soon

Twice Shy

The Shelter Series, Book Three

"Hello. My name is Micah, and I'm an addict. Any of the opiates—I'm not too picky. But I've been sober for ninety-two days."

"Let me guess," a grey-haired lady with a smoker's rasp said from two seats away. "You spent ninety of those days in rehab."

"And two in the hospital," Micah shot back at her. "This is my first meeting on my own. And I'm sure enjoying it so far."

"We're not here for your enjoyment," someone growled from behind him. Micah didn't even bother turning to see who was speaking.

Instead he addressed the man at the front of the room. "Isn't there usually a 'Hi, Micah,' chant right about now? Come on. I was really hoping for some chanting."

"Hi, Micah," the man said dryly. "We usually save the responses for when members share, not when they introduce themselves."

"Oh. How disappointing." Micah sat down. He was probably being an ass. Petulant, maybe. That's what Tristan would call him. Except Tristan wasn't talking to him, and for damn good reason. Not that remembering that inspired him to be any less petulant.

"If you'd like to stick around after the meeting, we can talk more," the man said. He seemed friendly, kind, maybe even gentle. Absolutely not the kind of person Micah wanted to be around, not when his head—his whole body—was buzzing like it was. Like he was composed entirely of bees, all of them angry and looking to sting.

But he managed to keep himself at least somewhat under control, and he nodded at the man like he was considering the offer. Then he slumped back down in his seat. And regretted it immediately, because he was way too restless to sit still. Way too restless to suffer through another sanctimonious damn meeting, another lecture about how it'll work if he works it, another empty argument trying to persuade him that he could still be something, still contribute.

He couldn't do it. He couldn't bore himself with another series of painfully earnest, totally humorless stories from his fellow inmates. Because he was still an inmate, out here, just as much as he'd been when he was in rehab. Stuck in a damn prison of addiction, facing a fucking life sentence.

Of course, that sentence might not be too long. Not if he kept drowning in his bottomless pool of self-pity, or if he was crushed under a mountain of his overworked metaphors.

That thought made him smile, just for a moment. It was the sort of thing Tristan would have come up with, back when their fighting was just play. And Shane would have been there, watching and listening, amused at first, then impatient. Trey and Becks, bored even from the start. Noah, so busy admiring Shane he'd barely even notice Tristan and Micah.

They were all still out there, somewhere. They hadn't visited him in rehab, hadn't even called or sent a care package, and the counsellor said it was because she'd told them not to. Maybe that was true, or maybe the counsellor was breaking her own rule about always telling the truth.

But even if they hadn't wanted to visit, even if they'd forgotten all about him, they were still out there, and that made it a bit easier for Micah to sit still. He might never earn his way back into their lives, but at least he could try. And the first step in that was going to these stupid meetings, one every single day for the first month. He wasn't sure he was going to get anything out of them—well, he was pretty damn sure he wasn't, considering how little attention he was paying to any of it—but at least it was one more hour out of the day, one more hour of sobriety to add to his total.

So he sat, trying to accept his new reality. His life wasn't going to glow anymore. He wasn't going to be buffered from reality. When he was in a boring place with boring people, he was going to be bored. That was just how things were when he wasn't high, and he wasn't going to get high any more. He *wasn't*.

About half way through the meeting he noticed the guy across the room, about his own age, looking vaguely familiar. That probably wasn't good. He was supposed to be starting fresh, leaving his old druggie friends behind, and that was all this guy could be. If he was something more, Micah would have recognized him with more certainty.

But then the guy grinned at him, threw in a conspiratorial eye-roll, and Micah smirked back before he knew what he was doing.

It couldn't hurt, could it? The whole point of these meetings was to find fellowship and support, after all. So if Micah made a friend, would that be so bad?

He tried to remember where he knew the guy from. Olive skin, high cheekbones—too far away to see his eyes, but Micah somehow knew they were green. Yeah, green eyes, dark lashes falling to cover them, then lifting back only halfway, too tired or too blissed out for full consciousness. If Micah had led a different sort of life, maybe he'd think the guy in his memory had just come, or was just about to, in a slow, languid sort of way. But in the life Micah had actually led, that look meant something else completely.

But that only made sense—who the hell was he going to meet in a Narcotics Anonymous meeting besides other addicts? And this guy had quit, obviously, and was trying to stay clean. Nobody would come to one of these meetings just for fun.

When everyone who wanted to talk was done, the guy leading the session read a page or two from his little brown book, and everybody nodded like they believed it all, and Micah saw the other guy looking down at his hands. Being polite about his skepticism, Micah figured, and followed his example. When the prayer started, everyone chanting along, Micah kept his mouth shut. There were groups that tried to work the twelve steps without dragging religion into it and he was definitely planning to hit those meetings, but they mostly met once or twice a week; if he was going to hit his meeting-every-day goal, he was going to be hearing more about God and prayer and all the rest of it than he really wanted.

Of course, compared to the pain of giving up smack a little God-talk was barely a mosquito bite.

The group hug was a bit much, though, so he dodged backward out of it, and started for the door. He was half-way there when he sensed someone walking next to him and turned his head to see eyes just as green as he'd remembered.

"You made it, then," the guy said.

And that was all it took to jar the rest of Micah's scattered memory into place. They'd been together on New Year's Eve, the night of the overdose that had sent Micah to the hospital and then to the rehab facility.

"Always a bit hard to be sure," the guy continued. "When someone disappears like that—did they leave the scene, or the planet?" His smile was easy and relaxed as they jogged up the stairs from the church basement. "Glad you were the first."

"Yeah, thanks." They stopped at the top of the stairs. "Sorry, man, I forget your name—that night's a bit hazy. And I guess I wasn't paying attention when they did the introductions."

"I'm Zach. We were at Moby's party." Zach shook his head. "What a shit show. You just got out, right? Do you know there were six ODs that night? Moby just about killed the guy who was selling for him, 'cause he fucked up and made everything way too strong."

Micah shook his head. He didn't want to talk about this anymore. Didn't want to think about it, didn't want to remember the ecstasy, the pure, soaring freedom that had lifted him out of his body, left the vessel behind while the contents explored the universe. Didn't want to remember that it had almost killed him, and absolutely didn't want to remember that he could never do it again.

"I gotta go," he said, and started for the door, but Zach caught his arm, then released it quickly when Micah spun around.

"Take it easy," he said. "I just wanted to know if you've got a job, yet. My brother's got a landscaping business and it's about to kick into gear for all spring clean up stuff. So he's hiring, and he's—you know, he's a bit less of a prick than most bosses would be. He'll give you a chance, if you want one."

"I, uh—that's supposed to be one of my tasks this month. Go to a meeting every day, go to counselling twice a week, and try to get a job."

"Be kind of nice to get one of those things out of the way right off the bat, right?" Zach's grin was encouraging. "He's picking me up, if you want to meet him."

Tristan had always said Micah was born with horseshoes up his ass. He'd said Micah got high because life was too damn easy for him and he needed to find ways to make it more challenging. Not exactly how Micah would have characterized things, but it was hard to argue with the general point. He had no employment history, no skills, and he'd been out of rehab for less than twelve hours. But someone wanted to give him a job, or at least a chance at one?

"Okay," he said. "Sure, I guess."

Why the hell not? Talking to this guy would at least be a couple minutes taken up, a couple less minutes to be thinking about finding a fix.

~*~*~*~

JAKE DESANTIS WATCHED as his brother bounced out of the church. Not alone.

Jesus Christ. Jake wasn't sure if it was a blessing or a curse, but Zach could find a friend anywhere he went. He seemed to *need* to find a friend, seemed unable to ever just be alone.

But on the list of things to worry about in regards to Zach, "excess sociability" was somewhere near the bottom.

Of course, "compulsive need to adopt kicked puppies" was a little higher, especially when, as seemed to be happening right then, the actual adoptee ended up being Jake instead of Zach. Zach had met this guy at a meeting, so the guy was an addict. Just what Jake needed more of in his life. But Jake kept a calm expression on his face as Zach led the other guy around the hood of the pickup and waited expectantly outside the driver's window.

For a moment, Jake thought about ignoring them. He could lean over, turn up the stereo, get distracted by his phone—just generally behave like a brother sometimes should, gently tormenting his younger brother. But he and Jake weren't playful like that anymore. They hadn't been like that for years.

So he hit the button to lower the window and waited patiently.

"Hey, man," Zach said with a too-bright smile. "This is Michael. Old friend of mine from way back. I just ran into him, and he's looking for work. I said you might be able to hook him up."

Of course Zach had said that. Jake looked at Michael, took in the dark, serious eyes, wondered if he caught a glimpse of something impish, something that suggested a sense of humor, then completed the inspection with a quick look down his body. Seemed fit enough. "It's pretty hard work. If Zach told you it was easy, he was lying, and if he keeps acting like it's easy and goofing off like he has been, he's gonna get his ass fired, brother or no brother. So if your plan is to get paid for sitting around like he thinks he's going to do, then you should find somewhere else to work."

"Hard work is fine," Michael said.

"You got any experience?"

"Landscaping? Not really. Used to mow my parents' lawn. My mom gardened, so I picked up a bit from her. But nothing professional."

Jake appreciated the honesty, he supposed. "Where you living?"

"Halfway house over on Military Road."

"Damn, you're getting the deluxe treatment, huh?" Zach interrupted. "Ninety day rehab, counselling, a halfway house—who's paying for all that?"

"My parents," Michael said. He didn't sound too thrilled about it. "My college fund, I guess."

Well, that would shut Zach up, at least. He and Jake really didn't discuss their parents. "You have a car?" Jake asked into the silence.

"No."

"So I'll give you somewhere to be, a bus stop or a Link station or whatever, and you'll be there *on time* for me to pick you up. You aren't there on time? I keep driving and you're fired. If I'm on my way to a job *and* I think I'm maybe going to be short a guy, I can't sit around waiting for you to maybe show up."

Michael nodded his understanding, so Jake shrugged. If the guy didn't work out, he didn't work out. He dug out his phone and took down Michael's number. "What's your last name?"

"Porter. And the first name's actually Micah." He glanced over at Zach, and Jake could tell from the look that the two weren't old friends, or at least not *good* old friends. Still, Micah tried to cover. "Sometimes people call me Michael. Like a nickname."

"Yeah," Jake said with a frown toward his brother. "Of course they do."

Zach knew he was busted and clearly didn't care. Because Zach was Zach, sure he could cruise through life on charm and enthusiasm, and Jake was Jake, the one left to pick up the pieces after Zach's disasters. And Micah, this new addition to their happy little circle? Probably going to be a disaster. Still, Jake tapped the contact information into his phone and said, "We start early. I'll text you tonight and tell you where to meet us. One chance. Clear?"

Micah nodded.

Probably about fifty-fifty odds of the bastard showing up the next morning, and way worse chances of him making it through a whole week of work. That was the way with junkies. But Jake could never forget that junkies had brothers, people who loved them and dreamed of their recovery. People who sat bolt upright at night, yanked out of a nightmare of the junkie *not* getting better, dying instead, lying in some damn flophouse with a needle and an expression of gentle surprise—

"Get in," Jake growled at his brother. Get into the truck, stay beside me so I know you're safe, let this be the time when the program actually works for you. Please. God, please.

But none of that came out in words. "Tomorrow," Jake said to Micah as Zach climbed in. And then they drove away, Jake leaving someone else's nightmare behind while he tried to get some kind of control over his own.

Other Books by Kate Sherwood

(all m/m – for m/f see Cate Cameron at
www.catecameronauthor.com)

About the Author

Kate Sherwood started writing about the same time she got back on a horse after almost twenty years away from riding. She'd like to think she was too young for it to be a midlife crisis, but apparently she was ready for some changes!

Kate grew up near Toronto, Ontario (Canada) and went to school in Montreal, then Vancouver. But for the last decade or so she's been a country girl. Sure, she misses some of the conveniences of the city, but living close to nature makes up for those lacks. She's living in Ontario's "cottage country"– other people save up their time and come to spend their vacations in her neighborhood, but she gets to live there all year round!

Since her first book was published in 2010, she's kept herself busy with novels, novellas, and short stories in almost all the sub-genres of m/m romance. Contemporary, suspense, scifi or fantasy–the settings are just the backdrop for her characters to answer the important questions. How much can they share, and what do they need to keep? Can they bring themselves to trust someone, after being disappointed so many times? Are they brave enough to take a chance on love?

Kate's books balance drama with humor, angst with optimism. They feature strong, damaged men who fight themselves harder than they fight anyone else. And, wherever possible, there are animals: horses, dogs, cats ferrets, squirrels… sometimes it's easier to bond with a non-human, and most of Kate's men need all the help they can get.

After five years of writing, Kate is still learning, still stretching herself, and still enjoying what she does. She's looking forward to sharing a lot more stories in the future.

Find out more about Kate Sherwood and her books at her website: www.katesherwoodbooks.com

Follow Kate Sherwood on www.facebook.com/kate.sherwood.79

www.ingramcontent.com/pod-product-compliance
Lightning Source LLC
Chambersburg PA
CBHW071242170626
46809CB00001B/56